D1269616

ALCHEMY
OF A
BLACKBIRD

ALSO BY CLAIRE MCMILLAN

The Necklace

Gilded Age

ALCHEMY
OF A
BLACKBIRD

A NOVEL

CLAIRE McMILLAN

ATRIA BOOKS

NEW YORK   LONDON   TORONTO   SYDNEY   NEW DELHI

ATRIA
BOOKS

An Imprint of Simon & Schuster, Inc.
1230 Avenue of the Americas
New York, NY 10020

The excerpt from Benjamin Péret's poem "Source," from Péret's *From the Hidden Storehouse: Selected Poems*, translated by Keith Hollaman (Oberlin College Press, 1981), is reprinted by permission of Oberlin College Press. All rights reserved.

Epigraph: A portion of the poem "You are Invisible. Go Visible." from *The Truth Is We Are Perfect*, by Janaka Stucky. Used by permission of the author.

First Atria Books hardcover edition July 2023

ATRIA BOOKS and colophon are trademarks of Simon & Schuster, Inc.

For information about special discounts for bulk purchases, please contact Simon & Schuster Special Sales at 1-866-506-1949 or business@simonandschuster.com.

The Simon & Schuster Speakers Bureau can bring authors to your live event. For more information or to book an event, contact the Simon & Schuster Speakers Bureau at 1-866-248-3049 or visit our website at www.simonspeakers.com.

Interior design by Kyoko Watanabe

Manufactured in the United States of America

1 3 5 7 9 10 8 6 4 2

Library of Congress Cataloging-in-Publication Data has been applied for.

ISBN 978-1-6680-0655-9
ISBN 978-1-6680-0657-3 (ebook)

For Remedios Varo,
in memoriam

and for

Mac and Flora,
may you always heed your call

". . . From the river of moth dust we float on at night

Hand in invisible hand saying
Go and be

Build your impossible fort full of secret magics
Designed to let others in"

—**"You are Invisible. Go Visible."**
JANAKA STUCKY

PART I

FRANCE

October 1939

CHAPTER ONE

Remedios had been looking for a friend like Leonora her whole life. She linked elbows and drew her close while they walked along the bank above the Seine, their legs syncing as they increased their pace.

"Have you been painting at all?" Leonora asked.

Months ago at the Exposition Internationale du Surréalisme, their paintings had hung near each other. That was how they'd met.

Remedios didn't want to admit that the only things she'd been painting were forgeries for Oscar Sanchez, who then sold them to aristocrats with more money than sense. She wasn't sure how Leonora would react to such a thing. Not because Leonora would oppose the illegality of it; Remedios had met very few people as unconcerned with convention as Leonora. And not because she'd object to Remedios taking the money; they all needed money. Remedios suspected it would be the inauthenticity of aping someone else's artistic style that Leonora would object to.

"Yes. Every day," Remedios said, leaving out exactly what she'd been painting.

"Me too," Leonora said, hugging Remedios's elbow to her side. Leonora smelled of cigarettes and an old-fashioned violet perfume that made a striking contrast to her generally rebellious attitude. "Daily-

3

ness is the most important thing. Creating that time every day for the muse to come through. Even with everything we're facing."

The muse. Leonora spoke as if she were on intimate terms with inspiration, as if her muse were a constant companion, like a well-loved pet or guiding angel, and not something smothered by faking another artist's muddy color palette and depictions of stolid masculine buildings.

Yellow leaves windowpaned the dark pavement, wet from an early fall shower. Remedios pulled Leonora toward a bouquiniste, one of those bookstalls that had lined the river for centuries. An old lady in a man's canvas jacket with a bright blue foulard at the neck, the vendeuse, smiled at them. Remedios was aware of the picture she and Leonora were creating—two young, fashionable women, some might even call them beautiful, untroubled in the face of war. Sometimes it thwarted Remedios to be thought of as just another pretty young woman. Today she enjoyed the buoyant image she and Leonora projected together, the fleeting sort of power it gave her.

Or maybe it was being with Leonora that lifted her, Leonora who radiated a unique kind of magic. Everything from the lazy accent with which she pronounced her French to the pendant from her Irish nanny that she wore around her neck was the product of an upper-crust British background she'd rejected with the blithe self-assurance of someone who had always had more than enough. She'd run away from art school with Max Ernst and come to Paris where her behavior quickly became notorious. Once, she'd taken off her shoes and painted her feet with mustard at a café. Another time, in the middle of a party, she'd taken a shower fully clothed and then attended the rest of the evening in clinging wet clothes. Max called her "la petite sauvage."

And maybe to seem a little savage herself, or maybe it was the coming crisp autumn air, or maybe because she'd been searching for a breakthrough in her own painting wherever she could find it, Remedios picked up a deck of tarot cards from the bookseller's stall. She needed something that would help her reach the next level of her art. She wasn't sure what her art was anymore, since she'd spent these last months imitating de Chirico's. She was still trying to decide if it had improved her skills or knocked the originality right out of her.

She'd come to Paris to be with her lover, the poet Benjamin Péret, who'd bombarded her with an arsenal of poems when they met in Barcelona. Poems so ardent that after two months she couldn't remember why she'd ever resisted him. This she had in common with Leonora. They were both in love with famous, much older, married, intellectual men. But while Leonora spent her time in a spirit of rebellion and pushing boundaries, Remedios existed in a state of perpetual searching and absorbing.

"Let me buy those for you," Leonora said, as reflexively generous as only those favored by fortune can be. "Nanny knew about these things. She told me you should never buy tarot cards for yourself."

"You had someone who taught you about the tarot, mademoiselle?" asked the vendor.

"Only a very little bit, but she taught me that."

"But this is a very old superstition, meant to keep women away from a source of knowing. Anyone who desires the knowledge of the tarot can buy a deck of cards for herself, can avail herself of that power." The seller turned to Remedios. "Buy what you wish, mademoiselle. No need to wait for someone to give you what you need. You must acquire your tools for yourself. You are the agent of your destiny."

And even though this speech was likely part of the seller's skills refined by years of surviving off the little stall, Remedios dug a few bills out of her deep pockets and handed them over. With her first touch of the cards her shoulders lowered, something settling in her, and she exhaled with the rightness of a key fitting into a lock.

THE SUN—
Sabina Cherugi

The Sun card depicts a naked, smiling child riding on the back of a white horse, a red banner unfurling behind him while sunflowers bloom. The sun shines down brightly, filling the upper half of the card. This is the card of illumination so that all can be seen and therefore put on a more solid footing. Something that has been in shadow comes into light and gains certainty. It is also the card of being comfortable with shining out and being seen. The card, like the child, says, *Here I am and here is what I bring.* The Sun offers a signal to consider what has recently become more visible and invites considered action to sharpen that clarity.

My family has owned this stall since the 1600s. Cherugi women have made a living for generations along the banks of this river selling secondhand books, and old maps, and other bits of aged and valuable paper. My family has traded in other, more secret knowledge too. My mother read the cards, and her mother before her, and her mother before her. Now I do too, though it is best not to advertise. Even before the coming threat of the Nazis, as superstitious and obsessed with the occult as I've heard they are, divination was always a word-of-mouth business for my family—our name whispered in kitchens and nurseries and on children's playgrounds.

I usually didn't sell tarot decks, but kept a few tucked away for customers who wanted their own cards, a rarity now. I'd heard that in Germany they'd started arresting fortune-tellers and astrologers regularly, and burning books by the heap. So I was a little surprised when the two friends arrived, and one of them homed in on the little bin of cards I kept under a folding table.

They could have been mistaken for a pair of glamorous sisters—dark eyes, thick hair, and delicately rouged lips. But the one who picked up the tarot had wavy, reddish hair, almost standing away from her head, alive with the fire of intellect and mental curiosity. I saw right away that the cards fit her. Then her friend said that old lie about not buying your own deck, and I had to speak up.

Of course she bought them. As I handed them over I said, "No power inhabits a deck of tarot cards beyond what you, as the tarot reader, bring to them. There is no doctrinaire meaning for any card and no authority on high handing down pronouncements. There is only your knowledge of myth and symbol. These things you may consider through the study of classical Greek and Roman myth, physics, all forms of mysticism and occultism, even psychology. You combine this with your own life experience as a Sagittarius and bring it to the cards."

How did I know she was a Sagittarius? A lucky guess, some call it; others call it intuition.

"You're an archer, and you have been aiming your arrow for a long while now," I continued. "Perfecting your aim, aren't you?" Anyone with eyes could see she was a young woman of promise and that she was in the knowledge-gathering phase of her life. "Before you let that arrow fly."

She told me her name then, Remedios.

"The remedy! Delightful. And you are one, aren't you? Not only to your mother who experienced loss before you." She looked at me, amazed that I knew this. But really, why does a mother name her child "Remedy" if she hasn't had a heartbreak in need of healing? "But to others as well."

"My sister," Remedios said. "She died as an infant. My mother never stopped grieving her. She prayed and promised Our Lady of Remedios that if she had another baby, she'd name the child after her. That's me."

"Know that your role with your mother is completed. You have remedied all that you can heal for her." I took my own tarot deck out of my pocket, where I kept it constantly. "Anyone who buys the cards gets a free reading." This I made up on the spot solely because I wanted to see what the tarot had to say about this Sagittarian woman. "Choose three cards," I said, handing over the deck. Remedios's friend drew in a breath. "What?" I asked, turning to her. "Did Nanny have rules about this too?"

"She did, actually," she said. She was not in awe of me, the friend. "She never let me touch her cards. She said only the tarot reader touches her own cards."

"Let me guess, you were a very small child when she said this?"
She nodded.

"I suspect your nanny's rule had more to do with keeping an unruly child from messing her cards than anything else." I turned back to Remedios. "Pick your cards."

The tarot is no mind-reading exercise. It does not offer easy validation to those who come, arms crossed in withholding, demanding proof of its accuracy. In its highest form, a tarot reading is a conversation between a person with a question, a trusted guide, and the universe through the synchronicity of the cards.

I give the querent the cards when I want to observe how someone goes about choosing. So much is learned from how they shuffle, cut, and pick. Some take their time quite painstakingly, some rush through the process, and some just hand me the first cards off the top of the deck with no preamble and then shove the cards back into my hands as if they're on fire.

Remedios took a breath, calmed herself, even closed her eyes. She split the deck and folded it over on top of itself, once, twice, three times. Then she chose a card at random from the middle of the deck, took the one off the top and the one from the bottom, and handed them to me. Only then did she open her eyes.

I flipped the cards over and laid them out on the wobbly folding table. King after King. King of Wands with his call to action, King of Cups with his emotions setting him out to sea, and King of Swords. I pointed to this last. "I knew he'd be here," I said. "Present in this reading as he is present in your life. A man of intellect. He lives in his mind." The girls smiled, nodding. "He has trouble getting out of his mind and into his body. That's where you come in." Remedios actually blushed when I said this.

"I want to learn," she said.

"Yes, and you are in the right place to do that. You are amassing knowledge from this man, this King of Swords, for a journey, lessons that will serve you throughout your life."

"I mean, do you give lessons? I want to learn this."

I'll admit I was offended for a moment. Did she think it was some simple mathematical formula that could be taught like an equation, $1+1=2$, without the need for insight or spirit? The tarot is a deeply personal practice. Anyone is free to adopt or ignore any meaning given to a tarot card or come up with her own. Personal definitions often offer the deepest insights. To the extent a card's meaning is widely adopted, it is because it is either useful or holds truth that resonates from reader to reader.

"The tarot is available to all and yet obscure," I answered, as if I was a hermit in the woods offering a riddle.

"I can't pay," she said. "Not with money. But I can barter." She reached deep into the pockets of her coat and withdrew a small black notebook. "Maybe you could sell them in the stand and keep the proceeds."

The little book was filled with sketches of life in the streets of Paris—pigeons, fine gentlemen, ladies of ill repute, and more recent soldiers. Each had a fantastical twist. The soldier had the head of a death-eating raven. The prostitute's legs were the posts of a bed. The pigeons had wind-up mechanisms and cogs in their breasts like a clockwork.

They were just the sort of thing I easily sold to tourists looking to take home a memento from the City of Light. I'd have torn them out individually and passed them off as my own, but there were no tourists anymore.

"I'm not sure I can explain my ways," I said. If she was easily discouraged, then let her be. "It's not rational, or linear. It's not something one can teach." I handed the sketchbook back. "Like art. Art cannot be taught."

"But that's what I'm always telling you," the friend said, shrugging into her.

"I attended art school, madame," Remedios said. "You're right, it cannot be taught, but natural abilities can be honed and guided, don't you agree?"

She made a compelling argument. "And do you have natural abilities in the psychic realm?"

The question was a test of sorts. Boast of her prowess and I'd know she was a fraud, claim she had no skill and it would be easy to refuse her. Admitting to one's own inclination to psychic abilities out loud and to a stranger was daunting.

"Some. Yes. Maybe," she said.

"Ah," I said, taking her hand in mine. "Then your first lesson is this. The tarot is like life. A set of cards to be played that rely on the skill, knowledge, and intuition of the reader to view the cards dealt, understand them, and react to them to the best of her ability. Like life, there is a random element to it, and like life, there is a synchronicity to it. And like life, what matters is the truth that can be glimpsed behind what is rather small and flimsy, in this case a card, and then what actions are taken in reaction to that truth. Understand?"

She nodded. They both did, swaying a little from side to side, a bit breathless.

"Bon, come back tomorrow. Then we will begin."

Chapter Two

Remedios rushed home past the Place Vendôme, past the statue of Napoleon atop the tall column now sandbagged and covered in scaffolding to protect it from possible bombing. She wished for her own scaffolding, her own armor to protect her. Even statues needed such things, but all she had was her red wool coat, the one she'd sewn herself in midwinter on the heavy black sewing machine hunched in the corner of the flat, abandoned by the prior occupants. She'd bought a half bolt of wool at a discount price from a tailor who'd closed his shop and left the city. The majority of Parisians had fled once France entered the war in the fall. Still there were those who hung on—like her, like Madame Cherugi, who'd been giving her lessons in the tarot nearly every day despite the news.

Leonora and Max had left months ago for the countryside, and she missed her friend who'd come to the tarot lessons with her. She imagined them now, blithely unaware of anything happening in the city. She'd heard Leonora and Max rarely put on clothes, painting naked all day so that they scandalized the villagers. She wondered if Leonora's carefree attitude was a remnant of her upbringing. If having been presented at court and coming from a landed and titled family allowed Leonora to believe that if the world descended into fire, it wouldn't scorch her. Max encouraged this naivete. He enjoyed

Leonora's youth and beauty unsullied by fears, or cares, or strife. Watching them, Remedios sometimes wondered if Leonora's nonchalance was natural or if she played it up for his benefit.

Her scrutiny of Leonora caused her to examine certain uncomfortable parallels in her relationship with Benjamin. Just today during her lesson with Madame Cherugi the subject of Benjamin had come up when they'd been practicing simple spreads.

"Ask a yes-or-no question," Madame Cherugi said, "and see if you can divine the answer. The tarot is usually not the best at direct answers, but sometimes it can add clarity."

Her mother, a devout Catholic who'd sent Remedios to convent schools and attended mass each morning during the forty days of Lent, would have been horrified to know her daughter was studying an occult practice. And so, much like that first time, each time Remedios picked up the cards she felt a centering—whether it was the result of this pleasing transgression or from the insights offered by the cards, she didn't know.

She'd asked if Benjamin, or the King of Swords as Madame Cherugi called him, was her one true love. She thought she heard Madame's exasperated sigh when she said this. Then Remedios pulled the Two of Swords in answer, which showed a woman seated and blindfolded, holding two swords crossed in front of her body.

"So that is a no," Remedios said, looking at the card.

"That is a block," said Madame Cherugi. "The answer will not be given at this time."

Now Remedios continued swiftly home from her lesson along streets where blackout curtains hung in every window, giving Paris an oddly muffled, cozy feel. She opened the door into the courtyard of her building, rounded the corner, and began to walk up the four flights to the apartment she shared with Benjamin. She knew what she'd find when she got there. She could hear it from two floors below—the rumbling of male voices. She didn't even need her interior key. The door was open, and when she stepped into her flat, she saw him.

André Breton sat surrounded, as he always was, by his intellectual admirers—Wolfgang Paalen and Victor Brauner, and of course Oscar Sanchez. They'd all made themselves at home in her home, the apartment she shared with Benjamin.

She'd read André's *Surrealist Manifesto* in art school. Everyone did. So it never failed to be a pinch-me moment when she found him in her flat. His friendship with Benjamin was a comradeship, a meeting of minds. André thought the thoughts, and Benjamin put them into practice in his poetry and in his uncompromising behavior.

"Dear Remedios," André called out as she entered the room. "Benjamin just stepped out for more drinks. Where have you been?"

She knew this was not a straightforward question, and she wasn't his dear. He regarded her as a novice painter who distracted Benjamin from his more serious work. What's more, he didn't care where she'd been. His question was a demand to amuse him, to say something surrealist.

In the past, she would merely smile until Benjamin came to her rescue with a witty barb.

But Benjamin wasn't there, and the circumstances offered no way to elude André's scrutiny. What would Leonora have said She of the outrageous gesture—something confronting or at least bizarre. Remedios reached for the first surrealist image she could think of.

"A cavalcade of cats alighted in my hair. I had to step into the hairdresser's to have them combed out."

"Well, next time tell those cats I said hello," André said with an approving nod.

Oscar got up and landed a deft kiss on each cheek and then to her surprise a quick peck on the lips. He'd always been as bossy with her as any older brother, and as protective too. When she first came to Paris, she'd been floating on a cloud of new love and sex, and it was

Oscar who'd cushioned the blow when she came back to earth. She still remembered the first time he suggested she forge a de Chirico. She'd laughed, assuming it was some surrealist joke.

"Look," he'd said, "if Benjamin had even two francs in his pocket, there'd be something new under the sun. You're going to need money. This is an easy way to make a lot of it fast. Your diet of coffee and cigarettes makes you look tired."

She refused outright. But over the course of months and as their financial situation became more dire, Remedios took Oscar up on his offer. Benjamin disdained such quotidian matters as employment, claiming a job was a bourgeois concept meant to stifle the creativity of the masses, and she had few other options for paying work. After she got over her fear of the illegality of it, she decided copying a master like de Chirico could only improve her skills, and she was always looking for ways to add to her abilities. De Chirico's rigorous line work, his far horizons, his masculine palette of muddy, muted colors were all in stark contrast to her own more feminine painting. She told herself this forgery was an exercise that offered dimension to her work and new skills to her repertoire, along with the money. And besides, Oscar provided a luxuriously ample supply of paints and canvases, which were becoming scarce.

Strangely, she'd found the hardest part to imitate was de Chirico's signature. It wasn't a flourished or elaborate scrawl, but the idea of signing another artist's name, the ultimate sham, stymied her. However, once she got the hang of it, she was able to paint never-before-seen masterpieces, all slightly different from their inspirations and all identifiable as de Chirico's. Oscar sold them quickly.

"Buyers think they're getting a deal because a war's coming," he said.

Tonight Oscar was at the apartment to pick up another fake. He'd been asking her to make them smaller, more portable, the better to travel with given that most everyone they knew was fleeing. To her dismay, Oscar took the most recent fake de Chirico off the easel where it sat drying and brought it to the middle of the room, flourishing it in front of André for his approval. It was all flat planes and plazas heading off into the endless horizon of infinity, and in the corner she'd painted a tiny shadow cast by an unseen woman fleeing just outside the frame.

"If I didn't know better, I'd think it was real," André said. "Quite bold, Oscar, to imitate a living artist. What if he stumbles across one of them? What if he sends the police after you?"

Remedios swallowed her reply that she was the one doing the painting, not Oscar. She often had this voiceless feeling around André, as if she couldn't speak up. It reminded her of a similar feeling she had around her mother—of trying to get her attention and then being terrified once she got it. Of needing to measure up, but not being sure what the measuring stick was.

"What do you think, Benjamin?" André asked as Benjamin returned, taking off his jacket and unloading the wine bottles from the bag. No matter if there was a war, the surrealists would find alcohol and tobacco. "Of your little sorceress faking these things with such skill." There was a touch of challenge in André's voice, and Remedios bristled at the word *little*.

Benjamin was silent for a moment. "De Chirico's become a hack. I hear he's making his own fakes and backdating them and then selling them himself since everyone likes his old style better. Imagine being so devoid of ideas, so devoid of life, that you don't move your work forward, just go back to what's popular and fake it so you can grub money. You ask me, he deserves it."

"He probably wouldn't even mind," Oscar said, nodding.

Remedios doubted this.

"It's money." Benjamin turned to André. "For food. And these things, these ideas, they don't belong to one person. Not to de Chirico, and not the dummkopfs Oscar sells them to."

"You're speaking German now? I'd rather bark like a dog." André grunted.

"They think they can own something that's really just an idea." Remedios spoke up, and the room grew disconcertingly quiet. "Or even more ethereal, an aesthetic. Those things aren't up for ownership. They've been brainwashed by a capitalist machine to think that just by putting their name on something in the same way a dog pees on a tree to mark it, they own it. Well, that's their folly." She always dreaded sounding like a provincial in front of André. The worst was if her voice trembled.

Oscar stood, slow clapping.

"So you're Benjamin's star pupil now," André said. "Good for you."

"Oh, let up, André," Oscar said, suddenly sour. "Give her a break."

Remedios felt heartened at Oscar sticking up for her, but chagrined too. Shouldn't it be Benjamin who stood up for her? But he never pushed back against André.

"Those are all Benjamin's ideas," André continued. "Are you trying to say she's ever had an original thought in her head?" She was used to André and his arrogance. They all were. No one was more intellectual, no one more cutting edge than he, except for maybe Benjamin. She'd tried to ignore it, but she always noticed it.

"Didn't she just say thoughts and theories aren't owned by any one person? Besides, we're doing a service," Oscar continued. "Helping people buy this stuff up, getting it out of France before the Nazis destroy it. Like this binge-buying American Peggy whatever-her-name-is that you introduced me to."

"Peggy Guggenheim," André said, slowly enunciating each syllable. "And have you forgotten you're selling imitations done by a student?"

"She's not a student," Oscar said. "Besides, it's heroic, even a little dangerous. The police could be after her in a moment."

Benjamin remained silent in the face of his two friends discussing his love like she wasn't there.

"Oh," André said, with a false levity. "Are you worried they'll come for her? Worried they'll lock up your golden goose? Or is it something more?"

Remedios waited in a vibration of anxiety as she watched this ramp up. They all did. André was capable of being coolly cruel when he wanted to be, and he enjoyed filleting people in public.

"Or are you worried they'll start arresting all the mistresses?" André said.

"*Mistress*—such a funny, uptight, hissy word," Remedios said, trying to lower the temperature and derail this train of thought. Things seemed to be swinging wildly off course, and she was, after all, the mistress André was speaking of. "What is a male mistress? A mister?"

"No, he is a lover," André said, eyes focused on Oscar. "A word based on action. But then one would have to actually take some action, wouldn't they, Oscar?" André then added more lowly and deadly, "Yes, we all know your secret. We all know you're in love with her too. You're just too scared to do anything about it, aren't you?"

Oscar, her old friend, wasn't in love with her. André was being ridiculous and territorial, somehow mistakenly thinking he was sticking up for his friend Benjamin.

It was at that point that Oscar hurled his glass—heavy-bottomed with a thin rim. It shattered into shards against the wall above Benjamin's and André's heads. A wedge lodged in Benjamin's shoulder. Splinters fell in André's hair. Later when she thinks of that night, she thinks of the last moment before all their worlds shattered, before their worlds were smashed and lay around their feet like the remnants of sparkling glass.

FIVE OF CUPS—
Oscar Sanchez

Three cups are spilled on the ground while a cloaked man stands before them, head bowed in sorrow or contemplation. Behind him, out of his sight line, two cups remain upright and filled. The Five of Cups is a card of loss or disappointment. However, the man can focus only on his spilled cups. He is unaware that two cups behind him remain intact. When the Five of Cups appears in a reading, it is a good idea to consider whether one has been brooding over a situation rather too long. It is a card for considering a situation from a new perspective and at the right time, if it is available, to turn and embrace authentically felt gratitude for what remains.

Yes, I threw the glass, harder than I meant to, and I regretted it the moment it left my hand. Did I love her? I suppose I did.

I'd been drinking since lunch. We all did in those days. I blame that, and I blame André and his extreme views—always more surrealist than anyone else, always more uncompromising than anyone except Benjamin. Frankly, I don't know how Remedios put up with them. I'd always been a little in love with her, ever since we'd been students together at the Academia de San Fernando in Madrid. She wasn't classically beautiful. You could find fault with each feature in her face. But when put together they created a harmonious sort of beauty—she appealed. And of course you had the feeling when you were around her that she radiated a special sort of energy and you yourself were caught up in it and revived by it.

It was why Benjamin had seduced her like a vampire, living off the spark of her enthusiasm. It's why I'd taken to mostly chasing after glamour girls and heiresses—rouged and bejeweled, the opposite of her. I didn't think I could stand a pale imitation of her fire.

We were free with our love in those days, and I don't mean physically. I mean as a group, love in camaraderie. Have you ever felt yourself a part of something larger than you? Ever felt that you were at the center of the only thing that was happening in the world at that time? We were a group with a vision and a mission as the world was setting itself on fire. A political cause, a religion, even a sports team would allow you to feel a taste of what we felt. Closer than family, more intimate than lovers, we wanted nothing less than to unleash what was hidden in each of us, to pull back the civilized veneer of an entire society.

I didn't think the glass would hurt anyone, not exactly. I thought it would smash on the wall above all their heads—dramatic and powerful, masculine even. Pathetic, especially in light of everything that happened. But André was always exhorting us to express ourselves freely, to be direct without the strictures of what was considered proper by society. Hurling a glass, you couldn't get more direct than that.

But how was I to know that the next morning they'd arrest Benjamin on charges having to do with his communism? That he'd spend his time in jail still picking shards of glass out of his scalp and worrying that his shoulder was infected? André came round and told me that, as if punishing me. He wanted me to try to get Benjamin out, but I told him there was nothing I could do.

But when I got news a month or so later that Remedios had been picked up too, merely for her association with Benjamin, I decided that in penance for that night I needed to try to help her.

I pulled in every connection I could think of—every two-bit royal I'd duped, every gallerist who might have some money squirreled away. It took me weeks to find out where they were holding her, a month, maybe more, before I had enough money to approach. In the end, amid the chaos, do you know that it was a simple bribe to the head of the night shift that got her out? He told me she'd be released by morning. "We're going to surrender anyway," the gendarme told me with a shrug. "What will it matter now?"

When I heard that, I didn't stick around, not even to make sure that she was freed. I paid the bribe, my debt then cancelled. The rumor was that the Nazis would be upon us in a matter of days, some said hours. It was then I fled, like everyone else, to the south, to a port, to Marseilles.

CHAPTER THREE

Remedios hadn't been searching for rescue amid her fellow evacuees walking south. She hadn't been looking for anyone as she kept her eyes front, reminding herself that every footstep forward was a step away from terror, from jail, and toward safety.

She'd been a prisoner for months, subjected to interrogations and privations and worse. She'd never been held captive by anyone or anything, and she spent the hours in her cell trying to fend off panic and calm a pounding heart. They'd questioned her, the back of a hand across the face when she refused to answer questions about Benjamin and his organizing. She'd lived in a perpetual state of uncertainty, filth, hunger, and boredom mixed with random interludes of minor violence. Then, early one morning the warden came, unlocked her cell, and walked away without a backward glance. She didn't need to be told what to do. Barely breathing, shoulders around her ears, she'd walked out and gone to the apartment only to find it empty and ransacked. She'd packed a suitcase with her few remaining possessions and started out on foot despite her exhaustion, fleeing south, thinking she'd form a plan as she walked along with everyone else who fled.

She'd been wary when the car pulled over, and then relieved when she saw who it was. Two women she recognized from parties at Oscar's apartment—American types she sometimes ran into who were searching for adventure and the bohemian life.

"Quick, get in," the passenger called as she leaned out the window and her friend slowed the Peugeot. "Before we're overrun."

Acting on instinct and not pausing to question, Remedios hefted her bag into the back seat of the car next to a pile of worn cotton quilts, jerry cans of gasoline, a crate of dusty geodes, and a matching set of monogrammed luggage. Then she climbed in.

"I remember you," the blonde driver said. "You're friends with Benjamin Péret and all those surrealists. I'm Mary Jane, by the way." She stretched her left hand over her right shoulder for a little back-seat handshake, all while keeping her eyes on the road.

"Remedios," she said.

"Oh, we know who you are," said the other one. "You're that painter. I'm Miriam."

The outskirts of the city fell away to farmland as they drove in grim silence, listening for the drone of planes and passing hollow-eyed mothers with their babies in rags, cars abandoned for lack of gas, bodies in ditches, roads filled with craters from bombing.

Remedios tried to get them to stop so she could give her seat to someone worse off, but each time she spoke up, the friends looked at each other and then Mary Jane silently accelerated.

Remedios slumped over the pile of quilts, trying to sleep amid the jouncing objects in the back seat—exhaustion hovering at the edge of her consciousness, but her mind on residual alert from faded fear. She feigned sleep to avoid talking.

They'd been driving awhile when Miriam said in a confidential voice, "This should be our last mission." She sleepily stretched her arms over her head. "Don't you think?"

"Agreed," Mary Jane said with a nod as she leaned toward the windshield to check the darkening sky. "But I'm not sure I want to leave." They were far enough from Paris that the danger of air strafing had lessened.

It must be nice to be American with an American passport and an American amount of money, Remedios thought. They had the reassuring capacity to book a ticket home on a ship and out of this reality at any point. It was all just an adventure for them.

"You know what Varian said to me, before we left this last time?" Miriam asked in a quiet tone that meant she thought Remedios was asleep.

"Some dreary lecture about how this was absolutely our last mission?"

"No. He said it was getting so we wouldn't be able to get out ourselves unless we absolutely wrapped ourselves in the American flag."

"Ha," Mary Jane said. "With nothing underneath."

"Don't be cheap."

"I'm not. I'm trying to be funny."

"Well, you're not."

"How would you know? You wouldn't know funny if it spit in your ear."

Their back-and-forth sounded oddly comforting to Remedios, as only two people absolutely secure in their mutual fondness could bicker like that and remain friends.

"Oh, you're awake," Mary Jane said, looking in the rearview when Remedios sat up. "How do you feel?"

"Exhausted," Remedios admitted. "And thirsty."

Mary Jane made a sharp right turn onto a rutted dirt road. She turned off the headlights as they pulled in behind a small rural chapel. "We'll sleep a few hours and start out again at daybreak," Mary Jane said as Miriam hopped out and found the black tarps and branches discreetly stashed behind a stone wall for disguising the car.

Mary Jane and Miriam walked assuredly into the dark, deserted church, up the aisle of worn marble pavers, and onto the altar made of the local limestone. The chill air held the lingering scent of incense long since burned and beeswax candles now snuffed. They veered and opened a small door at the side, and the three of them squeezed into the sacristy.

A basket on the floor was covered with a striped tea towel. The priests' vestments were piled in little nests on the floor like blankets. They weren't the first to use this safe room. Mary Jane locked them in. Miriam was already handing Remedios a hunk of cheese and a torn piece of bread. Mary Jane passed her a full canteen.

As they ate, Remedios started to ask how many times they'd done this, but before she could get the question out Mary Jane put a finger to her lips.

"They like us to keep quiet," she whispered, tilting her head toward the door and presumably their hosts.

They ate in silence, and then Mary Jane and Miriam covered themselves under the heavily embroidered robes and bedded down. Remedios followed suit, but the foreignness of sleeping under church vestments and the coldness of the floor, mixed with her nerves, made sleep difficult. She slipped a hand into her coat pocket, feeling the familiar card deck in its rough linen pouch. At the apartment, she'd packed a bag as quickly as she could and managed to shove her deck into her pocket. Thinking of Madame Cherugi, she untied its tattered ribbon one-handed.

She took a breath to center herself, a brief request to the universe, to the divine, to whoever was listening, that she might be given guidance. Was she safe now? What would she find in Marseilles?

She wormed her hand into the pouch, took a card from the middle of the deck, and held the card up to the stained-glass window. Faint, red-tinged moonlight illuminated the dim outlines of the Four of Swords.

"What have you got there?" Miriam whispered.

Remedios flipped the card around between index finger and thumb.

A knight lay on an altar or a sarcophagus in what looked like a church, a sword parallel under him and three hanging perpendicular above him, pointing toward his body. A call to rest, to meditate, to go within. The presence of the swords all around him showed that he'd just been engaged in a battle and likely would be engaging in another again soon. But for the moment, the resting knight looked at peace, as if he were napping. It had been one of Leonora's favorite cards. An odd choice, yes, but it reminded Leonora to calm the outside so the inner could embark on serious work. Leonora's view of any card was always so singular. Remedios wondered then if she and Max were still in the countryside, or if they too were on the move, fleeing.

"Is he dead? That doesn't bode well for the future," Miriam whispered.

Remedios crammed the card back into her pocket. Miriam could be forgiven for her clunky, literal interpretation. Given the circumstances, everything looked like death.

"They show the interior," Remedios said. How to explain the haziness that existed inside her head? That sometimes a card pulled at random could illuminate everything. She'd been searching for illumination for as long as she could remember.

"I guess people believe in stranger things than a deck of cards," Miriam said as she rolled over.

During those months in jail, Remedios had plenty of time to question what she believed. She'd spent all that time with Benjamin in the cafés, surrounded by his artistic, philosophical friends, absorbing, mouth agape, dazzled. The surrealist circle egged each other on to outrageousness with their theories about the desirability of irrationality, chaos, and the subconscious. And then they were all thrown headlong into those very things. Sitting in jail, she'd wondered if it had all been so much bluster. Sleeping in the safe haven of a sacristy made a jarring contrast with Benjamin's constant criticisms of the Church.

-‹‹‹◊›››-

It seemed to Remedios she'd just fallen asleep when Mary Jane was shaking her shoulder.

"We need to move," she said.

Delirious and practically sleepwalking, Remedios followed her out into the cold gray morning, lit up at the edges of the forest with a glow of pink and orange.

Standing in the stone courtyard, next to the now-uncovered Peugeot, was a woman in black robes with a paper-wrapped package in her hand.

"Sister, thank you," Miriam whispered, accepting the parcel.

"The last time," the nun said. "We must stop now. It's no longer safe."

"Yes, I understand," Mary Jane said. "Thank you for all you've done."

"Don't thank me," she said. "Thank our heavenly father."

They got into the car.

"Sure, I'll be thanking him," Mary Jane said as she reversed the car. Miriam handed out the stale rolls the nuns had packed for them. "I just hope I don't have to do it in person anytime soon, know what I mean?"

Miriam blew out an exasperated little laugh. "No," she said. "Not anytime soon."

The farther south they headed, the less crowded the roads became. Mary Jane, who had made the run from Paris to Marseilles more than a few times in the preceding months, kept to the back roads and seemed to know shortcuts that kept them away from the most congested routes. She was a steady driver and kept up a reasonable clip. At deserted spots, they pulled over to refuel from the jerry cans, stretch their legs, and relieve themselves.

As night came, Mary Jane made a sharp right.

"Let's not stop," Miriam said. "Let me drive if you're tired."

"They'll spot us. From the air. It's a perfect night to attack."

"I haven't heard a plane all afternoon. You sleep while I drive and we'll switch."

Mary Jane stopped the car. "You really want to get back."

They drove through the night, and when they reached the outskirts of Marseilles on the third day, Remedios asked them to drop her near the old port.

"But we know someone here. He's helping artists like you," Mary Jane said as she drove toward the hills and away from the water.

They pulled up to a path lined with cedar and plane trees leading to a villa.

"We'll put the car away and head inside," Mary Jane said as she steered around the back of the villa as if they'd just arrived at a country house weekend instead of a safe house.

When Remedios opened the car door in the coming dark, the air was alive with the sound of night insects. She inhaled, hefted her suitcase, and walked toward the light.

PAGE of WANDS.

PAGE OF WANDS—
Mary Jane Gold

The Page of Wands is at the beginning of his journey to understand how to harness his fire and wield his own power. A young person holds his staff of fire, or wand, as if he has just discovered it and is wondering over the potential of what it can do. Associated with the fire energy of movement and creation, this page is ready to make his mark on the world. When the Page of Wands appears in a reading, one might take it as a good sign that an enterprise in the beginning stage will go well, or that a freshness will return to a project in progress. The Page of Wands can also be a suggestion to call in more fire and creativity to one's life. This page holds the fresh perspective of a beginner's mind with the spark of the possible.

I knew who she was when we picked her up. I'd seen her at Oscar Sanchez's parties in the corner talking with all the most interesting women in the room. A painter, I'd been told. So I knew she was a good fit for Varian's villa.

Or should I call it my villa? After all, I'm the one who found it, and I'm the one who pays the rent.

I have a way of making things appear when I want them, but not like an abracadabra kind of thing. More like I'd been working for Varian Fry and his American Rescue Committee since I arrived in Marseilles, though *committee* is a bit much for an organization that was basically Varian and the three thousand dollars he'd strapped to his leg along with a list of artists and thinkers that a bunch of society swells in New York wanted him to save. When I found him, he was single-handedly trying to get visas for artists and intellectuals to get out of France. Things being what they were, he understandably prioritized the Jewish artists on the list first.

So I joined up and helped the people who sought us out who weren't on Varian's list. You'd be surprised how quickly word got around Marseilles that there was an American in town with money and connections working to help people leave. In any event, if someone wasn't on the list, Miriam and I figured out ways to help them anyway. We got people visas—both real and forged—secured passages, bailed people out of jail, and even gave them a little money to start a new life in a new country.

The police raided us twice, and after the second time I was thinking, you know, if only we could find a nice place, relatively out of town, where the police would leave us alone, maybe with a little more space so we could all stay together. Then the next day someone mentioned the villa to me—decent price, perfect location. That sort of thing happened to me all the time. My brother used to tease me about it when we were kids.

And what a relatively splendorous villa it was—three stories of apricot stucco that emanated a glow in the dusk. The arched windows enticed with candlelight from within, and the green lacquered shutters glittered like the wings of an insect. I mean, there was no reason we had to live in squalor, was there? The terraced gardens were planted with fragrant lavender native to Grasse that now struggled against the weeds, as the gardeners had abandoned us months before.

I parked the car in its hiding spot in the stables behind the house, and we let ourselves in through the back door. A shore break of laughter crashed over us from the dining room. Madame Nouget, the cook, raised an eyebrow as we entered. The kitchen was her domain, and she didn't like invaders.

In her neat chignon and bright red lipstick, Madame Nouget was a source of comfort and fear to me, not unlike certain of my mother's friends I'd grown up with in Chicago. Women who knew how to run a kitchen, how to organize their house staff, how to garden, how to serve a proper dinner, how to heal fevers, and never missed a thing going on around them. She'd come with the villa, a package deal.

"We brought a new one," I said.

We all turned toward Remedios, who stood there, one battered suitcase in hand, looking for all the world like a lost orphan and not at all like the glamorous artist I remembered from parties in Paris.

Madame Nouget wiped her hands on her pristine red-checked apron, with a practiced calm that came from having refugees show up on her doorstep at any hour of the day or night. She took Remedios's suitcase and led us out of the kitchen and down the candlelit, terracotta-tiled hall to the narrow formal dining room, where the walls were padded in dingy faux leather and the Fortuny drapes at the French windows hung in long shreds.

Amid the dim candlelight, a well-polished mahogany table bore the remnants of a dinner served on sturdy faience plates and at the head, as always, sat André Breton.

The room silenced when Remedios entered, and André leapt to his feet, tears in his eyes, which I found impressive. André never really showed much friendship to me or Miriam, or even Varian.

But he came around the table now, saying, "Remedios, my God." And planted a kiss on each cheek as if she were a long-lost relative. "We heard you were imprisoned under the Eiffel Tower."

She looked at Mir and me, over André's shoulder, and said to us, "But how did you know? I don't understand."

"We get intelligence sometimes." He gestured toward Varian, who rose to introduce himself.

"No, you two," she said, gesturing to Miriam and me. "How did you know to bring me here? How did you know he'd be here?" There were tears of exhaustion and confusion brimming in her eyes, and truth be told, I just wanted to hug her.

Varian came around the table then, wearing one of those baggy tweed jackets all Harvard men seem so fond of, and he must have been impressed by the effect Remedios had on André, too, because he actually bowed a little as he introduced himself.

"Varian's our knight in shining armor," I said, and then realized too late it sounded like I had a crush on him, which I didn't.

"We're trying to get people out as quickly as we can. I was sent with a list of names. Monsieur Breton's was on it, of course, as well as Monsieur Péret's."

"Benjamin? Do you know where he is?" she asked, looking between André and Varian.

Jacqueline Lamba, André's famous and famously beautiful wife, put a hand on Remedios's arm then and sort of dragged her to sit down. I was fascinated by Jacqueline, too, by the colorful gemstone rings she wore on each finger and the tiger claw necklace at her neck and the elaborate toilette she kept up. Even in exile her hair was beautifully coiffed, her nails lacquered, and she smelled like the new

Chanel perfume called only No. 5. I knew this because I'd spied it on the counter in the bathroom we were all forced to share.

"Benjamin's fine," Varian said. "He's here."

Remedios stood, but André placed a hand on her other arm.

"He's unharmed and living above a café in town." He smiled a little when he said it. "Can't you see it? Benjamin always did love a café. We see him every day. He's been out of his mind with worry about you. He's been trying to get news of you."

Madame set a plate of dinner before Remedios along with a glass of wine. Somehow, and I never knew quite how she did it, Madame Nouget would make a dinner out of our compiled ration cards that could last around the table, no matter who showed up and joined us. A loaves-and-fishes sort of conjuring that extended even to the candles alight in the wall sconces, the dark wine in the glasses, the yellow wildflowers in a low bowl on the table.

"You can see him tomorrow," André was saying.

"I want to see him now," Remedios said, ignoring the food, though I knew she had to be famished. "I'll walk if I have to. Or will you drive me?" she asked, turning to me.

"I wish I could," I said, and I meant it. "But there's a curfew."

"It's very strictly enforced," Varian said. "You're lucky you didn't get pulled over coming here."

"He'll be here tomorrow," Jacqueline said.

"You should eat," André said directly, as if ordering a child.

"How did he escape?" she asked, finally sitting.

"You know Benjamin. He bribed his way out of prison at the last minute before the surrender—cursing the guards, his fellow countrymen, and the entire nation of France the whole way. Somehow he even managed to drag the Church into it."

"Benjamin drags the Church into everything," she said, and then took a bite of food.

"Is it true?" Jacqueline asked. "Is there a secret jail under the Eiffel Tower?"

"I don't know. I wasn't under the Eiffel Tower," Remedios said, settling in to what I imagined was her first real meal in months.

"How long total?" André asked.

"I lost track of time in there, but it was nearly two months," she said after she swallowed. "They asked me a lot of questions about Benjamin and his political organizing. And about Spain. Toward the end more about—" She paused, a sideways glance at the rest of the table. "My paintings for certain clients."

André waved a hand at her as if waving away her troubles. "You can speak plainly."

"To show me, I think, that they knew about me, that they could bring me up on forgery charges if they wished."

When she said it, I began forming a tactful way to ask her if she'd try her hand at forging documents. We had a few forgers we worked with, but given demand, we could always use more.

"They could have brought you up on anything," Jacqueline said, a little breathlessly, I thought. "My God, you could have been killed. What was the worst part?" she asked, chin attentively resting in her hand. "What was the very worst of the interrogations?"

I thought Jacqueline's questions obtuse and in truth a little aggressive. They forced Remedios back into her memories of police officers yelling at her, and the threat of worse, I was sure. Jacqueline had put Remedios on the spot, reopened her wound, and then asked to watch it bleed. It seemed cruel to me and gave me the feeling that in Paris, Jacqueline hadn't liked Remedios much, though she probably would have denied it if put on the spot. Having watched them for months now, I'd realized that while André and Jacqueline were surrealists, they weren't libertines or really very political, despite all the socialists and anarchists who orbited them.

"Max Ernst is holding a vernissage here tomorrow, and he's bringing Madame Guggenheim around to look at the pictures," I said, trying to change the subject when it became clear Remedios didn't want to answer the question. I always liked it when Peggy Guggenheim came to the villa. It meant Madame Nouget made the most delicious little canapés to impress her.

"But Max is here too," Remedios said. "Is Leonora with him? Tell me everyone who's here," she said, closing her eyes for a moment as if in pain. "Tell me now. Everyone who made it."

"Max escaped," André said with a hint of pride in his voice. "When the armistice was announced, the head of the internment camp set them all free. We don't know where Leonora is. Max lost contact with her when he was arrested, but he's heard she's not well."

"Not well?" Remedios said.

"I don't know more, only that she was worried about Max. She started behaving strangely."

"Rest assured, we see almost everyone who comes through Marseilles, or we hear about them," Jacqueline said.

"Yes, it's Varian's job." André inclined his head toward the doorway. "And we continue to try to do ours, which is why I'm so glad you're here, dear Remedios."

"Max wants to show his work attached to the olive trees tomorrow," Jacqueline said, pulling the focus back to her. "You'll see Benjamin then. You should rest now. Can she have the Saint-Exupérys' old room?" Jacqueline asked Madame Nouget, as if the house were hers, as if she were the hostess ordering her staff. This I found the most irritating part of her personality. I was the one paying the rent; shouldn't that be my role? Or Varian's, since he was the one doing all the work? Or even André's, as he was the famous ringleader? But somehow Jacqueline had stepped in and acted like she owned the place. I had no idea how to wrest control away from her.

"Bien sûr," Madame Nouget said, and did I detect just a faint hint of disapproval in that answer? "I've just made it up now with clean linen. And if you give me your laundry," she said to Remedios, "I can have the girls start on it first thing in the morning. Your clothes don't look so far gone. I don't think we'll have to burn them."

Nouget and her girls could rescue even the most threadbare rags as long as they weren't infested with lice or worse. I saw it register in Remedios's eyes that we'd welcomed refugees in poorer shape than her, and it appeased me. Why was I doing all this if not to shelter people and in a small way help them find safety? Wasn't that something my parents' money could buy? Besides, few things were more heavenly than falling asleep in sheets laundered by Madame Nouget. This I'd learned firsthand, and it made me happy to think of Remedios having her first fully relaxed sleep in weeks or months tonight, safe with all of us under one roof.

Chapter Four

When Remedios awoke the next morning to the scent of baking bread, for a moment—and how disorienting this was—she thought her father would knock on the door and tell her to get dressed, that they were going to visit one of the aqueducts he designed. The clear quality of the bright midday light took her right back to her childhood in Catalonia. There would be a question for her father, as there always was during construction, about his blueprints. His expertise would be needed on-site. He'd pull her out of school and bring her along for company on the train. He always did hate to travel alone. He'd give her a blueprint to copy to pass the time and then critique her sketches when she was done.

"Things are only beautiful if they are useful, and they are only useful if they are right," he would say while pointing out a wobbly line, a perspective skewed, a radius not quite symmetrical.

It was just a passing moment before she opened her eyes, before she came fully into her room at the Villa Air-Bel, in the south, in unoccupied France.

And then the rush of knowledge engulfed her, inescapable and coloring the day going forward. She couldn't linger. She shouldn't relax. She needed to leave France as soon as possible. The thought of being detained again was always with her.

And finally another thought, the one that held her in place. She'd be seeing Benjamin that day.

The smell of the bread mixed with the scent of clean sheets, bringing hope. A pale blue bathrobe with white piping lay folded on the armchair next to the fireplace.

She wrapped herself in the robe, heavy Provençal cotton made soft from washing, with *JL* embroidered in tiny white script on the breast pocket. Jacqueline must have come in and left it while she was sleeping, which was both touching in its thoughtfulness and disarmingly intrusive.

Remedios went downstairs from the third floor to a quiet house, searching for a place to wash up. Madame Nouget emerged from the kitchen.

"It's nearly lunchtime," Madame said kindly, practiced at dealing gently with the exhausted.

Remedios followed her into the kitchen and sat at the broad wooden table while Madame prepared her a cup of milky coffee, which was really a mix of chicory and herbs and acorns, as coffee had become precious months ago, and a piece of warm, damp, fresh bread spread with honey. Madame also directed the two young girls who worked chopping and washing. There wasn't much meat to work with given rationing, but it looked like Madame stretched what she had with homegrown produce. Her herbal coffee was hot, the bread excellent, and for a while Remedios felt soothed as she watched Madame run her scanty kitchen with knowledge and competence.

The two kitchen girls, their movements made efficient through repetition, worked together as an appealing team. Remedios had never cooked much—her time had been taken up with painting for so long, her meals taken in cafés, that the idea of doing something useful appealed.

"Can I do something?" Remedios asked. "To help you," she clarified.

Madame stopped, her eyebrows raised.

"You know how to cook, mademoiselle?" Madame Nouget wasn't harsh, but she was used to artistic types with few practical skills.

"I don't," Remedios said. "But I'm a quick learner."

Madame wiped her hands on a scrap of an old flour sack, neatly hemmed to do duty as a tea towel. "Well, if you're a quick learner, then maybe you should come foraging with me."

The two girls stopped their chopping and gave each other a knowing look.

Something about this spurred Remedios. "Yes. I'd like to."

"Every morning at seven, mademoiselle." Nouget looked at her out of the corner of her eye and added, "If you're not sleeping off the wine." She picked up a basket and headed into the garden.

Remedios was left with her coffee.

"You should go," one of the girls said quietly.

"It's a big honor," said the other. There was a hint of a smile on her face, as if she were teasing.

"I'm sure," Remedios said with a shrug.

The first one dropped her knife in exasperation and said in a hushed, rather awed voice, "She's a legend, you know. This"—she gestured around the room—"is what she can do amid rationing."

The other was nodding, and together they told her, with many interruptions and diversions, that they were all in the presence of a skilled master—that before the war the house had been filled with buckets of flowers, local and rare cheeses, starched linens, floors gleaming with beeswax.

"And even when the family left, she kept up her standards. Even in war."

They hinted that she had other talents as well.

Nouget came back then, her basket filled with greens, and began washing them at the sink.

Remedios pondered what she'd been told. "I'd like to contribute," she said finally. "I don't have money. I don't know how I'll stay." She felt tears spring to her eyes as she said it. Really, she was going to need to get a grip on herself, but she'd played brave for months now. In prison crying only brought the guard's mocking, and in the car with Mary Jane and Miriam she'd wanted to match their hearty courage.

Madame's face softened. "André and Varian have resources for people in exactly your spot. Varian's made a whole job of it. Now you come." She hustled Remedios out of her chair, the kitchen girls averting their eyes from the emotional display.

The only bathtub in the villa, zinc with swan's-neck faucets, was in the bathroom next to the kitchen. Madame handed over a fresh cake of verdant green olive oil soap de Marseilles. "Make it last," she said. "I don't have much more." And she left Remedios to an hour of piping-hot water and steam. Later, Remedios wouldn't think of occupying the tub for that long, but on her first day, she couldn't control herself. She gingerly lowered herself into the hot water with relief, with the release of being safe, and with the physical pleasure of bathing in clean water. The transforming water and the cleansing soap, the exhaustion after being in a state of siege all led to an unfurling as she fully gave herself over to tears, fists at her mouth, so as not to be overheard in the kitchen. Letting herself go, knowing she might not have another chance at this level of privacy, she cried until she was wrung out.

She crept back to her room wrapped in Jacqueline's robe, eyes red from crying and everything else red from scrubbing. Someone had lit a fire in the little fireplace with the marble mantel, her meager things unpacked by invisible hands and put away neatly in the armoire, her filthy clothes taken and presumably being brought back to life. The coat she'd hand-stitched, the nap brushed clean of grime, hung on a hook on the back of the door, and a quick hand in the pocket confirmed her tarot deck was still there.

She brought them out now. Sitting on the freshly made bed, the faded quilt tucked tightly. Today she shuffled them overhand, placed them on the eiderdown at the end of the bed, cut and pulled a card.

Temperance, a huge, white-robed angel poured water from one chalice to another. One bare foot in a stream, the other on solid land, with a bright sun shining in the background.

Permission and a rescue in that sparse room, a way out of the chaos she'd been living in, because how else did Mary Jane and Miriam find her among all the thousands evacuating Paris? They pulled up next to her as easily as if they'd spotted her on the Boul Mich. What was that, if not the intervention of an angel?

A soft knock on the door preceded Jacqueline leaning her head into the room. She'd somehow managed to pin little pieces of colored glass in her hair, her necklace of tiger claws gleaming. She looked part warrior, part ethereal angel, and a perfect companion for André Breton, the lion of surrealism.

While Jacqueline waited in the hall, Remedios dressed in the few clean clothes she'd rescued from the apartment in Paris. Then she followed Jacqueline down the stairs and through the enfilade of rooms.

"Puffy," Jacqueline said, ever the grooming perfectionist, patting under her own eye and looking sideways at Remedios.

"I didn't sleep well," Remedios lied as they entered the library.

The vaulted ceiling was covered in ancient frescoes of mythological scenes, and a long refectory table ran down the middle of the room with three chairs on either side. It looked like the sort of place where monks would illuminate sacred manuscripts. André had clearly claimed the room as his own, a pouch of his tobacco on the table next to an overflowing ashtray and the fug of pipe smoke in the air. He'd made himself as comfortable as an insect naturally burrowing into its preferred habitat. The Russian novelist and activist Victor Serge sat opposite, hunched and scribbling in his rushed, myopic way, as if he might be carted off to jail at any moment, even from a safe house in the South of France.

"I've sent the message boy to bring Benjamin back before Max and Madame Guggenheim get here," André said without looking up. The villa had yet to be outfitted with a telephone. "I heard you were awake and refreshed."

It gave her a sudden skip in her chest to hear Benjamin spoken of so casually. As if they'd just sent out for the newspapers or a quart of milk. Benjamin would be here soon.

Madame Nouget came in then and set up a platter of chicken liver pâté with chopped hard-boiled egg and toast points at one end of the table. One of her girls from the kitchen brought in a tray with wineglasses. They were prepping for Madame Guggenheim's arrival. As Madame Nouget fussed and arranged chervil around the plate, it dawned on Remedios that Madame Nouget was doing this to impress André. Jacqueline sensed it too and seemed amused and protective of the cook.

André uncorked the wine. Even in war, France would have her wine. Miriam polished the glasses with the hem of her blouse. Victor Serge looked up from his writing and took the first canapé off the plate.

More from wanting something to do than from any desire to help, Remedios picked up a glass and rubbed it with a napkin. Nouget frowned at her, Jacqueline smirked, and then Remedios heard footsteps on the red-waxed tiles behind her.

A wide and genuine smile lit Benjamin's face as he picked up his pace and came into the room, ignoring everyone's greeting and embracing Remedios in an all-enveloping hug. Leaning back to look at him, she felt the same zing running through her as when she first saw him years ago on the train platform at the Gare de Lyon in Paris.

She'd checked her lipstick twice that day as the train pulled into the station. A quick peek in her dented compact and then she blotted her lips on the back of her hand, a waxy open-mouth kiss that she'd rubbed into her already humming skin.

He'd been easy to spot on the train platform, a tall bald man who stood a full head above the travelers around him. New love can create a bright bubble of interiority, a private universe impenetrable to the world even at its most ugly. Benjamin's reserved facade gave away no notion of the inventiveness of his poems or his passions. Through the smoke and drear of that Paris platform, Benjamin radiated a sizzle of intellect covered over by the thinnest veneer of restraint. She always marveled that no one else could sense how thin that veneer was. Couldn't the people hurrying past them in their drab woolen coats see, like she did, that with the slightest tug they might expose the passion that lay beneath his rumpled facade of control?

At the villa now he looked thinner, with darker circles under the eyes, and his reserved aura remained intact despite the hardships he'd endured. Or maybe not, because he leaned down and kissed her full on the mouth with an uncharacteristic display of luxurious affection that made the kiss that much more delicious.

Not only had war and evacuation made André and Jacqueline her friends, but for a moment it had smoothed over every hurt between her and Benjamin, that night Oscar smashed the glass, everything. He somehow remained what he'd always been, a tall intense man with a private fire that burned only for her.

Now, in this beautiful villa in the South of France, they found each other again as the sound of a car rumbled up the drive, delivering Max Ernst and Peggy Guggenheim, and someone offered Remedios a glass of wine. Benjamin had been in prison. She'd been interrogated. She'd fled Paris. He'd escaped the camps. All of this had transpired, but in that single moment none of it seemed to matter. Her lover was in her arms again, a long journey complete.

IX

NINE OF PENTACLES—
Peggy Guggenheim

A woman in a walled garden wears a splendid robe, a hooded falcon resting on her arm. Pentacles, symbol of material and earthly abundance, surround her, as do lush plants. She is immersed in luxury and abundance. However, her falcon, a symbol of the spirit and the soul, is hooded, artificially blinded. This woman's bird does not soar. She is alone in her luxury, walled off, and blind. She could be a woman who has everything in the world but love. She could be a woman who has pursued the exterior world of the material to the exclusion of knowing her interior self. She could be a woman who needs to free herself from something so she can truly fly. The Nine of Pentacles is an invitation to consider your blind spots and a gentle reminder to live a fully integrated life.

I could feel the Villa Air-Bel vibrating with excitement when Max and I stepped out on the terrace. But there's often a sense of excitement before a big payday, isn't there?

"The American heiress Guggenheim!" André Breton stepped forward with a clasp of his hands to embrace me. He ignored the look I gave him. Max smirked next to me.

I'd met Max Ernst in Paris only briefly. He'd been in love with Leonora Carrington, and I ran into them sometimes at Oscar Sanchez's parties. A natural salesman, that Oscar. He dealt in Max's lesser works, little collages and sketches. I still have a few of them. He also tried to sell me some rather suspect art that I never got near, no matter how low the prices.

But Max was with *me* that day in Marseilles, and brought me to the Villa Air-Bel, yet again, in hopes I'd buy more art. As André confirmed with his little nickname for me, they were all in on it.

It's not like I didn't know how Max viewed me, but I was powerless when it came to him. He was long and lean with icy eyes. Really his skull was probably perfectly formed under all that gorgeous white hair. The genius inside was most appealing to me, though. I guess I have a type. The only thing my lovers—Samuel Beckett, Yves Tanguy, Constantin Brancusi, and now Max—have in common is their genius. Well, that and a certain emotional reserve; some might call it disdain. I've had enough psychoanalysis to know that I choose challenging men. Challenging through his silence, that's my very German Max.

But I couldn't begrudge Max his show that day. The Nazis had banned him, putting him on that list of theirs, along with Picasso and so many others. Idiots. Didn't they realize it was a badge of honor to be called a degenerate? But it meant the galleries holding Max's work in Paris wouldn't be able to show what they had. It meant his prices tanked. It meant he wouldn't have money coming in for the foreseeable future.

Hence me. Hence the vernissage. Hence my checkbook.

There was an additional buzz in the villa today, a celebration that I quickly learned had nothing to do with me. Another artist had found her way to the villa and was being sheltered. Remedios Varo was her name—a Spanish painter who had been living in Paris with Benjamin Péret, which should have made me like her.

But it was Max's face when they told him she was here that soured me.

"She's here? She made it?" His reserved Germanic demeanor fell away, and his smile was pure joy as he said the thing that I'd associate with Remedios from here on out. "If only I could tell Leonora."

Max lived with Leonora in the countryside before he was arrested and imprisoned for being a German. After he escaped, he'd gone back to their farmhouse to find her gone before he'd been arrested yet again. He'd been released during the chaos of the armistice and circled back to the farmhouse a second time, where he managed to pack up their paintings and leave with them in the middle of the night. I'd even bought one of Leonora's paintings in a fit of . . . what exactly? Wanting to keep Max close?

Leonora seemed to hover over us wherever we went, and now her friend was here. Leonora, it seemed, could not be escaped.

"Do you know where she is? What happened to her?" Remedios asked Max. And how I hated the assumption—the assumption that Max was the repository for all news of Leonora.

"She left a note in the farmhouse saying she'd gone to Spain and to meet her there," Max said in a lowered voice. "I haven't been able to find anyone who's been in touch with her."

"I hope she's all right," Remedios said, and from the tone of her voice I figured they must have been quite close. "I'm so sorry."

"Thank you," Max said, and I noted the intimacy of him accepting condolences on Leonora's behalf. "Oh, you should know Remedios," he said, turning to me as an afterthought, suddenly remembering I was there, that I was the reason for this little soiree in the first place. "She's a great friend of Leonora's. They used to study the tarot together in Paris."

"Study is a strong word for it," Remedios said.

She had thick red hair, wide-set light brown eyes, and a prominent nose that she held with a confidence that yet again had me rethinking the surgery I'd had on mine at age nineteen. I'd never liked my nose, and liked it even less now that it'd been butchered. But on Remedios, her wide eyes and large nose made her look like a fawn, and quite a self-possessed one, as her gaze didn't waver as she shook my hand. She had an outward-going energy that met you. Young to be so self-possessed, then again I thought everyone was self-possessed in those days, or at least more so than I was. Benjamin hovered about her, protective and smitten.

"Tarot. Are you a fortune-teller?" I asked, in a slightly teasing tone.

I could see my comment displeased Max, but Remedios only smiled good-naturedly. "Not at all. I follow my curiosity where it leads."

"The tarot is a source of the random and unknowable, much like a woman," André said, joining us. André liked to be the center of any gathering. "The archetypal, the mystical, the symbolic—all these things are of interest, aren't they, Peggy?"

Something like the tarot was just the sort of slightly silly thing André would champion and then imbue with meaning. Yet if I'd learned anything from André, and from Max, it was to be open-minded.

"But you must bring your cards out sometime and give me a reading. Give readings for us all," I said, trying to sound expansive.

With that they all fell silent.

Max sideways-hugged Remedios up into his armpit in an awkward show of protective chumminess. "Did you manage to bring anything with you?" he asked her.

"My cards? Oh yes," she said.

"I mean paintings to show. With me."

We all fell silent, and from the look on her face, I wondered if she'd ever shown her work before. If not, this would be quite a first public exhibition alongside Max Ernst and in front of André Breton, not to mention the others.

Because we'd managed to form quite a well-rounded party for the afternoon. The Romanian painter Jacques Hérold was there with a glass in hand, nibbling on toast points. The Cuban-Chinese painter Wifredo Lam, who had designed posters and leaflets for the Republican cause in Spain, had arrived wrapped in someone else's summer-weight coat, two sizes too big for him. Victor Serge was joined by his Italian mistress Laurette Séjourné, who also insisted on calling me "the American heiress Guggenheim" until André quietly took her aside and told her it was just a joke and to knock it off.

I felt a little sorry for Remedios then.

"Oh, please bring them out," I said, hoping to sound encouraging. "I so enjoy looking at new things. And Max always knows what I like."

She let my request hang there for a moment in the bright southern sun, and I realized that rather than encouraging her, I had forced her hand. She left without another word through the French doors flaked with crackled varnish and into the villa to get her paintings.

The housekeeper brought out a bottle of Lillet that she placed on a grimy iron table.

Remedios was back before the drinks were all served, with two small canvases. She must have run up the stairs.

"The only things that fit in my suitcase," she said. I was reminded that she'd just fled Paris, that she was likely still exhausted.

"Put them here," Max said, giving her prime place on a wide tree next to the largest of his paintings.

Her work was small, finely wrought, and clearly effortful. An empty corset covered in white vines and thorns lay on its side, as if its wearer had just discarded it.

"Wonderful," I said. "Just marvelous." It was the type of filler praise I often offered while thinking. Some works needed time to grow on me, and some I needed explained to me.

I stepped back, and she stepped forward. "What's the title?" I asked.

She seemed lost for a minute, in reverie, as if she too were seeing her work for the first time. "*Memories of the Valkyrie*," she said quietly. She had technical brush skills, that was certain.

"And this?" I asked. It was smaller. A little jewel of a painting of eyeglasses on a table looking into a set of glass eyes, the background with the flat horizon of a de Chirico. Both glasses and glass eyes were filled with the taut intelligence of a question. If the Valkyrie was ice, this painting was fire. They made a pleasing pair together. The harsh midday sun served them well as it brought out the small nuances and texture.

"How much?" I asked. "For the pair." Thinking if I bought them both, she'd give me a bargain.

She looked at Max, flummoxed, and I realized she had no idea how to price her work. My heart picked up as it always did at the thought of a bargain. Perhaps I'd be her first sale.

André came forward then, and I thought he might help offer a price. He glanced at both pieces.

"Keep painting, little one," he said, patting his hand on her shoulder. "Keep painting."

I took a second look then. Was her work too student-like? Despite his arrogance, André really did have impeccable taste, the best.

Maybe I needed to start focusing on quality. Maybe less of these new unknown artists and a little more of the old guard to add gravitas and heft to my collection. I'd asked the Louvre to store my pieces in Paris before I left. The director laughed in my face, called my paintings a bunch of junk, and then, as only a Frenchman can, propositioned me. Needless to say, I turned the narrow-minded snob down. But the nightmare of stashing the collection in a friend's barn near Grasse had proven burdensome. It started me thinking about rounding out my collection a bit.

"You really are getting quite good," André said to Remedios, puffing his pipe. And that seemed to be the final verdict. He took my elbow and steered me toward some new collages by Max.

Months later, when Max and I are safely in New York, he'll get a desperate telegram from Varian Fry asking for money to get Benjamin and Remedios out of Marseilles. They will be the last ones left in the villa and funds will be low.

"Well?" Max will simply place the telegram on my desk. We will have been fighting. The arguing will start right after we marry, and I'll feel that I can't get anything right, that he can barely tolerate me, that he is counting the minutes until he can get away.

So this request will be welcome, at least here is something I can do that might please my new husband.

"I've always said Benjamin's very surrealist." I'll nod.

Then I'll cable enough money for the both of them to escape, hoping that it actually makes it.

I always regretted that André swayed me from buying Remedios's paintings that day in the garden.

CHAPTER FIVE

Remedios lit her own cigarette. The chatter from the crowded tables in the port café encroached on her thoughts, making it hard to concentrate on what Benjamin and André were saying. Around her refugees and natives alike discussed the only things that really mattered in Marseilles—papers, visas, ship bookings, and waiting.

She lit another cigarette before she'd finished the first.

Benjamin stopped her hand as she brought the freshly lit smoke to her mouth. "What is it?" Even after their time apart, he was alert to the smallest changes in her emotional weather. He picked up her half-smoked cigarette still smoldering in the messy glass ashtray and raised his eyebrows as if to ask, "You're leapfrogging cigarettes now?"

She shook her head at him. "Tired."

"What? Is everyone tired now?" André said peevishly as he poured the last of the wine into his own glass, draining the bottle. Benjamin and André seemed determined to re-create the atmosphere of the Café de Flore right here on the terrace of this port café. They'd re-create it in a cardboard box on the side of the road if they had to.

Benjamin watched her for one minute more, as if reassuring himself of something, and then turned back to address André's new, and apparently genuine, desire to hold a séance at the villa if only he could find a psychic.

In response Benjamin stabbed at the air with the half-smoked cigarette, condemning Victorian-era superstitious practices and defending chaos.

In Paris she'd sat by the hour, mouth open, listening to André and Benjamin talk. She'd felt that she was, just for a moment, in the white-hot center of the universe and nothing of interest was happening anywhere else in the world. It was why people came to the cafés and requested a table near André's—to hear him speak about any thought that came into his head, to eavesdrop essentially.

But today she felt like a barnacle on the hull of these men's intellects, sometimes far out to sea and sometimes lulling listlessly in the harbor. Hoping to distract herself, she dug her tarot deck out of her coat pocket.

In Paris she and Leonora would sometimes slip a card out at discreet intervals during afternoons like this, each showing the other what she drew as a new way to think about the ideas swirling around their heads. They'd excuse themselves to go to the powder room or quickly duck into an alley while André and Benjamin walked ahead of them.

Today, she figured André and Benjamin were so absorbed in what the other was saying that they wouldn't notice as she slipped the cards out of her coat pocket and under the table. She untied the pale grosgrain ribbon and slid them out of their pouch.

"What've you got there?" André asked, leaning over. She looked up to see both men focusing on her.

She brought the cards above table height and began a deft overhand shuffle—dropping the cards from one hand into the other.

"May I?" André placed his palm out faceup, a demand.

She reluctantly placed the cards in his hand.

"I've seen these. A lot of garbage." He packed the cards together and then cocked his arm back as if to hurl them into the nearby water.

"Don't!" Remedios reached over as Benjamin braced his friend's forearm.

"We're in the birthplace of the tarot. And this is the deck you choose?" Andre lightly tossed the cards on the table where they landed in a jumble. "The Marseilles is the deck I prefer. Descended straight from the royal courts of France via Egypt. Or so they say. This other one you use is only fit for the trash can."

Maybe it was irritation at the self-satisfied cocoon André seemed to walk around in that made her slide her plate aside, tidy the cards, and fan them out facedown on the white marble table. "Pick one," she said, a hint of defiance in her voice. The look Benjamin gave her was half pride, half panic.

"They're really more like a toy, these cards," André said with a dismissive wave at them. "Shall I call you Lady Esmeralda?" He reached over quickly and automatically to choose a card. Remedios grasped his wrist, stopping him.

"No," she said. "Like you believe."

André smirked. "Oui, femme sorcière." He re-chose with care, sliding a card facedown across the table. Remedios flipped it over, the Hierophant reversed.

André nodded and then swept a hand palm up between them as if to say, "The stage is yours." The card showed a priest on a throne holding a stylized scepter in one hand, two bald acolytes facing him.

Remedios felt a surge of power run through her. She'd be telling André something for once, not the other way around.

"The Hierophant sits on his throne of tradition and formalized learning. When he is right side up, he is all about structures and hierarchies. His two supplicants attend him and hang on his pronouncements. When he is reversed, he becomes a rebel character, subverting accepted thought. A reversed Hierophant turns the world upside down, not just for himself, but so others can see things differently. Your desire to get at the subconscious, to turn everything on its head, calls the known universe into question. The reversed Hierophant turns learning inside out."

It was an accurate read; even André would have to admit that. Benjamin slowly, solemnly winked at her.

"But that is very basic," André said. "What does it mean for me? What does it mean for my life?"

"It is you," she said. "It is your life."

"And here's you," he said as he chose a card quickly and flipped it over—the Empress. Remedios considered the Empress a powerful creator—a female paragon of sexuality and fecundity, Venus incarnate and the goddess of harvest. When she came up, Madame Cherugi said to consider pleasure and abundance and how open we are to those energies in life. But Remedios didn't aspire to be some lady bountiful, man seducer, procreator. She was an artist, same as Benjamin, same as André, really.

"That's not really me," she said. "Not at all."

"Don't sell yourself short. Of course it is, or at least you have the potential, little one. You're actually quite appealing, you know?" Why did André always tether women back to sex, really it was so tiresome and small, she thought. For all his cutting-edge theories, his ideas about women were conventional, embarrassingly so. She had yet to get him to admit the contradiction in this.

Benjamin sat smoking his cigarette and observing them as if watching a play, as if his best friend and his lover didn't concern him personally.

André always made her feel like this, like a girl, like a novice, un-heard and unchanging. And Benjamin was always silent, whether out of agreement or laziness, Remedios could never be sure.

"These cards, like little cartoons if you ask me." André swished them around in a circle on the table. "Makes me want to make my own deck." He leaned back. "What do you think?" He pointed at Benjamin.

Benjamin shrugged. "It makes more sense than a séance, if that's what you're asking."

He pointed to Remedios.

"Different suits, I would think." It never benefited anyone to hesitate in front of André, who prized the automatic above all else.

"And what would you recommend?" he asked, focusing on her as a person for the first time all afternoon, it seemed.

"Flames, not wands. Dreams, obviously. Knowledge. And wheels." She'd learned to give him a quick answer or nothing.

"Not wheels, revolution," Benjamin said.

"Better," André said, pointing his pipe at his friend. "We'll ask Max to help illustrate, of course. I think the project will appeal to him. Victor Brauner would be good too."

Remedios was silent, flipping through cards. They were talking about creating something—painting and drawing it into life. She was still too daunted to speak up, to suggest that she be involved, to breach the impenetrable wall of theories and knowledge that Benjamin and André built around themselves.

"Oscar Sanchez might help," she said.

"Remedios," Benjamin said lowly. She looked up at his tone, thinking he was objecting to her mentioning Oscar. The night he'd thrown the glass remained unmentioned between them.

Instead, a pair of gendarmes had entered the café, passing by some tables, stopping at others to check papers. One of the terms of agreement between the Nazis and the Vichy government was that the French state must "surrender on demand" anyone, citizen of any country, whom the Nazis were interested in for any reason. It meant that the Germans made the French police conduct raids to find potential degenerates, refugees of all types, and anyone who the Germans could argue didn't belong in Marseilles.

André made it a habit to sit at the back in any café, the better to watch who came to his table to pay homage and who didn't. That day in Marseilles, Remedios was glad for the habit.

"Go out the back, now," André said calmly. "Into the alley."

"Now," Benjamin said, scooting his chair so that his back was to the police in an attempt to shield her from view.

As a foreign-born refugee, Remedios was always in danger during one of these inspections. Her Spanish citizenship marked her out as an assumed Republican, and therefore a communist. She'd been interrogated once. She didn't plan on being jailed again.

If she got up casually and pretended she was going to the bathroom, the police wouldn't notice her. Benjamin and André stayed seated. Despite their notoriety, as citizens of France their papers were in order. By staying seated, they called less attention to Remedios.

She rose slowly, put her hands in her pockets.

"Go," she heard Benjamin say. "Now."

She looked back for only a moment to see a policeman weaving through the tables.

"Arrêtez!" he called as she turned to the back door. "Mademoiselle, stop!"

She broke into a run then, as did others who had gotten up at the same time. No doubt they all faced similar problems with their papers. They sprinted through the back door and fanned out in the alley, hoping to disperse the police. It was just her luck that one of the gendarmes followed her, whistle in mouth.

Shoppers going about their commerce cleared her path, paused to watch her run, some even cheered her on, but none intervened.

The crowded streets were covered in bumpy cobblestones, barely wide enough for a car. The fortified walls of the old city had withstood more than the world's current tip into madness, more than one lady being chased through the streets. They wouldn't, however, survive the Nazis, who months later will level the neighborhood with dynamite when the Vichy government falls.

She was slowing, her chest cramping, but facing certain arrest, thoughts of her interrogations in Paris gave her a second wind. That's when she passed a printer's shop, one of the few still open in a city known for its exceptional printing houses.

She ducked in, wheezing, looking for a place to hide.

"Be with you in a minute," came a cheerful, unseen voice.

A piece of old fabric printed with a pattern of sprigged mignonette hung in a doorway separating the front of the shop from the back. Remedios ducked behind it.

A woman in a smart wool suit looked up surprised but understood the situation in a glance.

"In here," she said, opening a closet door, paneled into the wall.

"Madame, merci," Remedios said, but the vendeuse put a finger to her painted lips as they heard the bells above the front door jingle.

"With you in a minute," she called in the same chipper voice, betraying nothing as she gently closed the closet without making the latch click.

Remedios heard boots and then the voice of what could only be the policeman.

"A woman ran in here."

"I wish, monsieur," the vendeuse said, a smile in her voice. "Business is slow. No one needs printing right now. But perhaps the commandant might?"

He walked directly toward the back, and Remedios heard him shove the curtain aside.

"Monsieur, is this not still France? You come barging in here . . ."

"Yes, this is France, or have you forgotten? In the window you have a picture of President Pétain and a photo of Admiral François Darlan on either side of a copy of *Les Misérables*."

"Ah, a man of literature. One finds so few of them nowadays," Madame said coquettishly.

Silence. Remedios tried not to breathe, her heartbeat throbbing in her ears. She heard his boots turn a circle around the room and then pause in front of the door to the closet, mere inches from discovering her.

"Despite what you might think, we're not all heathens, madame," he said, as if he was speaking directly through the door to Remedios. "We know the plight of many. But when they run, and run in public, we have no choice but to give chase. It's better if they let us do our jobs and look at their papers. It is then we can make decisions. We are not so heartless as some may think. We are still Frenchmen after all."

He paused a minute more. She could hear him breathing after their run through the streets, and she braced for the door to be flung open, papers demanded. But then she heard his boots walk toward the front of the store.

"Be careful of the messages you are sending, madame. Au revoir."

And with that the bell above the door rang again as he left the shop.

Remedios waited in that black space, and when her eyes adjusted she saw neatly stacked shelves of boxes of playing cards embossed with gold foil, marbleized backs with tight paisley patterns or stylized grids. She heard heels clicking on the wooden floor, and then the door opened, the light momentarily blinding.

Coming into the room, framed posters and billets hung on the walls showcasing the printer's work and creating the atmosphere of a showroom mixed with a bookstore.

Standing there, Remedios felt she was back in Paris in the little shop that sold Benjamin's chapbooks and her sketches.

"These are beautiful," she said. Perhaps the shop needed an artist to illustrate billets or design posters.

She was about to offer her services, when on a low shelf she saw medieval-looking illustrations in primary colors and the flowing script on a box—*Tarot de Marseilles*.

The shopkeeper was smart to be discreet with them. The tarot was potentially revealing, uncontrollable, and most often a tool of women. All things that both repulsed and enticed the Nazis, it would be reckless to display them where a German officer might stroll by and see them in the window.

"Someone just mentioned these to me."

The vendeuse clapped her hands once. "I knew it! I can always tell when someone is called to the cards."

"I have a different deck," Remedios said, realizing she'd left her cards in the café and hoping Benjamin would save them before the police confiscated them or André threw them into the Mediterranean.

"Here, we are famous for the Marseilles deck." Madame took the box from Remedios, popped open the top, and spilled out the brightly colored cards on a display table. "I'm not surprised you prefer the Rider Waite." The vendeuse reached down off a low shelf and brought out a crisp, new box of the cards Remedios recognized. "Since you are an artist and all."

Remedios hadn't mentioned that she painted, hadn't asked for work yet. "What gave me away?"

"My family has been printing tarot cards here for the last three hundred years," the shop owner said, ignoring the question. "Give or take a few. Shall we see which deck wants to work with you? I'm Madame Carvon, by the way." She offered a well-manicured hand, and Remedios admired the heavy gold rings on nearly every finger—one a circle of leaves, one an enormous ram's head, one a gleaming pearl, one a signet with an indecipherable scrolled monogram. This last one, old gold and finely engraved, reminded Remedios of Leonora. Not that Leonora wore much jewelry, but it was the sort of thing that looked like it would belong to her. Leonora would have loved Madame's shop. Madame took the Marseilles deck and placed it on the drafting table facedown next to the Rider Waite deck. "Try and see."

Remedios picked up the Rider Waite deck and shuffled.

"As I'm sure you know, the first twenty-two cards of the deck make up the Major Arcana, or the revolutionary journey of the soul," Madame Carvon said. "From the Fool and his divine beginning to the

World when a sequence is fulfilled. Now, shuffle like this," she said, picking up the Marseilles cards and sliding them over each other end to end, from one hand to another. "So they all stay upright. Like life, tarot is difficult enough without having to deal with the reversals."

"I thought reversals meant the opposite of the meaning when it's right side up."

"Can be. Can also mean something is out of reach but about to come forward. Can mean something has just been present and is now receding. In any event, I find reversals less useful than the meanings of the upright cards. The four suits, as you know, are similar to playing cards—cups representing emotion, flow, and the heart; pentacles representing the material world, the physical, and the body; wands representing fire, creativity, and sexuality; and swords representing intellect, thought, and the brain. These are the Minor Arcana, and they speak to the specific and transcendent along the journey of life."

As Remedios shuffled in the new awkward way Madame Carvon had shown her, she tried to think of a good spread. "One card for now, one for the past, and one for the future."

Madame's heavily ringed hand formed a fist on the table. "Is that what you really want to know?" She opened her fist, waggling her hand in a questioning motion.

Remedios took a breath. As she was beginning to learn, the quality of the question related almost directly to the quality of the answer. Benjamin came to her mind. "One for the situation, the left for what's influencing it, the right for where it's headed."

Madame pursed her lips in a doubtful little moue and said, "Better."

Remedios handed Madame Carvon the shuffled deck and Madame fanned the cards out facedown on the table. Remedios took a breath, centering herself, keeping Benjamin in her mind as her hand hovered over the cards, asking them to work with her, seeing which ones called to her.

"Bon," Madame Carvon said quietly.

Remedios slid three cards out: the Sun, the Two of Cups, and the King of Swords, in a line from left to right.

"The Sun on the left shows you were meant to shine, to be seen, to radiate out the nature of yourself. It is safe to do that now, to be seen by all."

"After being chased by the police?" Remedios said. "I would prefer to hide."

"Not so literally," Madame said with a little cluck in her voice. "You have been hiding your light under a bushel." She pointed to the card on the far right. "Perhaps this is the problem—the King of Swords, an older man who surrounds you. What?" Madame asked, seeing the look on Remedios's face.

"I always get that card in relation to him, mon amour."

"That is his signifier then. He's quite rigid, isn't he? But in some ways, not so much," she said a bit slyly as she pointed to the middle card. The Two of Cups. Two lovers facing each other, sharing a cup between them. "You think this is a card about him," she said, pointing to the King. "But it's not. It's a card about you. About union with your true self."

Remedios tilted her head to the side, considering.

"In your work specifically," Madame continued. "In your painting. You have not worked since you came here to Marseilles."

"Do the cards tell you that?"

"No, I don't need the cards for that. No one can work right now unless it is working to leave. But you are getting ready for a time of great production. I can't tell for what purpose, but you have lots to say." She flipped the stack of remaining cards over. "Let's see what's at the base of the pack. The Four of Pentacles." A man sat gripping a pentacle in a tight embrace, each foot resting on a pentacle and one crowning him. "You have been stifling yourself for so long that you risk cutting off access to a part of yourself, like a tourniquet too tight and left too long."

"Which part have I been stifling?"

"The artistic part. The flowing part."

"I sketch daily." Though she'd had to scrounge materials, using newspapers and magazines before Max and André cut them up for collages.

"That is your technical skill. Here." She pointed to the Two of Cups, the man with a cup. "He represents your skill, your training. But she"—she pointed to the woman receiving his cup—"she is the artistic spark and spiritual explorations. This card is calling you to a union of the two. When you do"—she snapped her fingers—"a fusion, a joining."

Madame Carvon leaned over and slipped the card into the pocket of Remedios's skirt. "I carry certain cards when they call to me." Madame's alert face scanned Remedios's features. "To call it into existence. With other cards, in other circumstances, it gives protection or provides guidance, and sometimes it is a goal to steer toward."

"Thank you," Remedios said. "For the reading. For the insights."

She readied herself to go. Her father's words came to her—leaving a bookstore empty-handed was the mark of a true philistine. "How much do I owe you for the reading? And maybe there's a book I can buy. . . ."

This last seemed to offend Madame. "It's not exactly the sort of thing you can learn from a book." She gathered up the Marseilles deck and put it back in its box.

"How much for lessons then?" Remedios asked.

"For you? I'm sure we can work something out. I always have work for a skilled artist." Madame gave the box a crisp tap on the top with a red lacquered nail. "There is knowledge behind the symbols—that, I can teach you. I can explain the traditional meanings of the different cards. What is more difficult to explain is how they fit together with each other in a reading. There's no agreed-upon meaning when two or more cards are put in relation to one another. That is the part that comes from you. Linking the cards together is where your knowing comes in." She handed the deck to Remedios.

"They're beautiful cards," Remedios said. "But I prefer my deck." She handed the Marseilles tarot back to Madame. "The Rider Waite speaks more to me. I've always admired the skill of whoever painted it."

"I can't say I blame you for preferring the Rider Waite. The artist who created it is from England, did you know? Pixie Colman Smith is her name, a woman with the ability to see the unseen, to access different worlds, and entranced in a deeply psychic life, as you can tell from the quality of the illustrations." Madame paused as if considering something and then pushed the Marseilles deck back into Remedios's hands. "Come back tomorrow and we'll start your lessons. Bring both decks with you and we'll begin. Consider it a gift."

THE MAGICIAN—
Pamela "Pixie" Colman Smith

The Magician is the ultimate alchemist, transforming all that the world has to offer into a unique creation. Each suit in the tarot—cups, swords, pentacles, and wands—awaits him on his workbench and serves as his raw materials, his prima materia. He is a conduit between the potential of the world as seen in his left hand pointed to the ground and the realm of the divine as seen in his right hand raised to the sky. The infinity symbol over his head shows his limitlessness. He has the skill and knowledge to manifest works of great power and great art into the world. If the Magician comes to you in a reading, he is a harbinger of pure potential and transformation. He is a reminder that all of us carry within us the power of the alchemist's vessel.

I cross the dusty street against the flow of traffic, lift my skirt to avoid a flattened horse dung, and pause for a trolley to pass. I can hear my father's voice in my head.

"Pixie," for he always called me Pixie, "London is filled with filth and hurry."

Father preferred trees to trolleys, and I can't blame him. The City is an olfactory experience, and scents have become intrusive of late, assaulting me up my nose and sinus passages until they lodge in my brain and linger behind my eyes. I can almost see them, and I've taken to trying to paint them, hoping for release, that by making them manifest I might transform them from a vision behind the eyes into the tangible on paper.

Just last night I'd had the image of a magician in my head, one hand raised to the heavens calling down divine inspiration, the other pointed to the ground, channeling up the sense experiences of the world. The vision persisted for so long that the only way to rid myself of it and get a little sleep was to paint it. I'd put a few finishing flourishes with pen and ink on the watercolor this morning and then put it in my portfolio to show to Arthur Waite.

I'm late for a meeting with Arthur, head of the splinter faction of the Golden Dawn. He's asked me to meet him at the Fleet Street tavern he prefers. It's grimy and dark, and he used to come here with Yeats before all the bickering started.

I suspect that's what Arthur wants to discuss with me. He is breaking off from the Hermetic Order of the Golden Dawn, which has always been a society for the study of esoteric knowledge—the kabbalah, astrology, alchemy, and the like. At least that's how William Butler Yeats described it to me when he first invited me to a meeting.

"Come with me already," Yeats said, and because he was famous and a poet and my friend, I said I'd go. He introduced me to that group of ritualists and ceremonialists—all very strict and routinized with their rites and formalities. I enjoyed it. I guess I did. But it wasn't what I'd been expecting. It may seem naive, but I'd been searching for access to knowledge, had hoped for a revelation of mystery, at least some direction for my own magical inquiries. Instead I'd found a rather uptight group of former clubmen who'd managed to turn the whole thing into a hierarchy. What was that aphorism about British men? If stranded on an island, the first thing they'd do is form clubs and begin excluding each other.

I haven't quit the Golden Dawn. It would be too socially awkward to leave, but I don't let it eat up my time either. Lately I've needed to focus on making money.

Arthur hinted at the potential for some work in his note asking to meet, otherwise I would have ignored it. Arthur has always been prosperous and has used his bourgeois lucre to fund all sorts of speculative endeavors. But now I wonder if our meeting is only to get me here so he can lobby me to join his new reformed group.

I suspect Arthur's ideas for reformation of the Dawn are less about the hierarchy and more about prohibiting certain carnal rituals that members like Aleister Crowley have angled to introduce into the proceedings of late. Something, I know, Arthur would not approve of at all. He hates Crowley. And while I'm no prude, I too steer clear of Crowley and his fascination with sex.

I readjust the leather portfolio under my arm. Arthur is familiar with my watercolors, so bringing samples is superfluous. Working on stage sets for months has me neglecting my personal art and leaves me feeling that I must prove my artistic credentials, even to an old friend.

Each stage set I design is more elaborate than the last, which is why the work keeps coming. I was already under contract when dear Yeats came wanting sets for his new play, *Where There Is Nothing*. I refused, saying I was already engaged. But then he clasped my hand, that forelock hanging down over his polished glasses, and said, "You alone seem to understand what I want in a design, Pixie." Yeats gets the producers to pay me well, so there's that too. For this I put up with his tight timelines and his last-minute changes. It's left me with little time for my personal work.

Arthur's already seated when I arrive, at a table practically in the window that he's chosen because everyone will see us. He's ordered us each a pint of lager, though I don't care for beer. I settle in anyway and take a sip, not wanting to reject a gift from a potential patron and glad that I won't have to buy my own drink.

"Have you seen Yeats?" he asks with no preamble.

"No," I lie. Arthur has never been able to hide the petty jealousies he keeps under lock and key. They pressurize there and escape under speed, so they can't be modulated with manners.

"I hear he's back in Ireland now until his next play opens," he says.

I merely nod, let Arthur think Yeats is out of town. Maybe it will grant him some peace.

I unwind the shawl around my neck and wrap it around my shoulders. Dressing in a hurry this morning I'd twisted a turban over my hair, slung together a neckful of messy amber beads, and wrapped myself up in the shawl I'd fallen asleep under last night.

"It smells in here." I pull the shawl over my nose. Cheese and old beer mixed with the vetiver of men's cologne create a haze almost guaranteed to provoke a headache.

"You can see smells now?" Arthur asks with annoyance. My synesthesia, my ability to see sound, was the topic of a Golden Dawn meeting last year and is the basis for nearly all my paintings. As far as I know, Arthur has never been the subject of a Golden Dawn meeting.

"No, but that doesn't mean it doesn't smell." I release my shoulders, and my shawl drops. I'm wishing I'd suggested somewhere else to meet—a tearoom where we might have had something warm instead of beer. I trace the scars in the worn oak table, thinking of lemon curd and clotted cream, wondering how soon I can leave without seeming impolite.

Arthur chats to me about acquaintances, people and places in common.

"So," I say, hunching down in my chair. I wish Arthur would get on with it. I'm already short and making myself appear small has always given me a certain feeling of protection and power, strangely enough. "You have me here," I say, almost in a crouch.

"Yes, quite," he says, straightening. "I had an idea, and in thinking it through I realized you're just the person to help me."

I brace for the recruiting to his side in the drama that is the breakup of the Golden Dawn.

"I've recently obtained some papers, from a dealer in esoteric texts."

Arthur's library is famously large, his collection of occult texts famously complete. This is not at all what I was expecting.

"They originally came from the back of a little shop in Marseilles and have passed through a few hands. I bought them at auction for an extortionate price. Marseilles being the birthplace of the tarot as we know it, this pile of notes has proven most illuminating. The most complete work I've ever seen on the different aspects of the Major Arcana, filled with knowledge not previously known."

The few meetings that still brought me to the Dawn were the discussions of the tarot. Arthur had been studying the Major Arcana ever since the British Museum put its recent acquisition of the Sola Busca tarot on display last year. We'd gone together to see it as it dated from 1490. And while Arthur was intrigued by the major cards, the deck was the first set with illustrated minor cards. In the Marseilles tarot, which we all use, the minors looked like regular playing cards.

"Not Egyptian in origin at all, despite what Monsieur Court de Gébelin said all those years ago." Arthur becomes expansive under our shared interest. Grateful this meeting is not to talk Golden Dawn politics, I brighten and unfold.

"The Greek link back to Pythagorean numerology and Euclidean geometry? A bunch of nonsense," he says.

"But the universal laws, the rule of seven, projective geometry?"

"Pythagoras still has things to say about that, but these papers really confirm that the Marseilles tarot as we know it evolved out of the French and Italian courts, most likely as a collective base of knowledge over many years and influenced by Renaissance theories on alchemy. And I'm now in possession of a set of notes that will illuminate the hazier aspects of the Major Arcana. That will revolutionize it, rectify it."

I imagined Arthur leaving the Sola Busca exhibit and marshaling his book vendors to send out their antennae in search of rare books or documents about the cards. When Arthur follows a thread down a trail of research there's little stopping him, and he has deep enough pockets to be as thorough as he wishes. What must that be like? Clearly he's made significant discoveries if he wants to issue his own deck. The idea immediately appeals, even as it sounds like an overwhelming task.

"And so I was thinking," Arthur continues. "I need someone to do the illustrations for the deck. Under my guidance and scholarship, of course."

Now seems like the right time to slide the folder of sketches and watercolors across the table.

"What does 'under your guidance' mean?" I ask.

He opens the folder and flips through my work. Without looking up he says, "I'd leave the court cards completely to you." Each suit in the Minor Arcana has court cards, much like a playing deck—page, knight, queen, king, along with an ace.

"That's seventy-eight cards, seventy-eight different paintings," I say.

"Seventy-nine if you count the back of the deck. You'll want to design the back of the deck, won't you?" he says, picking up the watercolor I did just last night and sliding it across the table. "Of course I'd pay you."

I blush at this. Is it because he's called me out for being concerned with money? Well, isn't he too? Isn't that how he amassed his riches, by paying attention to such things?

Or is it because he knows how close I live to penury, despite all my work? It's evident to everyone, isn't it? Wrapped as I am in threadbare shawls and dusty beads.

When he names his price, I hate him just a little.

"It's a big job for not a lot of cash," I say, trying to appeal to his sense of fairness. He's offered me a low price while he sits there with his well-trimmed mustache and his thick Irish wool jacket. He's a clubman through and through, and like all clubmen, he knows when to spend and when to save. He knows exactly where I stand in relation to him for this negotiation, knows who has the power and that I do not. He's made all these calculations and come down to a bargain price. This is the thing that bothers me most about my place in the world. Would that I had the confidence of most men I meet, not to mention their money.

Money is really such a silly, useless thing when you get down to it, a mere piece of grimy paper passed through many hands. But I can't deny money is full of energy. It's exchanged between people, after all, and carries the remnants of that transaction with it, transformed into a useful tool. Life is undeniably easier when you have some money and very hard when you do not.

"I'm intrigued by your project." I shift in my seat, the chair suddenly hard and uncomfortable. "But what if you don't like what I decide to do? Will the cards be subject to your approval?"

"That you have knowledge of the tarot, the hermetic in general, is why I asked you. We can discuss each card before you start. But dear Pixie." He takes my hand across the table, a surprisingly intimate gesture from the usually controlled Arthur. "I like all your work. I can't imagine I'd make any changes to what you create."

I silently sip my beer with my free hand.

"Fine. I'd be willing to let you have full discretion over the Minor

Arcana too. The entirety of it." He rubs a thumb across my knuckles, laying it on so thick that I suspect he has no other options. "I know you're the right person for this job."

I wait a beat more to see if any more money is on offer. Complete control over the minors is intriguing. As far as I know no one has ever illustrated the minors except the Sola Busca. The blank slate tempts me, a way to express all that I've been learning in the Dawn, and all I've been studying on my own these last years. He's offering a place to alchemize it all, a holding vessel for my knowledge.

I take another sip of bitter beer, take my hand back, and then I agree. After all, it's a chance to do something I know I'll enjoy, get paid for it, and work with a friend. I say yes too much. I know this.

What I don't know is that it will take me nearly two years to complete all seventy-nine illustrations for the deck, and that when it's published Arthur will call it the Rider Waite tarot deck. Waite for himself, Rider for the publisher, and omit my name completely. When I object, he'll look at me dumbfounded and state he paid me the agreed-upon price for the job for which he engaged me. He'll imply that my wanting my name on the deck is like the bricklayer wanting his name on the building.

I'll add my sigil, though—a small symbol of my initials on the corner of each card. A last-minute flourish before I turn in the final proofs, already hideously late. Arthur will say nothing about this, exasperated by my delays and wanting to finally get them to the printer.

I'll sell the originals of each card through my friend Alfred Stieglitz's gallery in New York. At least they will fetch something. Stieglitz and his wife, the artist Georgia O'Keeffe, will be amused when I gift them each a deck of the cards.

Years later when I retreat from London for the mystical landscape of Cornwall—for moor, and sea, and rock-face cliffs—I'll stop cursing Arthur for making his money and garnering fame. Neither of us had known how popular the cards would become, and I have found my contentment with space to do as I wish. I paint. I listen to music. I take in boarders here and there, mostly Catholic priests on vacation as there is a church next door. They let me play the organ, which keeps beautiful music close and all the visions that brings me.

That doesn't mean I'll give up my cards. When I painted them, I intended they'd be of help to me first, then anyone else who might find them handy. They helped me finally fulfill the thing I'd been always searching for—an entry into the unknowable, a revelation of the patterns that the world repeats to me, to all of us at every moment, revealing the truth lying just on the other side of all that is around us. I'd wanted to create a tool for making this accessible to me. That others found it useful was an additional satisfaction.

Arthur released a little book with the cards, his guide to the tarot, as impenetrable as any of the writings of the Golden Dawn. Arthur exasperated me in this; I admit it. I'd painted those cards to be picked up and used by anyone without any specialized knowledge, to provide a path to the self and the inner unknowable realms we keep hidden even from ourselves. They weren't meant to be simple, but they were meant to be accessible. Arthur's little book only confused things with his bombastic scholarliness and self-important theories. But I wish him no ill will. He has found the fame and notoriety he has always wanted. I have found something more.

The cards have proved to be a portal for me and for so many others. More than this, they have provided a path, a way to gain insight— from which is derived choice, from which is derived freedom.

That's all I ever intended—to banish fear, to embrace courage, and to touch what divine energy I could while living close to a wildish place.

CHAPTER SIX

In addition to Remedios's daily lessons with Madame Carvon, dinner each night in the crumbling Villa Air-Bel was the anchor to her days.

André would sit at the head of the table and embark on long monologues about the importance of art, techniques to access the subconscious, and how to shed the confines of society to get straight to pure thought.

His lectures lifted her out of their present circumstances and back into her old Paris life so that when dinner was over, she'd look up at her surroundings, fully expecting to walk out into Saint-Germain-des-Prés. Benjamin and she used to sit with André at the Café de Flore with as many as twenty people surrounding them, tables and chairs pulled up, to listen to André's thoughts, as if at any moment he might launch a new artistic movement. Waiters brought hot coffee and threaded through the tables so fast that she imagined they had wheels instead of legs—easily spinning past, never dropping their trays.

Remedios tried to tell André one night that his talks took her out of herself, if just for a moment. She offered it as a moment of truth and as an attempt, as always, to be seen by her lover's hero.

André had turned to her with a rare smile of true fondness. "Everything we do here, dear Remedios, is to outwit the anguish of the hour."

In the close environs of the villa, every room was used, every bedroom occupied, and refugees lined the hallways waiting to talk to Varian from daybreak until Madame Nouget shooed them out before dinner. People were always milling about the downstairs parlor, smoking in the gardens, propped up against a wall in the hall, waiting their turn.

Max and Peggy had moved into the villa, taking the largest bedroom on the first floor with doors that opened onto the terrace. Peggy pinned the same large diamond brooch to the different cocktail dresses she wore for dinner each night, ever the overdressed American.

Yet even with the new arrival of Max and Peggy, topics of conversation could become stale among a group that sat down for meals together every day and lived communally. The staleness made Benjamin irritable, and he would transform for a time into what André called "the Grand Inquisitor of Surrealism." He'd go around the table interrogating each person in turn like a surrealist Socrates, searching for a fresh idea. If you had to give up day or night, which would it be? (But what do you mean give up? they'd ask. What do you mean give up? he'd retort.) What color would you choose to inhabit for a week? Are you a clock or an owl? Are insects our overlords?

On nights when Benjamin couldn't think of any more questions, André would start the games. André was a skilled ringleader and organized diversions like cards and cribbage and those that required what he called the "synchronicity of the universe," such as blackjack and poker. But his particular fondness was for parlor games, and among those le jeu de la verité, truth or dare, was his favorite. He went around the table, gesturing with his glass at each of them in turn—which did they choose, truth or dare? The question never put to André himself, as he controlled the activity.

That night, he started with Remedios because Benjamin always enjoyed it when Remedios was chosen, as she always chose dare, which she did again that night.

"You," André said, stroking his chin in exaggerated pondering. "Must make me a tarot deck."

Damn André with his mind like an elephant, she thought, he never forgot a thing. Of course he remembered the tarot conversation at the café.

The table erupted—it wasn't fair, and wasn't that kind of a big dare, and how could he expect someone to undertake all that work?

"A card then," he said, leaning back. "To start my deck. You decide which one."

The terrace doors were open to the night air, and the insects buzzing brought to her mind their exoskeletons of armor perpetually gleaming and intact. Benjamin slid one of the little notebooks that lived in his pockets along with a tiny gold screw-top pencil toward her, and she began sketching a beetle that had been scuttling in the corners of the room all evening. She wished she'd had something to try to render the colors, but with chiaroscuro and shading she managed to convey an idea of the shiny carapace.

A beetle upside down, his multiple legs folded over one another and tethered in a spider's web, her version of the Hanged Man.

She slid the notebook across the table to André.

"Et voilà—the Hanged Beetle," she said. "His hard shell reinforces the message of the Hanged Man—that one must cease struggle, that trust is the only way to true wisdom, that even when in an uncomfortable position, enlightenment and growth are possible."

"You and your insects," Benjamin said.

"Insects are delicate and easily smashed, yet heavily armored and weaponized with stingers and poison beyond their tiny size," she said.

"Insects are quite savage," André said. He rose to rustle in the faded drapes that blew in listlessly on the evening breeze. He emerged with cupped hands and deposited something on the thick faience platter in the center of the table.

A pair of insects were locked together in the middle of the platter.

On closer inspection, they were a pair of praying mantises copulating. As everyone watched, the female turned and bit the head off her mate to a rousing cheer from André, who had somehow managed to spy them there in the drapery folds. "I've been watching them circle each other all through dinner."

"Your constant terror, isn't it?" Remedios said to laughter around the room, because of course the praying mantis centerpiece was signature André provocation, his way of whistling past the gallows.

"Your constant instinct," Benjamin said and cupped his crotch. "We have to be careful of our insect rulers. Look at how they behave."

"Perhaps she's under duress," Peggy said as the insect continued working her powerful jaws. "At being put on display. What can be the evolutionary purpose of it?"

"Evolution? Science?" André said. "We've had enough of those, haven't we? With the guns and the bullets and the technologies of war. This is instinct." He flourished his hand. "Pure and undilute. We can't overcome it any more than they can."

Madame Nouget came in then with a dish of dried apricots and a bottle of local cognac she'd managed to barter for from a nearby farmer. Benjamin poured out the glasses and distributed them around the table.

When he sipped his own, he reared back in his chair. "But this is horrendous," he said, and held the glass away from his body in offense. It was new and sharp and though not like cognac at all, it wasn't bad.

"Keep your voice down." Remedios shushed him, hoping Madame Nouget hadn't heard as she closed the pantry door. "It's hard to find such things. Don't discourage her."

"I don't care anymore if I discourage her," Benjamin said. He'd had more than his share of wine at dinner. The room fell silent. "Why can't I call something horrible if it is? Why can't I speak the truth? This whole place is awful. The whole world is fucking awful. Why are we not talking about it? Why are we sitting here playing parlor games as the world goes to shit? Why . . ." He turned to Varian. "Do I have to apply to Mexico for a visa? Why can't I go to the US like everyone else?"

That afternoon Remedios and Benjamin had been working through their options for asylum with Varian. He'd told them that given Benjamin's connections to the Communist party, there was no chance of a visa to America.

Now Varian removed his tortoiseshell glasses and dropped them onto the table with a clatter. He rubbed his face, his exasperation evident to everyone in the room.

"To be clear," Varian said, slowly. "The Mexican government is offering full citizenship to Spanish refugees, to Remedios. Citizenship, do you understand, Benjamin?" he asked, rare annoyance in his voice. "The time you'll waste applying for a visa to the US that you'll never get could prove crucial."

Madame Nouget came in then to collect dirty dinner plates, the cracked walnut shells. Her face was tranquil, but she must have heard Benjamin's complaints.

Remedios hopped up to help her.

"I went to Mexico once," André said to Benjamin reassuringly. "A most surreal place."

"Shall we all go out in the gardens?" Peggy asked, rising. "Have a moonlit walk?" She was always up for movement of any sort. "They can't take that away from us, can they, Benjamin? Do you know I heard only today in a letter that Churchill has been consulting Aleister Crowley?"

Remedios was impressed by Peggy's intuitive reading of the situation. Benjamin secretly loved a good gossip, and information about Aleister Crowley, the wickedest man in the world and occult figure of scandal, would easily draw him in. Besides, all of them longed for news of any type. "He's a desperate drug addict now, that's what I've heard. Heroin. And so old," she continued.

She took up Benjamin's arm and led him out onto the terrace. They all listened as Peggy's voice wafted in through the open doors. "Those Nazis are all horribly superstitious. Can you imagine? A charlatan like Aleister at 10 Downing Street . . ." Their voices faded as the rest of them got up to reconvene outside.

Remedios placed her pile of dishes in the deep trough sink in the pantry, and when she came back, she found Max sitting in her seat.

"Surprise," he said flatly, and there was a sinister edge to his tone. Or maybe it was just that he, too, seemed constantly annoyed and on edge. Peggy kept him within earshot always, almost as if he was a pet or a child. Though if it was Peggy who held Max's leash or the other way around, Remedios couldn't tell.

"I've just had a letter too," he said. "Leonora's in a sanatorium." His voice was quiet. "In Spain. It's supposed to be a good one."

Remedios came and sat across from him. "A mental hospital?"

"Apparently she had a hard time after I left." And this annoyed Remedios because, as she was learning, Max would place himself in the middle of any story.

Remedios sat back, floored by the idea of her friend sick. "But she's all right?"

"I don't know. I just heard a tidbit from a friend who knows a friend who helped her get to a hospital outside Madrid. She had a breakdown, quite a bad one. They told me where she is."

The thought of Leonora in a hospital, a mental hospital, was incompatible with the vibrant Leonora whom Remedios knew. She felt as if the world had been rearranged. It couldn't be true. Perhaps Leonora was sheltering there. Waiting, like they all were, for her chance to escape. "Can I write to her?"

Max shrugged. "Of course. But I wish I could go see her. I need to go help her." In all the time she'd known him, Max had always been an aloof and taciturn character. She supposed that was part of his appeal to Leonora and to Peggy. But now she saw a crack in the facade, and behind it a beating heart. "Her family"—he said the word with distaste that made his disapproval clear—"has sent her old childhood nanny to fetch her, I guess."

Leonora had referred to her nanny so often that the woman had become a mythic figure in Remedios's mind. From the way Leonora spoke of her, Remedios got a picture of the woman as part Irish grandmother and part Celtic mystic and not at all the sort you'd send on a reconnaissance mission in the middle of a war to fetch a daughter in trouble.

"Look, here they come," Max said, straightening himself.

Peggy floated in and stationed herself behind Max where she leaned down and draped her arms around his shoulders. "What are you two talking about?" she asked next to his ear. Remedios wondered if she was drunk.

"Art," Max said curtly enough that it defied her to ask more questions.

"Well," Peggy said in a false cheery tone. "I certainly approve of that."

THE MOON—
Nanny Mary Cavanaugh

Navigation at night with no light except for moonlight requires the compass of inner knowing or else it can feel like fumbling in the dark. The Moon card shows the wildness of the wolf and the tameness of the dog, along with the crayfish surfacing from the watery unconscious to a pathway at night. The path exists, but it is in otherworldly silver light. The Moon card is the bell of intuition ringing, and its sound waves rippling up into the conscious mind. It is a reminder to call upon inner knowing. When the Moon card appears in a reading, a request is being made to look deeply into the subconscious and to be led by intuition to the best of one's ability despite the obscure path.

When they asked me to go find Leonora, they called me, as they always did, Nanny Carrington, their name, not mine. Despite this, I leapt at the chance to help my dear girl, never mind the crossing in a fetid cabin belowdecks. Even that level of discomfort had required some string-pulling by the Carringtons. England was at war after all.

Agreeing to the mission made me seem braver than I was, but I'd agreed out of love. I raised Leonora like my own, that one, and I hadn't seen her in years. I kept up with her through the clandestine letters she sent to her mother. They were in correspondence, though she hid that from her husband. No one was to speak of Leonora in front of him since she ran off with that painter. It was like her father had become some white-bearded king from a fairy tale.

Information hard to come by given wartime, so I hadn't been too concerned when Leonora's letters stopped. That is, until a letter from the British ambassador in Madrid arrived saying that Leonora had made it out of France, but that she'd become ill and he thought it best to send her to a hospital for psychiatric patients in the mountains. He wrote that she showed up saying that Madrid was the stomach of the world, and she was sent there to aid its digestion. She had a suitcase filled with shredded newspapers as evidence of its rot. She was only twenty-five.

When the Carringtons tell me this, I assume it's because they're about to leave, to go to her—their own child, sick and in need of care. But instead I try to keep the surprise off my face when they ask me to go get her.

They explained, as if this made up for them sending me, that the scoundrel Max Ernst had been imprisoned. It's that piece of information that convinces me to make the trip. I doubted Leonora could handle such a thing. Max was old enough to be her father, and likely acted like one too. His removal and her escaping a country at war by herself would strain her resiliency, and now she was in a sanatorium.

Years ago when Leonora announced she was leaving for art school, I'd gone to her room after dinner. Her mother asked me to check on her. There'd been a fight at dinner. There were often fights at dinner. Her father red-faced as he slammed cutlery on the table, raised voices we could hear even in the kitchen.

"Nanny," Leonora said in a warning tone when I knocked on her bedroom door that night. "Don't come in here."

"Why not? Are you ill?" I creaked the door open a sliver. Party dresses glittered in a neat line, untouched on their hangers, including the snow-white satin she'd worn when she'd been presented at court. Everything else lay strewn about the room, trailing out of a tweed-backed suitcase.

"You're here for them, and you can't play both sides. This is where childhood ends," she said, taking up a stack of books and then setting them back down absentmindedly. "You're here on their behalf. You're one of them."

"You think I don't know what's in your head?" I said, slipping inside the room, closing the door behind me with a quiet click. "You think I don't know what you'll do?"

"What will I do?" she asked. Standing there in the middle of a mess, defiant and determined, she looked exactly the same as she had as a toddler with a sweet gripped in her fist.

"Great things," I said. "You convinced them to send you to art school. If you can do that, you can do anything."

She crossed the room and hugged me then, a sparkle of a tear in the eye. She was always the most engaging child—part fey, part wild. "To have been in your care is one of the great good fortunes of my life, I think," she said.

But she was a charmer—impulsive, generous in a way that couldn't be dimmed in her. Her appeal was as much a part of her as the modulation of her voice, or her quoting long swaths of poetry the tutor made her memorize. Her parents had tried to instill their overly formal ways, trying desperately to hide their upwardly mobile background. There's no zealot to anything, even upper-class pretensions, like a convert.

"Here," I said, crossing to her and opening her palm. It was why I'd come to find her. I placed the silver in her hand and closed her fingers over it. "The Celtic cross for protection."

"Oh, I couldn't possibly," she said, looking down at the cross with the halo at the top.

"It's not fine silver," I said. I'd bought it earlier in the week in town. "It'll tarnish, which is all the better. Means it's been used. Take it now, and if you can't accept it, think of it as a loan until I see you again."

"It's beautiful."

She crossed to her dressing table, draped in flounces of silk and lace, and started digging through drawers. They were like Ali Baba's cave, those drawers, full of gifts she received from her parents, from other relations, most of it jewelry and all of it unworn, still in its boxes, tossed into the drawers and forgotten. "Oh, why do I want that fiddly stuff all over me, Nanny?" she'd say. She unearthed a sterling silver chain, just waiting for her in that cache of loot. She threaded the cross through, clasped it around her neck, and dropped it down the front of her blouse, where it would sit next to her heart.

"Thank you, Nanny," she'd said.

—⟨⟨⟨◆⟩⟩⟩—

It wasn't too hard for me to imagine that Leonora had a breakdown. Despite her courage, or because of it, she was always getting into things over her head. It was her hard stubborn streak mixed with her dreamy ideals that did it—an unmanageable combination.

When I arrived in Madrid I was taken straight to the ambassador, more strings from the Carringtons. The ambassador directed me to a town up north.

"It's lovely there," the ambassador said as he filled out my travel passes, punctuating each with a stamp from his stamp pad. "You'll like it. It was a great favorite of the royal family," he said, as if I was a pleasure-seeker heading out on vacation and not a nanny who had never been outside the British Isles sent to fetch a daughter who'd lost her mind in the middle of a war. "I do hope she's all right."

His office seemed a hive of activity. The phone ringing as a secretary periodically came to the doorway, holding a handful of telegrams, waiting for him to be finished with our very brief meeting. "She was quite unwell when last I saw her," he said. "Her friends who brought her here said she'd been living by herself in the French countryside consuming nothing but orange flower water and fasting until she hallucinated." He handed over the papers with a smile. "Came to my office saying Madrid was the intestines of the world and that she was in charge of helping it digest the evil around us and set the world to rights. Then she ran up to the roof. We were all afraid she was going to jump." He told me this in the straightforward tone of an attaché briefing his superior. At the shocked look on my face he said, "Do give the Carringtons my best, would you?" And he dismissed me without another word.

The police at the train station gave my papers the merest glance and a cursory look at my face. Age does have the advantage of acting like an invisibility spell sometimes.

When I arrived, the hospital looked proper enough, housed in an authentic former castle in a parklike setting, which fit in with the resort town. As a representative of the Carringtons, I was shown in to see the director, Dr. Mariano Morales.

After pleasantries and an overbroad explanation of Leonora's situation, he brought out from a drawer in his desk a white linen pouch tied with a leather knot and a pile of envelopes, their tops neatly slit, bearing a return address of Max Ernst in Marseilles. When he placed the pouch in my hand, I could feel a set of cards inside. "She was sent these."

"You open her mail?"

"We collect all our patients' mail. We find that ensures nothing outside hinders the therapeutic relationship. Look inside," he said, nodding at the pouch, "and you'll understand why."

They were fortune-telling cards inside, brand-new and practically shimmering with life force. Who would send such a thing to Leonora in a hospital?

"There is a note," the director said, and slid it forward on the desk. I slid it back. "I don't read Spanish, señor."

"Of course," he said in his slow English and began.

Dear Leonora—

Max, who is well and free and living with a group of us here
in Marseilles, told me only today about what happened to you.
I haven't been able to stop thinking about you and wishing
you well. I have recently taken up study of the tarot in a little
printer's shop here, and it has ignited new thinking. My teacher
prints decks in her shop, and I thought you might like to have
one. Madame Carvon (that's my teacher) says a set of cards can
often be useful for healing. I send you heartfelt wishes on the
wings of a griffin for your speedy recovery.

Your friend—
Remedios Varo

I tucked the cards into my handbag. I knew what they were. I left Max's letters where they were, untouched. "When can I see her?"

"And this," he said, bringing forth a glassine envelope. I spilled the contents into my hand—the Saint Brigid's cross, tarnished black around the edges from wear, but still glinting.

"She's due for an injection now. You might wish to view it as then you can reassure her parents." He said it with pride, as if it was a boon to his hospital that he treated the daughter of a fancy English family and there might be more Brits who'd lost their minds coming to him for cures. "She has been refusing food as well, so we've had no choice but to put her on a regimen of milk-sopped bread and bed rest."

Later, I would try to block the horror show from my memory. They strapped her to the bed, naked, and injected her with Cardiazol meant to shock her mind back into sanity. All I saw was her writhing, her tears, her convulsions, the seizure, her eyes rolled back in her head, covered in sweat, a wooden spoon in her mouth so she wouldn't swallow her tongue. She'd lost weight, and her ribs jutted underneath barely visible breasts. I stood there openly weeping, ashamed to be blubbing in a room of strangers, though everyone was focused on restraining Leonora and not on my tears.

When it was done, I followed the doctor out of the room and stopped him in the hall with hushed questions about what I'd just witnessed. He was supercilious and then domineering as my questions became more pointed. He stated that this was the best, most scientific treatment currently recommended for Leonora's condition and that the Carringtons were well aware of what it entailed. As a means of intimidating me, he mentioned the price, as if I'd be cowed by the expense, as if money made it effective.

It wasn't until the next morning that they let me see Leonora alone in her room, which was really just a bare, windowless cell.

She was subdued, exhausted, wrapped in a tattered robe. She'd been bathed and her dark hair washed but not styled, so it lay on the pillow in a fluffy corona.

"What are their plans for me?" she asked on her back, staring at the ceiling, not looking at me.

"Prim." The childhood name her family called her, like all good nicknames, was the opposite of who she was. "What have they done to you?"

Leonora turned her head and looked at me blankly as if she'd never known me. "If you're here to take me back, I'm not going."

"But what they're doing to you. Do you think it can possibly be helping?"

"It's helping."

"Dear, can you know that? Watching it . . . it was ghastly."

Leonora turned her eyes back to the ceiling.

"Wouldn't you be more comfortable at home? Where you might recover more fully. Out of harm's way. With an English doctor at least."

"If my parents wanted me back, perhaps they should have come to get me themselves instead of sending the paid help."

Her words hit me like a slap. Of course she wasn't herself. She'd been ill and was weak from the injection. Certain indulgences had to be extended.

"Between Dr. Morales and my father," she continued, "I'll take my chances with the doctor any day." She rolled and turned her back to me so she was facing the wall.

I moved to sit on the edge of the bed, as I did when she was sick with fever as a child. I heard her sob then and reached out for her shoulder, but she shrugged me off.

"Dear one," I said. "You're not in your right mind. Come back home where we can take care of you."

"Don't you see that if I do that, I'll die?" She rolled toward me, eyes red and nose inflamed. "You know more than anyone that going back there is a death sentence."

She'd always been dramatic. It was part of her flair, her charm. But when it combined with her stubbornness, I had to keep my annoyance in check.

"You need rest," I said.

"I need safety," she said. "They're not the same."

I tried for a few more days. Leonora had no more treatments that

I saw. But it was clear I wouldn't be able to make her voluntarily come with me anywhere, and the thought of forcing her seemed both cruel and unfeasible. I'd need help, strong help, to take Leonora anywhere she didn't want to go, and where could I find it? Could I really travel with Leonora like some sort of prisoner? Faced with these options, I did the only thing I could do. I left. I'd give Leonora's parents a full description of the hospital and the treatment and the advice that someone with more muscle and a colder heart than mine be sent to bring her back.

I saw her once more to say goodbye. They'd given her sleeping medication, which vexed me as they knew I was leaving that day. They could have waited until I said goodbye. I could have waited until she woke up. But I was ready to leave that hellish place, and so I went in to see her.

I left her with the only things I could think to give her—I set a picture of us together with her brothers on the terrace at Hazelwood. I thought it might remind her of who she was, where she came from, and that she had people there who loved her still. I put the Celtic cross next to it. Silly maybe, but I thought that if ever there was a time she needed protection, it was then. And I left her with the set of tarot cards and the letter from her friend. How could it possibly harm her, I wondered, compared to what she was going through?

CHAPTER SEVEN

As the months went by, Remedios reinstituted a lost routine from childhood: the siesta. Benjamin claimed he was working on a new poem while Remedios napped. Everyone knew the real purpose of their afternoon interludes. Everyone left them alone.

Within the walls of the room, she and Benjamin had come back together again. At first awkwardly with tentative touches and pauses and now with passion, returned to each other.

André's quote came back to her; she'd been living with it in her head for weeks now. Outwit the anguish indeed, she thought as she lay dozing in linen and blankets that smelled of homemade soap and sex. Those afternoon moments had been one of the few times she could fully relax in the villa. Their room became a private oasis. Yet the minute she stepped out of their room, even to go to town for her tarot lessons, the world came flooding back in.

It came rushing back now, as water raced in the pipes in the walls from the WC down the hall and Benjamin walked back in, took a card off his bureau, and dropped it onto her bare shoulder.

The invitation was on heavy card stock with a tiny monogram in unobtrusive light blue from a countess with a villa near the old port, likely owned by her family for generations.

"Let me unpack my tiara," she said. She was always trying for one of Benjamin's smiles in those days. They made her feel like she'd been given a handful of fairy gold—buoying and then dissolving into dust.

"She's not like that," he said. His quick defense made Remedios wonder if this countess was funding one of his causes. "She's an intellectual," and with that she wondered if he'd been sleeping with her.

She turned the card over, familiar with this type of countess. In Paris, Benjamin seemed to collect them. The countess likely thought having a revolutionary poet like Benjamin Péret at her parties made her seem avant-garde and chic. Benjamin cultivated her for financial support for his magazines and for introductions to her wealthy friends. Even without meeting her, Remedios was certain this woman had no idea what Benjamin's poems meant. The countess knew his poems were rough and profane, which she mistook for passionate. When Remedios had first arrived in Paris, she'd wondered at Benjamin associating with such persons. She'd since learned all his friends cultivated these types of connections. Max and Peggy being the most recent example.

"The Countess Pastré," he said, nodding at the card, "is helping Varian get people out. She's bankrolled quite a few. She's friends with the Saint-Exupérys." *So that's how Benjamin met her*, Remedios thought. "She's the one who suggested their speaking tour in America to raise money for the Resistance."

"So it's a political mission, this countess's party?" she asked.

He leaned over his bureau, studying himself in the mirror. "Do you know what I saw before . . ." Benjamin's voice trailed off, and she waited for his choice of words describing his imprisonment. This was the first time he'd mentioned it in all their reunited days together. "Before I left Paris?" he said, his euphemism for being arrested and jailed. "In the window of Cartier on the Champs-Élysées? The jeweler? A gold yo-yo. The child's toy. I thought Duchamp had started designing for them, but then I saw a man on the street with one. A grown man with a solid-gold child's toy."

"The French are extravagant. This is new?"

"Not all the French. Not me." He took up his tie, hanging from the bureau drawer knob. "And some of them need to be guided to put their money in a better place than yo-yos. So maybe that's something I can do."

She rolled over and snuggled deeper into blankets that smelled of them, suddenly exhausted. She wanted to sleep now, side by side in a space to dream and rest.

"The champagne's good," he said, coming to sit next to her hip. "And there's lots of Noilly Pratt, that's where the money comes from."

"A vermouth countess, very French," she said into her pillow. She could imagine Benjamin there, holding court, entrancing with his theories and his poems about sex and decay.

"There's real food, even sweets." He paused and then doled out the pièce de résistance. "La Baker is rumored to be staying with her."

She rolled back to face him, impressed. If the goddess Josephine Baker graced the countess's villa, Remedios would go if only in hopes of a glimpse.

"And I don't need to tell you our situation is dire."

He'd always been like this, able to compartmentalize his political beliefs and meet the moment without their encumbrance. He walled off the unpleasant and then used people to his advantage. Of course knowing some rich aristo could only help them in coming days if they needed money or connections, or even a place to stay. Of course going to her party and shining would only benefit them.

But it made Remedios nervous, because if he did this with others, did he do it with her? Did he reserve the true parts of himself for André, or some other lover, and show her only what he thought she wanted to see?

"Rosa," he said, the nickname he'd given her when she'd first arrived in Paris. His rose. She hadn't been able to articulate the small frisson of irritation that surfaced in her when he first used it. It placed her separate from him, opposite almost. As an object to be admired, not a fellow artist and certainly not a fellow thinker. But how does one object to being called a beautiful rose without looking churlish? She'd grown used to it. As if sensing her mind spinning, he said, "I've missed you so much." He leaned down to kiss her then, a gentle kiss of comfort and pleading. "Come with me. We were separated for so long, I don't like to let you out of my sight for even a moment now."

And with that, she softened a bit. "So I'll go." She wanted to, not because she missed parties but because she missed feeling normal again, missed feeling that they were artists, intellectuals, creators heading to see friends and patrons—not prisoners, not refugees, not exhausted people. Life continued somewhere—perhaps on a parquet floor in a countess's ballroom.

"Excellent. And Rosa?" he said as he tossed her skirt to her across the bed. "Don't wash."

"Does that make you Napoleon in this scenario?" she asked.

Benjamin smiled. "That makes me a Frenchman."

Remedios stepped into the countess's party and admired the vista of red-tiled roofs in shadow leading down to the port still glinting in the sun below. The floors shone with wax. Not a speck of grime marred the concertina windows. Voluminous sprigged white cotton curtains were held back by sumptuous pale blue silk cording. Blue-and-white vases sat on pretty little tables in charming groupings filled with forced flowers because apparently the florists were still operating in France. The skill and money involved in creating this level of immaculateness wasn't something Remedios aspired to, but some people would still make a grasp for escapism, for joy even, in the face of looming chaos. She'd seen this kind of defiance in Paris as the Panzer divisions lined up on the Belgian border and the opera still played, and before in Barcelona when the cafés remained open while Franco's forces tear-gassed the streets.

A maid in a starched apron put a glass of champagne in her hand,

and she had to bow to the countess's talents. A woman who could conjure this sumptuousness in the middle of chaos had formidable skills.

She took a gougère off a passing silver tray—warmth of black pepper and tang of Gruyère cheese on her tongue.

Across the room, a woman who could only be the countess wore an aqua-blue and mustard-yellow net confection likely designed by that favorite of all the surrealist patrons, Schiaparelli.

Peggy and Max were there, of course, surrounded by those who wanted to be near Max's genius or Peggy's money. Peggy wore a necklace of tiger claws. She must have bought it right off Jacqueline's neck, which struck Remedios as rather triste in its blatant emulation. Peggy bought everything that caught her eye.

Remedios was wearing her smartest black skirt along with a boxy, sack-like jacket she'd stitched in Paris trying to copy the severe and clean-edged lines of Chanel.

She watched for a moment as the countess introduced her guests to each other with practiced ease. Middle-aged with a tiny, well-controlled potbelly, she emanated an air of gravitas, but the effect in the frothy dress was of mutton dressed as lamb. Net added bulk where it should have streamlined, and chiffon hugged where it should have skimmed. If Remedios had royalty levels of money, she would have opted for a real Chanel. Clothes made for living without fuss. The jersey Madame Chanel used added a certain subversive flavor to her clothes. Madame Chanel had convinced wealthy women to shell out for glorified men's underwear fabric, something that surely would have pleased Duchamp had he focused on it.

Remedios leaned down and snapped the head off a gardenia in a low arrangement. Something tangible, something real, smelling of glamour and silvery evenings. She put the flower in the top buttonhole of her jacket.

"Meet an up-and-coming painter," Benjamin said in a forced voice as he took her by the elbow and propelled her toward his patron.

The countess offered a soft hand with nails buffed a clean pink. She smiled thinly, staring at her flower now gracing Remedios's jacket. "Delightful," she said flatly, and then swept Benjamin up on her arm and took him to introduce him to someone on the other side of the room, leaving Remedios stranded. Any thought of asking if Josephine Baker would be joining them was gone.

Despite her snubbing and the stiff formality of the evening, a party like this in the middle of a war was something quite surreal. Glass in hand, nibbling on a second cheese puff, Remedios watched as another clutch of guests arrived, as the maids circulated, as more champagne was brought up from the cellars below. Across the room, her lover chatted, raising money for his causes and full of purpose. A whole night lay before her in a royal villa. For a moment she felt lucky. She was with Benjamin again, and even if Spain was in tatters, even if the Germans had marched on the Champs-Élysées, even if she knew they had to find another country, to be there at that moment at the beginning of a party, she felt the slightest hint of relief. As if a spell had been cast that evening taking them all back to a time before the war.

Left on her own, she followed the flow of guests into the drawing room, and as she rounded the corner she stopped and then consciously righted her face. She'd done such a good job that even she was fooled for a moment. She wasn't sure the painting was hers until she was standing right in front of it and then remembered every stroke of painting it. Hung with pride in a conspicuous spot, next to a window where it would catch the afternoon light, was a de Chirico. One of her de Chiricos. Oscar sold them off to unsuspecting rubes, and he never told her to whom. Remedios felt her heart speed. She'd painted a long alley of classical columns, and at the end, barely visible and only hinted at, was a woman in profile, as if waiting for the viewer. Remedios had spent a good amount of time mixing the colors to get the earthy tints that marked a true de Chirico. It was a good forgery, yes, but it was a forgery nonetheless. Anyone who had ever seen a real de Chirico would surely know it was an imitation. She was a lesser artist copying a greater one—that left gaps in the work.

"I told you we'd be fine," a voice said behind her.

She turned and Oscar Sanchez himself stood before her, a smirk on his face. "Everything will be fine," he said in a lowered voice. "Stay calm."

"You're here," she said, embracing him with a halfhearted air kiss on each cheek. "How long have you been here? How do you know the countess?" She squeezed his arm. "What the hell is this?" She inclined her head toward the painting.

Oscar hadn't looked well when she'd last seen him in Paris the night he'd thrown a glass at Benjamin, the night before all hell broke loose, but he looked better now. His black hair drooped in his face, but it looked clean, and the thin little mustache he always wore, in the manner of a rake, was precisely trimmed. "I'm staying with the countess," he said. "She's an old friend." He nodded to the painting and then leaned in close. "It's like a boardinghouse here. You wouldn't believe the bed-swapping at night. But you look well." He leaned back, taking in her measure. "And you smell fabulous."

"Chanel No. 5," she lied, thinking of the bottle Jacqueline kept in the bathroom.

"Smells more like eau de Péret if you ask me," he said with a grin.

"Has Benjamin seen this yet?" she asked, ignoring his comment, though it made her twitch as it was intended to do.

"No, and don't tell him. You know as well as I do that he never can keep a secret."

"When did you sell it to her?" Remedios asked.

"Sell me what?" asked the countess, appearing at Oscar's side. "I see you're admiring my de Chirico. Dear Oscar here helped me acquire it."

For just a moment Remedios thought she might ask the countess how much she'd paid, to see just how big a multiple Oscar made off the sales. But of course, such a question would be rude and strange.

"What do you think of it?" the countess asked Remedios, a bit aggressively.

Oscar almost choked on his drink and came up coughing. Remedios willed her face to look calm regardless of the countess's interrogation.

"I always enjoy the perspectives in a de Chirico. It's like its own world, brings to mind the cities in Hieronymous Bosch," Remedios said.

"Everything brings to mind Bosch for you," Oscar said.

"Well, he is a favorite," she said.

The countess was staring at her. "I've been told, by someone who has an excellent eye, that this is a fake."

Remedios turned red. They both looked at Oscar. For the countess to call him out so aggressively made them all fidget, but then money and status sometimes allowed the privileged to ignore manners.

Oscar laughed nervously. "Countess, what are you saying? Of course it's a real de Chirico."

She nodded. "That's what I told my friend. And I told him I am on good terms, on very good terms you might say, with the commandant. I said he shouldn't say such things, or I'd have him reported for false accusations." She smiled brightly while delivering the oblique threat. It didn't escape Remedios's notice that she could also report a forgery to her good friend the commandant as well.

A commotion at the door caught the attention of all as a man walked in carrying a cello followed by staff carrying his chair and a small table.

"Ah! My treasure," the countess said, and hurried off in a rustle of netting.

"He takes breakfast in his room, and then practices till after lunch," Oscar said in an awed whisper. "I haven't actually seen him. But the house is full of his music."

Pablo Casals, the most famous cellist in the world, a Spaniard who famously hated Franco, walked in, trailed by two men who busied themselves with adjusting his chair, placing a table next to it just so, and attending to other solemn duties. He had a bald head and wire-rimmed glasses and a pipe that stayed in his mouth as he spoke to the party now crowding into the drawing room.

"I'd like to play a piece that I've played since I was a child. It has meant different things to me at different moments in my life."

Remedios's heart was still beating from what the countess had said. "Oscar, she suspects. What are you going to do?"

But Oscar merely put his fingers to his lips as Casals took up his bow and a hush fell over the gathering.

The energy shifted in the room, as it will when a creator at the height of his powers takes up his tools for calling down the divine.

He was framed under an arched doorway, and his pipe remained in the corner of his mouth as he began the Bach cello suites, puffing out little plumes of white pipe smoke that caught the fading sunset as he bowed.

"He said he won't go back to Spain until Franco is defeated," Benjamin whispered, coming to stand beside her and Oscar.

"Does he have a choice?" she asked.

"Franco would like him back," Oscar said.

"As a little pet." Benjamin tilted his glass, draining it. "Dictators aren't immune to art and music. They just think they can buy it, possess it."

"Or ban it. As if that's going to destroy it," Oscar said.

"Hitler is actually destroying art. Burning it."

"Especially our art," Remedios said.

Oscar leaned back and looked at her in shock. "*Our* art?"

A woman standing next to him in fine pearls and a diamond ring shushed him. "Really, you've talked through the whole piece so far," she hissed.

With his bow and strings, Casals gave voice to the collective dread and hope in the room as they all waited for an escape from looming war. His bowing was as expressive and precise as it had ever been. He'd kept ahold of his art, his discipline, his expression in the face of upheaval and despair. Remedios envied him this and wondered how he managed it. Was his cello a refuge, or did he need to force himself to retain some semblance of normality, the defiance of an expert refusing to dull his skills? She felt buoyed witnessing it, a moment of inspiration. Her painting, even if it was a forgery, reminded her that she was, indeed, a painter still and that she possessed technical skills. She might keep them up, might paint, might sketch, might even write. She must do something to keep herself from atrophying.

"He's planning to give a public concert in the square," Oscar said when Casals was finished. "Come, let me introduce you to some other people, those who will want to buy *your* paintings. And I don't mean"—he lowered his voice—"the de Chiricos." He tilted his head toward two gentlemen and then took Remedios's arm.

"Oscar, I haven't been able to work. No one has."

"Doesn't André have you all creating collages and paintings in the gardens at the villa? That's what I've been told. You must still create, you know. Like Casals practicing his scales."

She looked over to where the great musician was surrounded by admirers as he placed his pipe in a crystal ashtray and accepted a glass of champagne.

"He's a genius," she said. "I can't."

"Well, you must. Remedios, when will you learn that?"

"I can't force. I don't understand how you do."

"You forced those de Chiricos well enough."

"Keep your voice down." But Oscar only put a hand between her shoulder blades to propel her toward two prosperous-looking men in the corner. "They don't buy art based on what it looks like," he said into her ear as he frog-marched her forward. "They buy art based on what they think of you, so be as outré and artistic as you can be, all right?"

The pair of old men with waistcoats stretched tight looked like they were somehow managing to profit off the war. She dreaded talking to them. It was the countess who saved her.

"Everyone," the countess said as she flicked a buffed fingernail on a crystal champagne flute, "I'd like to thank dear Pablo for that exquisite music. It reminds us that we need an oasis of beauty and expression in these dark times. I want to thank you all for coming here to what has been a place of refuge in the arts for me, and I hope for you as well." Remedios tried to catch Benjamin's eye across the room. Clearly, the countess enjoyed playing the patron. "And in the spirit of the evening, I was hoping we might persuade Benjamin Péret now to grace us with one of his poems to make our night complete."

Applause and cheers of "yes" and "hear, hear" sprinkled around the room along with "Of course, he hasn't actually written anything new." This was from Oscar, who enjoyed taunting anyone. Benjamin loathed this sort of thing, performing like a parrot, and following Casals was daunting. That Benjamin didn't refuse her outright was a testament to her past generosity.

Most of Benjamin's poems were obscene with liberal scatological references that would make an odd mix with the sublime cello concert they'd just been gifted. As Benjamin came to stand next to the countess in the middle of the room, her closed-lipped smile radiated triumph at having him bend to her will.

He took a sip of champagne. "This is something I've been working on," he said and began.

It's Rosa weather with a real Rosa sun
and I'm going to drink Rosa with a Rosa meal

until I fall into a Rosa sleep
dressed in Rosa dreams
and the Rosa dawn will wake me like a Rosa mushroom
in which Rosa's image will be seen surrounded by a Rosa halo

He said the last while looking right at Remedios to cheers from the room and a sour face from the countess. Remedios wished she didn't blush, and to hide it and hopefully to show the whole thing as a touch ridiculous, she bobbed a little curtsy. The gardenia in her buttonhole fell out onto the floor. She didn't know why she curtsied like that. Benjamin had placed her back again where he preferred her—muse and lover, not a fellow artist, not a skilled painter. He came across the room, scooped up the gardenia, and presented it to her. She was very much aware of the image they were creating—he the great poet and she the ingénue, the inspiration, the flower. He'd again revealed his role for her, and feeling as powerless as she always did before him, she bowed and accepted the bloom.

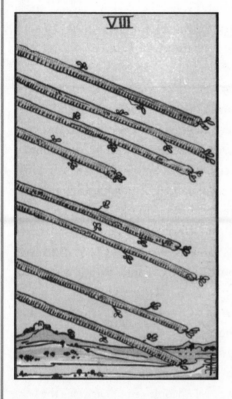

EIGHT OF WANDS—
Marie-Louise Double de Saint-Lambert, "Lily," the Countess Pastré

The Eight of Wands is a call to movement both physical and mental. A message is coming, and it will arrive soon. A question might be cleared up or a situation made plain. It might be a literal message, or it could be arriving from the higher parts of consciousness or the intuitive mind. But bottom line, information will be coming in fast. The key is how one decides to act once the information arrives. Action based on information is more than reflexive reaction. It is an active step forward with choice. When the Eight of Wands appears in a reading, pause to consider information coming your way. If action is warranted, consider whether it serves your highest interest. The Eight of Wands is a reminder to be reflective in the face of any news, rather than quickly reacting. The Eight of Wands reminds you that there is always a choice in dealing with information, even if it feels like spears raining down out of the sky.

I watch Benjamin Péret present one of my flowers to his amour across the living room of my family's villa. The girl has a layer of brash confidence that grates on the nerves. Though I suppose it shouldn't, it's so thick it must be a disguise for insecurity. I'd feel insecure too if I were wearing those plain clothes, a boxy black jacket and a rumpled skirt, both clearly homemade and too warm for the balmy evening. And the girl had felt free to pluck a bloom from one of my bouquets, as if she's strolling through a meadow or something. Yet after Benjamin recited that poem, a new one I've never heard before, making an ass of himself for love in front of everyone, could she lack confidence in anything? She looks as grave and alluring as a renegade nun with a vibrant slash of crimson on the lips that gives her away as being no religious sister.

Oscar Sanchez complained to me only this morning over breakfast that I can never see things for what they actually are. Yet I have suspected for months that the de Chirico he sold me is a fake. I can see *that* for what it is.

Yes, I called out the fake to put Oscar in a pickle, and why not? They should know I'm not clueless.

Oscar has cultivated his charm such that he can be forgiven for these things. The "de Chirico" was a bargain even as a fake, and I know he used the money to help ferry people out of Paris. It's the least I can do, turn a blind eye to his fraud. It's a beautiful painting in its own right, very well done, and the frame is handsome too. I enjoy it. I've always wanted a de Chirico. Does it matter if it's real? The only people who'd guess it's a forgery are me, Oscar, and somehow, I don't know why, but Benjamin's little amour, who stood in front of it with the strangest look on her face. Who knew she was an expert in de Chiricos? Or perhaps she knew it wasn't real and enjoyed the surrealist dualism of it. Or perhaps she had something to do with it. I wouldn't put anything past Oscar.

Despite his occasional swindles, Oscar is the best breakfast guest in the world—full of gossip and insights, and I don't want to lose him. He's always been a dear friend, and the poor thing has become a bit piteous of late. His face is drooping down the left side due to that disease he has. Just this morning I thought to myself that he's starting to look a bit like a halibut. He'll need friends as he deteriorates, and we're old friends, he and I.

This morning over toast and coffee, Oscar said I have what he calls "romantic ideals" that cloud my vision. When Benjamin recited that poem tonight, I thought Oscar might be right.

I've given Benjamin money for his underground magazines, and I gave what I could to Varian Fry and the American Rescue Committee. After that, Benjamin hit me up for his more political causes. I know most of those donations are turned into weapons and ammunition for the French Resistance or the Republicans in Spain. Given how things are going, it might not be wise to support such causes.

My husband has been writing me from America telling me I should join him in New York City. It's touching he's so concerned for my safety. He never seemed concerned with anything I did when we lived together.

Most everyone I know has fled. It's why I host the soirees, a mix of whoever is left in town and these stray-dog artist types who are attracted by the food and wine. And of course I feel it is my duty as a Frenchwoman to shelter a genius such as Pablo Casals. So when Varian told me Casals and his family needed a place to stay, I took them in immediately. He's a Spanish Republican, and therefore a person of ideals. I have a soft spot for those types.

The same with Josephine Baker. The girls in the kitchen tittered with excitement when I offered her a refuge. Even they knew about the Venus of Paris, such is her fame. The girls brought her endless cups of coffee, very strong as she liked it, in my best porcelain cups, along with tiny cakes they'd bake especially for her as if they were making offerings to Isis. They vied to take her underpinnings to wash, marveling at the fine silk and lace.

As long as I have a staff, my money can be of some use. As long as I have bottles in the cellar, I can evoke a turnout. I draw the line at entertaining German officers, though Josephine suggested that I might get information for the Resistance that way. So far no one has brought a German to these parties, but I fear it's only a matter of time. And what then? Kick them out? Serve them treats? Both options are unthinkable.

I take a sip of my family's vermouth and put a hand to my chest, anchoring myself to the two burnished coins I carry in my bodice next to my heart.

My mother gave them to me the night before my wedding. "They're a lovely little thing to seek direction from." Old, solid gold, and handled so often the heads and tails are nearly rubbed off. One side has what looks like Latin phrases, though they're too faded now to read. On the other side, I can faintly make out a fine old Roman nose.

"Your grandmother used them to cast lots and her grandmother as well. Shake them and focus on your question. Heads is always yes and tails is always no. If you get one of each, there are two ways of looking at a situation."

When she'd left, the first thing I asked was if I was doing the right thing marrying my husband—one heads, one tails. How right that had turned out to be.

There are times when I need them near. When I keep them stashed in a pocket. When I cannot stop asking them questions. Recently, I've kept them next to my heart so they are accessible at any time of day. Will the Germans succeed? Does Benjamin fancy me? Should I leave France? Tomorrow? In two days? Next week? Now?

I cast the coins three times just this morning asking that last question. They all landed heads.

My housekeeper tried to hide her relief when I told her to start crating the valuable paintings for shipping to America and to get the good furniture ready to be stored in the basement. I had no intention of calling off the party that night, though. I thought it rather heroic to stay in a city in danger of imminent siege, supporting art and intellectuals until the end. But it was smart to start preparing for the worst.

I'd been loitering in Marseilles, hoping for a little diversion with Benjamin. But now, having seen him with his jeune fille, I realize I've been merely a patron. I exchange my empty glass of vermouth for a glass of champagne off a tray, feeling a bit tipsy as I watch Benjamin and his lover begin their adieus. The first ones to leave the party, and as conspicuous as if they've announced they're going home to get in bed.

I touch my chest and feel the reassuring weight of Mother's gold coins. Three yeses in a row, six times those old Roman noses came up facing me. I am ready to leave Marseilles. Perhaps I'll offer to take messages to New York for Varian Fry. I could even ask the maids to sew them into my underthings. Josephine Baker instructed them on just how to do it before she left.

CHAPTER EIGHT

As summer turned to fall, Remedios would wander to the back of the house in the late morning to chat with Madame Nouget in the kitchen after the cook returned from foraging.

In that sun-dappled room of warm wood and worn marble, Nouget looked as confident and competent as any old chemist at work in her apothecary as she unloaded a basket of foraged greens and herbs. Remedios watched, hoping to learn the processes and techniques through which Nouget transformed the most meager raw material into a feast.

Remedios always entered the kitchen with the excuse of wanting a glass of water or a cup of tea, never anything too complicated that would add to the cook's labors. Then she stayed and tried to make herself useful by washing herbs, chopping vegetables, even scouring pots. When there was nothing else she could help with, she brought out her pencil and her sketchbook and tried to fade into the background while Madame worked.

Nouget disapproved of Remedios pitching in at first and warned that she didn't want to be mistaken for one of the kitchen maids.

Remedios shrugged. "At least I'll be doing something useful."

As the young maids came less and less to the villa because they were needed to help their own families, Nouget began to accept Remedios's help more readily.

In this way Remedios gained skills. She watched as Madame braised tough cuts of beef and salted the latest catch that the fishmonger brought to the back door. Huge bubbling copper pots of both stews and laundry simmered on the stove, as Madame was a stickler for cleanliness. She said it saved time in the long run to keep everything clean, and she was a great believer in boiling linens. But Remedios was most interested in the teas and tinctures Madame made, some straightforward salves for chest congestion or mint tea for indigestion, but others more complicated. Remedios asked about the exact uses for them, but Nouget would only say they were for her personal use.

Remedios had begun sketching a portrait of the cook.

"You are always watching me," Nouget said one day as Remedios sat sketching at the wide, scarred kitchen table. "Wanting to know more about what I do."

"Yes," Remedios said, not lifting her eyes from the paper. "Taking something in the raw form and making it into something else. Making something from nothing. That is what fascinates me." Remedios turned the sketch toward Nouget and slid it across the table. Paper was hard to come by, and she'd resorted to using old newspapers and whatever scraps she could find. Nouget had shown her how to boil it down to paste and stretch it on a mold and deckle to make rough rag paper, which Remedios then sewed together in the absence of glue. It provided a pleasing texture to her images.

"This is your form of alchemy—your paints, your sketches, your paper. You don't need to learn mine," Nouget said, sliding it back with a small nod of approval.

Remedios was familiar with this type of logic. Her father had been in charge of her education, and his strategy had been to keep her so busy with books and drawings that she'd never learn how to cook and thereby, under his logic, would never be asked to. He hadn't been able to keep her away from his mother-in-law, who'd taught her to sew, but he'd kept her out of the kitchen. In doing so, he'd ensured his daughter wouldn't be trapped. Yet the strategy left Remedios unable to make the most basic food for herself. It was why she was as fascinated with cooking as with making money through her painting. She wanted to be self-sufficient, to support herself in every way possible.

"I'd like to learn so I can feed myself," she said.

"Did your mother never teach you?"

How to explain her mother? A remote figure obsessed with the church and service. She took no interest in Remedios's artistic abilities, save for the one portrait Remedios did of her grandmother, her mother's mother. She'd painted Doña Maria Josefa with her sewing needle and hoop in hand—the only piece of art her mother ever praised. The rest her mother professed incomprehensible, and with those pronouncements had relegated Remedios and her education to her father. If her education had been entrusted to her mother, she'd have learned the lives of the saints and the catechism and little else. Her mother's highest ambition for her daughter was that she become a nun.

"Will you be going to see Madame Carvon tomorrow?" Nouget asked now, breaking Remedios's reverie.

Remedios's daily tarot lesson with Madame Carvon provided routine and a reason to leave the close environs of the villa.

"Yes," Remedios said, a bit startled. "Do you know her?"

"I have a basket for her. Would you mind delivering it?"

"Of course," Remedios said, interest piqued, trying to formulate a question. Why? What for?

But Madame Nouget merely picked up her knife and returned to her chopping.

QUEEN OF PENTACLES—
Madame Marie Helene Nouget

The Queen of Pentacles sits on her throne of earthly abundance cradling her pentacle, her life force. She is connected to the physical, meaning both the world around her and the world of the body. She is the keeper of the home and hearth and takes this responsibility seriously. She will always have a pot of something delicious bubbling on the stove or something welcoming baking in the oven. She is a keeper of traditional feminine crafts, a highly skilled domestic nurturer, and an alchemist who can create a home and haven wherever she goes. She is an expert gardener who excels at planting seeds, nurturing them, and caring for them as they grow.

If the Queen of Pentacles appears in your reading, consider where in your life you are in need of nurturing, nourishment, rest, and the comfort of home. Consider ways to create this feeling for yourself. Or is there a part of you, perhaps long neglected, that is in need of this archetypal kind of maternal loving care? The Queen of Pentacles invites you to look at the concepts of nourishment and caretaking in your life.

In the mornings while they sleep off the wine, I take to the hillsides and forage—culinary herbs for dinner, medicinal herbs. I also keep my eye out for refugees in need of food and blankets, for Resistance fighters who need information and connections, and for German soldiers. I haven't seen any of the last, but there are always rumors. They're about to overtake us. Those stooges in Vichy are just a front anyway. Soon the Germans won't even bother to pretend Pétain isn't a puppet. I spit on the ground at the thought of him, older than I am, ancient.

I didn't expect Remedios to show up this morning. I'd invited her months ago and she never came. But I asked her to take a basket to Veronique Carvon, the bookseller, yesterday, and I know it piqued her interest.

Years ago we used to have a circle of women, thirteen of us, a coven an inquisitor in the old times might have called it before burning us all at the stake. But we were merely friends, of all ages, each with her own knowledge in herbs, or kabbalah, or the stars, or simply in how to direct attention and focus. Carvon joined, offering her knowledge of the cards.

But that was years ago, before the war.

Now Carvon and I exchange forged documents buried in the bottom of the basket. Passports, exit papers, visas that I hand off to Varian for his clients. I bring her Varian's payment under a bunch of herbs along with information and new requests. Carvon's shop has become a hub for fake documents and falsified passports.

These exchanges with Carvon fortified me and gave me courage in the face of uncertainty. But they required that I made special trips leaving the villa. It wasn't until now that I realized Remedios could be our go-between. I'm kicking myself that I hadn't thought of it earlier, but something about her when she first arrived was so fragile and exhausted that I'd left her alone to gain strength.

Carvon and I were doing what we could, helping in the face of madness. Could we save them all? We could not. But we could save some of them, and to those few it made all the difference.

"Is this milkweed?" Remedios asks now, holding up dogbane she's pulled out by the taproot.

"No, and it's quite toxic. Bitter if you taste it. I'll show you real milkweed if we find it. The pods are good for soup. Though never pull it in late summer. The monarchs lay their eggs on the undersides of the leaves. And so few monarchs find their way to France, we don't want to discourage them do we?"

Trying to explain my herbalism sometimes reminded me of when I'd ask my grandmother to teach me to cook. She'd sigh at the magnitude of verbalizing the million little choices she made based on a lifetime of experience, and instead just say, "Make what you like."

My heart had broken open just a little that day in the kitchen when Remedios told me she'd never learned to feed herself, at least not properly. The misguided protection of a father who wanted her to be more than a wife. A conundrum of sorts, since the man presumably had a wife of his own, didn't he? And what did he think of her?

But no matter, if Remedios wanted to learn how to nourish herself, I'd teach her.

She follows behind me, noting what I pluck and what I pass by. We walk uphill to find purslane growing in cracks between the rocks and ramps in a clearing in the woods where enough light can get to them. I abandoned the formal gardens at the house as soon as the boys left. Nothing but a bunch of ornamentals anyway, good for a show and nothing more. I'd had to go to the woods to find anything useful.

Borage and chervil I find in clumps. These, with a bit of wine that's gone off, make the toughest cuts of meat edible. I gathered young nettles and mint for tea for the aviator Saint-Exupéry and his wife Consuelo before they left, as they were both prone to indigestion. They assured me it wasn't my cooking. But I suspected they were unused to my hearty peasant fare and strong flavors, and their manners were too refined to mention it. Consuelo was a countess after all. My tea was an apology of sorts as well as a remedy.

Sometimes after a rain I find mushrooms, chanterelles and hen of the woods, enough to flavor pigeon stew or even make an entire side dish.

Everyone in the house gives me their ration cards, which I aggregate and then take to the market. Madame Guggenheim comes into the kitchen and slips me extra money. It made me like her, despite her hoarded wealth, despite her loud honking voice that carries across the terrace. Her largesse has allowed me a few luxuries like nicer cuts of beef, a wheel of cheese I once made last for a week, one time a whole lamb.

A crowd converges for dinner no matter what I serve, and I can make things stretch around the table. Dinner is the main event of the day, and they linger over their wine while cracking dark walnuts and nibbling croque fruits, a combination of almonds, dates, and whatever dried fruits come in on the ships from Tangier. I used to make it to sell, but I started setting some aside for the villa. And why not? We all need a reprieve. When I presented a few simple roast capons done up with forest herbs the other night, André Breton called me a surrealist and proclaimed my medium was gastronomy.

I like André the best.

I know which herbs to add to things—a dash of echinacea in their tea when the fog rolls in to keep the damp away, a bit of chervil in the stew to stoke the inner fire, a salad with bitter greens to keep their guts in order. They think me a fine cook, but come to me with other needs as well. Sacred basil for uplifting the heart. Oregano oil for dealing with various fungal infections. We all need fortification now. We all need a place to rest for as long as we can, a place to recoup, recover, and gain strength for what lies ahead.

When Remedios and I return from our forage, we lay out the herbs to wash and dry. The windows are open above the sink and warm spring air envelops us.

"Do you have anything that might help with . . ."

"Are you unwell?" I ask, concerned she might be pregnant.

"It's not for me."

"Oh my dear, it never is."

She smiles at this. "It's for a friend. She's in a, well, she's in a mental hospital. I sent her a deck of tarot cards, but I thought maybe you might have something I could send her as well."

I sigh. If the woman was truly mentally ill, there was little I had that might help her.

"She had a sort of break," Remedios continues. "After her lover was arrested. I think it was too much for her to bear. She's in a hospital in Spain."

Something in Remedios's voice makes me ask, "Did you see any signs of this in her before? Did you suspect she might have trouble in this way?" If she were an artist like all these surrealists in the villa, any one of them might be deemed insane given the art they made.

Remedios shakes her head. "No, I was shocked when I heard."

"There likely is nothing wrong with your friend," I say. "So often what gets called illness, sickness in women is actually a quite rational reaction to atrocity and evil. I think I have something here."

I wouldn't give the friend anything to ingest. Lord only knew what kind of horrific medicines and treatments they were already subjecting her body and mind to. I pull out a substantial sack of dried lavender, clary sage, motherwort, and dried balsam fir tips.

"Tell her to sleep with this under her pillow until the next full moon and then burn it." At least this wouldn't hurt her further.

Remedios hefts the sack. It's bigger than her palm, smaller than a book. "Thank you. What do I owe you?"

"Owe me? My dear, you owe nothing to no one. Remember that. But if you want to balance the energies of giving and receiving between us, come foraging with me again. I can always use your help."

For a moment we are smiling despite friends who are ill, a war at our door, a house full of refugees. The lightness in the room is palpable when Jacqueline finds us.

"Are you having a party?" she asks. "When there are people lining the halls trying to escape death?"

The way she talks to me, I wonder if she realizes the power I have over her food, over what she consumes. Many times I've thought of slipping a little something into her tea.

She asks about putting cots in the downstairs library. "I've managed to convince him," she says. André had claimed the entirety of the library for himself, excluding anyone he deemed unintellectual—a group that included Mary Jane, Miriam, and the local mayor who'd come out to greet him, celebrity to celebrity, and promptly had the door shut in his face.

But Jacqueline has convinced André to give up his lair in favor of sheltering more people in the library. "That's why we're here—isn't it?" She gives a pointed look at Remedios washing the herbs. "To help more people. Not have dinner parties."

"Of course," I say.

"Boisterousness is disconcerting to the waiting refugees," she says, as if she isn't a refugee as well. "Perhaps a little less time tucking lavender under the pillows," she murmurs as she swings back out the door.

It's on the tip of my tongue to say back, "Perhaps a little less time with the maquillage for some." But Remedios saves me.

"We must remember what André said, Jacqueline," she calls after her.

Jacqueline stops and turns, eyebrows practically at her hairline with surprise.

"Everything we do here is to outwit the anguish of the hour," Remedios says with a little lift of her chin.

Jacqueline gives a nod before she turns and leaves my kitchen.

CHAPTER NINE

Remedios buttoned her skirt the next morning, dressing to leave for her lesson at Madame Carvon's.

"Get a pack of those tarot cards for André today, would you?" Benjamin asked from the bed where he lazed, smoking and reading pages from Victor Serge of a novel in progress in French. "He'll like that."

A unique request, it didn't escape her notice that Benjamin was engineering ways to endear her to his best friend.

Remedios leaned over the bureau for a quick swipe of the nub of her dwindling lipstick in the mirror. "With what money?" It came out annoyed. Madame Carvon had already gifted her the deck that she'd sent to Leonora in the hospital. Funds were running low, and they'd need everything they could scrape together to start a new life, wherever that may be.

"Open that drawer," he said. "There's a false back. Push near the bottom."

She felt back over his socks and T-shirts to the back panel of the drawer and pushed gently. The top flipped forward, and a tidy packet fell out.

He rose from bed and came to take the wad of bills out of her hands.

"Here," he said, peeling off a small stack.

"You've been hiding this from me?"

"Found it when I was putting things away. Get a pack of cards for yourself, why don't you?"

Left behind in haste and surely needed elsewhere, the bills were dirty. "Shouldn't we give this to Madame Nouget?" she asked. The cook would put it to the best use.

"Whoever hid it didn't."

The aristocratic Saint-Exupérys had occupied the room before them; perhaps they had so much money they didn't miss a small stash like this. Somehow she doubted it. Cash was a universal that eased the way for anyone, regardless of rank.

"I'll give the rest to Nouget today," he promised, but returned the money to the back of the drawer and pushed the false back into place. Scratching his balding pate, he headed down the hall to the bathroom.

What might she do with a little money? They'd always been struggling—even in Paris, and here Benjamin had a stash he'd kept private. She supposed she should be grateful; money usually slipped through his hands like water. That he'd held on to it showed their situation was dire indeed.

Yet he hadn't thought to share.

While he was gone, she carefully snuck out a few more bills. Extra money was always a smart idea.

-⫷⫸-

She was late and sweating, her coat too heavy for the suddenly warm day, as she hustled toward her lesson. Her home-stitched creation looked as shabby on the streets of Marseilles as it had in Paris. Remedios still loved clothes, despite a war, or maybe because of it. She made notes for potential coat alterations in her sketchbooks—a dart or a seam to smarten things up. Changes she might manage by hand sewing but never seemed to get around to actually doing. Like everyone, she was searching for a strong enough diversion in this town of waiting.

She swung into Madame Carvon's shop to the tinkle of the bell overhead as Madame came out of the back as groomed and snappy as ever. No matter how much care Remedios took with her appearance before she came, she always wound up feeling unkempt next to the sleek Madame Carvon.

"Pétain has announced a visit next month. Raids will increase," Madame Carvon said. "They want to show they have control." She reached out for the basket. "Given how obsessed the Germans are with ports, I can't imagine we'll remain independent for long." As she took the handle, she tilted the basket and two vials of Nouget's tinctures rolled out, along with a note that Carvon studied quickly and then slipped in a pocket.

"Are you ill?" Remedios asked. It was out before she could moderate the intrusiveness of the question.

Madame didn't seem to mind and merely shook her head. "Nouget's a brilliant herbalist. These are merely an insurance policy of sorts—one to stop pregnancy, one to aid sleep and . . . other things. I hope I never need them."

Remedios was horrified. "Surely it's not going to get as bad as that."

"I'll leave soon. But not just yet. I still have things to do. That's where you come in."

At the inquisitive look on Remedios's face, Madame continued. "I believe you have skills in the area of forgery. That's what you used to do in Paris, non? Nouget told me." She was walking toward the back of the shop, Remedios forced to follow.

Nouget knew she was an artist, but how had she figured out the forgeries? Nouget knew everything apparently.

"My forger has just left. Escaped. I helped him leave, but now that means I need someone new to help with documents."

"But I only ever copied large-scale paintings in Paris, and I stumbled over the signatures. I'm not sure I can be of any use."

Carvon was impatient. "You'll try, Remedios. We all must do what we can. We didn't ask you before because it was clear you needed rest and my man was excellent. But now there's no choice. If Benjamin weren't so famous, you might have been able to fake your own papers and get out faster."

In the back room on the worktable lay an authentic document granting exit from the free zone. It was typed, with an impressive faded red watermark in the background and a multitude of different blue and black stamps across the whole of it. Next to it, Madame had placed a rough piece of paper for Remedios to practice her skills. "Start with this." Watercolors, oils, and pigments for tempera were placed next to a display of brushes, one so fine and small it had only three bristles. "I don't need to tell you paper's precious, so you'll work out the kinks before I move you on to the real stuff, d'accord?"

"What about the signatures?" Remedios asked, immediately fretting over her previous struggles to replicate de Chirico's.

"I have someone who's very good with the ministère de l'intérieur's signature, has access to the right kind of typewriter too."

Remedios shrugged out of her red coat and laid it over the back of a chair, ready to get to work, to try. It was daunting, yes, but not impossible, and this back room where she'd already sought refuge once before felt safe.

"Oh, before I forget." Remedios took the wad of bills out of her pocket and plunked them down. "André wants a Marseilles deck," she said.

"André Breton wants my cards." As Remedios suspected, not even Madame Carvon was immune to the fame of André. "Bon." She folded off two bills and handed the rest back.

"No, you keep it," Remedios said. "Let me repay you for some of this." She gestured around. "The knowledge you've given me."

Madame put the money into her pocket without protest. "This will come in handy. You start on that, and I'll be right back," she said with a crisp click of her heels to the front of the shop.

While Remedios had found pleasure in duping the rich and proving her skills were as good as a master's, now she felt fueled with purpose. The tiny three-bristled brush intrigued her. She was used to working with small, precise implements, but this would provide another level of detail. She wondered if Carvon would let her keep it.

It took her four tries to get the watermark right. Mixing a tint with the same watery paleness as the real thing was tricky. The stamps were easier. She'd been bent over, face close to the paper, her back beginning to ache. Straightening, arching her back, her eyes were drawn to a low shelf of dulled Moroccan leather-covered books with faded gilt lettering. Madame Carvon had loaned her books from the front of the shop, letting her treat the shelves like her own private library as long as she didn't break the spines. Remedios had been reading Gurdjieff on Madame's recommendation. His theory of the Fourth Way intrigued her—a way to harness body, mind, emotion, and spirit to access the unseen realms.

Remedios's father had thought that a civilized house, no matter its grandeur or modesty, should have a library. He filled his with engineering texts, illustrated botany guides, books in the universal language Esperanto that he'd mastered, and a deeply individual mix of novels and treatises on ephemeral topics guided only by the interests of his curious mind. In that handsome, chilly room he would sit at his drafting table working on his engineering renderings. As a child, she could hide in his library during the siesta as long as she didn't make noise. He allowed his daughter unsupervised access to any book on the shelves save one.

The small, ancient-looking red leather-bound volume emblazoned with *Tarocci* on the spine enticed her when she was about twelve years old. It fit perfectly in her palm, the exact size of the deck of cards it described.

"Not that one." She looked up to see her father watching her. "In deference to your mother, not that one." He'd plucked it out of her hand and reshelved it on the highest shelf. One she couldn't reach, even with the ladder. Then he handed her a copy of Edgar Allan Poe's stories, outrageously scary for a twelve-year-old. But the *Tarocci* book wasn't forgotten, and she speculated that it must be filled with something heretical and sinful since her mother revered the Church above all.

Of course she climbed the shelves one night and got it down. Of course she read it. Putting it on the highest shelf practically had been a dare.

It was filled with diagrams and complex illustrations of a deck of cards that when shuffled and laid out in particular sequences could foretell the future and illuminate the past.

Now, in Madame Carvon's back room amid her secret stash of books, Remedios tilted what looked like the same book toward her and off the dusty shelf.

Madame came beside her. "A collector's item. My father had a set of notes that went with it, but he sold them long ago."

"My father had it in his library. I wasn't allowed to touch it as a girl, but I read it anyway, barely understood it."

Madame smiled. "These things often come to us when we're ready. It's quite valuable." She pressed the volume into Remedios's hands. "I think you take this one next. Though, of course, I can teach you more than any book."

Remedios objected. If it were valuable, she didn't want to be responsible if something happened to it. Yet Germans were burning books by the heap, and perhaps in giving it to her, Carvon meant to protect it.

"Keep it as payment for your labors." Madame gestured toward

Remedios's work on the table, tilting her head to the side. "Not bad, but not convincing either. You see here? It becomes a bit irregular. Precision is the answer."

"Things are only useful if they are right."

"I suppose," Carvon said. "But come, you've done enough for today." She began tidying the paints away. "We will begin our study of the swords suit."

At the look on Remedios's face, she said, "You didn't think we'd stop with our studies?"

Remedios wanted to say, well, yes, she did. Since she was needed now to forge documents, since raids would be increasing, since she had the book now, since everything was ramping up in tighter and tighter circles.

"Take out all the swords and lay them on the table. I'll join you in a moment," Madame Carvon said, heading to the front of the shop to speak with a newly arrived customer.

The book was calling to her as Madame didn't allow her to take notes during their lessons. Carvon thought the lessons should wash over her and what was meant to be retained would stay. "This is not some precise science," she'd say. "This is the indefinable. You take what is meant to go with you because it hits you deeply. The rest is . . ." She fluttered her hands. "Writing down notes blocks the channel from coming in, your inner knowing from being heard." It meant that when Remedios left for the day and walked around the corner out of sight of the shop, she'd scribble down everything she could remember from the lesson on scraps of paper and fill her pockets with notes that she then crammed between the pages of her homemade notebooks.

It also meant that Carvon quizzed Remedios periodically during the lessons to make sure she was retaining.

"The five," she said when she returned, picking up the card with a soldier standing on the battlefield. Two swords hefted on his left shoulder, and another in his right hand pointed into the ground. In the background two foes have turned their backs, their swords lying on the ground, useless.

"Blockage and setbacks."

Madame nodded, letting this paltry answer slide, and picked up the seven.

"All sevens bring lessons, learning, and critical insights. The four different suits show four different ways of going about this."

After a moment Madame said, "But you are not retaining today."

"No," Remedios admitted.

Carvon shook her head. "Let's have a new lesson." She reached for a sheet of paper, thin linen, textured and refined. "Write down what's distracting you." She rolled an enameled pen her way.

Remedios picked it up and wrote "leaving" in peacock-blue ink.

"You might consider being specific, because magic has a way of rebounding on you."

The word *magic* stopped Remedios.

"What do you think we're doing here?" Madame asked at the look on her face.

"I want to leave here for a safe haven where I can do my work in peace," Remedios said.

"So write that at the top of the page. I desire to leave for . . ."

Remedios did as she asked.

"Bon. Now cross out all the vowels and all the repeated consonants."

She was left with DRTLVFNHWK.

Madame Carvon took up her own pen. "Now create the sigil. A symbol, made up of these letters but put together like a monogram or a crest and shrunk down." Madame began sketching, her ink viridian green. "Until it is no longer recognizable as letters or for what it is." She sketched the letters on top of one another in a looping script. "You're an artist, yours will look better than mine."

When Remedios hesitated, Madame continued. "The power to transform is naturally within you, Remedios. Bring your artistic nature and play with it until it's a symbol."

Remedios began enhancing and simplifying; cave paintings and hieroglyphics came to her mind.

"Bon," Madame said when it was finished. "Now you draw a circle around it. Then we charge it."

"How?"

"Energize it. Attach a strong emotion or feeling to it. Love, laughter, pain, crying, or sorrow—any of these will work. But the easiest way to charge it is to focus on it while you please yourself."

"Sorry?"

"Physically. You must love yourself, and at the height of pleasure you must concentrate on your sigil."

Remedios wasn't a prude, but she blushed nonetheless.

"Yes, this is usually how it's done," Madame said with an efficient nod.

It was just the sort of thing André would love, Remedios thought. A new path into the subconscious laced with sex, but as bold as she encouraged herself to be, she didn't think she could explain this to André over dinner.

"Must I be alone?" she asked, thinking of Benjamin.

"It's easier to concentrate if you are alone, but if you have a lover who is willing . . ." Madame shrugged and pursed her lips. "You could have it with you in bed. Perhaps you should draw it on his shoulder," she said with a smile. "Or his forehead."

Remedios smiled at that.

"After it's charged, you must destroy it and forget about it. Burn it, bury it, but make sure it's gone and then put it out of your mind. It's only when you've forgotten it that you will find it has worked."

Remedios felt discouraged then. There was no way she could stop thinking about leaving. Even if she could silence her mind for a moment, a million different people and reminders of her desperate state encircled her at the villa.

Madame nodded as if reading her mind. "You might not forget the wish, but you will forget what you have done in furtherance of this desire."

Remedios twisted one side of her mouth up in doubt.

"Try and see," Madame said. "What else do you have to lose?"

That night after dinner and games when they were getting ready for bed, she told Benjamin what she'd learned that afternoon. He smiled wide, a little teasing. "Well, sorceress, let's enact your spell," he said as he took her hand and fell back on the bed.

The next afternoon as she headed to the shop for her lesson, she took the long way to Madame Carvon's, dropping the sigil in the harbor, hoping the sea might take it to that safe haven she'd been dreaming of, that soon she might follow. She watched it become saturated, then sink, then rise on a current, then sink a bit more until she could no longer see it. Then she headed toward Carvon's shop. As she watched the paper fade in the dark water of the harbor, she tried to remember—how had she phrased the sigil? Had she used the word *desire* or *want*? The exact words floated away as she hurried along down the street.

THE HIGH PRIESTESS—
Veronique Carvon

The High Priestess is the keeper of esoteric learning and intuitive gifts. Sitting on her throne, cloaked in blue robes, she is the symbol of divine feminine wisdom. Behind her, the curtain of consciousness obscures universal knowledge. She holds the Torah on her lap and wears a cross on her chest, with a crescent moon at her feet signifying her connection to the great monotheist traditions. When the High Priestess appears in a reading, she is a call to listen both to deep intuition and to consider scholarship and study for purposes of soul advancement. She points the way to gaining formal knowledge, internalizing it, and synthesizing it with intuitive internal knowledge. In this way wisdom becomes accessible.

If the High Priestess comes to you in a reading, she is a call to look inward and to apply acquired knowledge to become comfortable with the unknowable, the ambiguous, and the mysterious in life.

My family has operated a printing press here for three hundred years in the same shop, the same spot. But this, I fear, is coming to an end. Every night I pull tarot cards, and three have repeated over the last week—the Tower of change, the Knight of Pentacles calling me to prepare, and the nightmare of worry that is the Nine of Swords.

Remedios landed in my shop months ago needing to hide from the police, but what she really needed was the opposite. She needed to be seen. She needed to come out of hiding. And she needed a guide. When she picked up the tarot cards, I knew they were meant for her. She'd found the first signpost along her path.

Madame Nouget told me she's a painter. That's what initially intrigued me about her, and I'd be lying if I didn't admit that I'd suspected her artistic skills could come in handy.

The day she started forging papers for us satisfied my hunch.

The *Tarocci* book has been with my family since the shop opened. Usually I hide it, and it's certainly not for sale. But I'd felt called to put it in the back room for the first time when I heard that Paris fell. It felt like a protective talisman for the other books, for the shop, for me. Silly, I know. But now that things are looking dire, it's better that she take the book with her and use it than for it to sit dusty on the shelf—its secrets unused, or even worse, destroyed. Perhaps it will provide protection for her too.

Our time together shifted in the following weeks, from learning the tarot to drawing freedom into reality by creating exit papers. She got quite good at it too. It was a month or so later that, unbeknownst to her, she delivered her last basket.

Madame Nouget had put tinctures in the bottom and a luxurious bushel of mint on top. But there was something else in the basket. It was a tiny slip of paper, "Remedios is next" written on it. "She'll have real documents. Péret can't travel on a fake." Varian didn't let people know when their documents had come through until they had. I supposed he'd learned the hard way that disappointment under the current circumstances could be crushing. She and Benjamin would be the next to leave, and soon.

I was planning to close the shop anyway. I'd made my plans to flee. I didn't tell her this because I hated long goodbyes and because you never knew where information flew once it'd left your lips. She'd tell them in the villa maybe, and they might tell someone else, and next thing you knew there'd be complications, an order from the police that I could not refuse. Better this way. Better that she come for her next lesson and find the shop shuttered. A bit brutal, yes, but these are brutal times.

When we said goodbye that day, as if it were any other day, I knew it was the last time I'd see her.

I felt the need to impart some wisdom, something she could take with her on her journey going forward. I picked up the tiny three-bristled brush she favored, my finest, and one that'd been in the shop for as long as I could remember. I put it into her hand, clasping both her hands in mine.

"Remember, there is nothing outside of the cards. What matters is what you can excavate from your own soul. Release what you can and make it manifest in the world. There's nothing more important than that."

Remedios was silent, looking me in the eye, and then to my utter surprise she leaned forward and kissed my cheek very quickly, a seal and a benediction. Her eyes were serious, a little wet, then she squeezed my hand and was gone.

PART II

MEXICO

1941

CHAPTER TEN

When they landed in Veracruz, Remedios slipped a bunch of Madame Nouget's lavender and rosemary out of her pocket and dropped it in the dirt as she stepped off the wharf. The dried leaves mingled with the dust of a new country. She'd picked them in the hills of Marseilles while on a foraging trip, drawn to their scent and what Madame Nouget taught her about their qualities, lavender for healing, rosemary for remembrance. She dried them, tied them with kitchen twine, and brought them with her on the *Serpa Pinto* to ground the watery days at sea. She hadn't anticipated that at night, lying in her cot, she'd hold the bundle to her nose to mask the scent of unwashed bodies and people being seasick in buckets. All of them down in the hold while the ill and injured rightly took the staterooms on a luxury ship packed to three times its usual capacity. She offered the herbs back to the earth now to acknowledge a rough crossing and to greet a potential sanctuary. She offered them back with thanks.

The ground swayed under her feet as if she were still on the boat. The crowd of people hauled baggage, trunks, and parcels from the ship. A delegation of local officials greeted the refugees on the pier along with a mariachi band wearing black evening clothes glittering in the strong afternoon sun. The sight of welcoming smiles and cheerful music brought an unexpected lump to her throat after living for so long in a country that didn't want her.

She and Benjamin hefted three suitcases between them—hers with all her handmade clothes, such as they were, Benjamin's with the books that seemed to attach themselves to him wherever he went, and the third filled with art. That third suitcase she never let out of her sight.

They joined the flood of passengers walking toward the town's plaza. As she walked, her nerves began to settle, blood returning to her unsteady legs. Walking refreshed her, as much as someone who had spent a week on a ship dabbing herself with homemade lavender water could feel refreshed. The fierce blue of the sky, the high stucco walls of the fancy merchants' houses, and the uneven road made her feel as if she were walking back in time on some medieval pilgrimage in her homeland of Spain and not as if she were walking into her future.

Despite her exhaustion, Remedios felt the energy of novelty. The trees were different here, the streets, the smells; it enlivened her. She'd been forced into change for so long now that it felt comforting, even as she landed in a new country with nothing but a suitcase. When they came to the zocalo, the cathedral and the arched portals of the arcades along the sides reminded her of Madrid. A raucous mix of music from competing mariachi and marimba bands gave the square the feel of a party. Under the arches boys played dominoes, women sold food, and men hawked cigars, which Benjamin wasted no time in changing money for and buying.

Women in pristine white dresses with dense colorful embroideries at the collar and a flounce of clean white lace at the hem sat on blankets spread on the paving stones. Mangoes and chayote were displayed on woven mats, tiny charcoal grills cooked goat meat, white cheeses glistened on banana leaves. The displays did their job, enticing Remedios to buy. The vendors noted her interest and called out.

"Señorita pájaro! Hey, el cuervo!" They teased her for her black skirt and plain black blouse, calling her a blackbird and a raven. It was a shock and a balm to hear Spanish in the streets again. Her native tongue after years of French, a confirmation that yes, this could be her home.

She leaned over the wares spread on a rough-woven horse blanket. Seed pods, dried grasshoppers, common clamshells, bits of red string, all of it radiated energy. As tired and grimy as she was, even she could feel the purpose emanating from the trinkets, turning them into treasure.

She slowed, and the vendors gathered, each outdoing the other.

"Health and harmony, señorita," said one, brandishing a bundle of dried sage that looked like flaking skin.

"Energy and vitality," said another, waving an immense white feather.

A tiny vial of holy water was offered in an open palm. "Sprinkle this on your true love."

"Protection and boundaries," one said, holding up a single rusted railroad spike.

"For peace."

Peace. The word stopped Remedios. Grounding her in place as a familiar word will when spoken at the right moment, like an incantation. They'd spoken of peace all the time at the villa, as a collective experience that was coming soon, something that could be attained and restored. But this now was a different word, one meant solely and personally for her. Peace.

As Remedios stood surrounded by vendors, she realized she had no proper Mexican money. Varian had procured everything for them in the end—exit papers from the Vichy government, travel papers through Morocco, visas into Mexico, and a small amount of French francs to establish a life upon arrival.

Still the seller who'd stopped her held up a dipped candle, glowing with yellow beeswax and scented of honey. "Light this and you'll see the inner realms where true wisdom and the unknowable secrets lie. That is the way of freedom. Freedom, you understand, is the only way to lasting peace."

Remedios dug into the pocket of her skirt, bringing out a few franc notes.

The woman took the bills. "I'll change your money for you," she said, tucking it away in her bodice and then wrapping the candle in old newspapers. She was used to dealing with foreign denominations.

"Before you burn, you must carve into it. Understand?" She handed over the parcel. "Everything you are leaving behind. Everything you seek freedom from. You must release it and be free."

Remedios took the wrapped package from her. Could it be that easy? "Todos?"

The woman smiled, understanding. "Just a letter or a symbol. As best you can. Your intention will be enough."

Benjamin called to her from up the street. He'd found a cantina he liked. He waved her on, and she hustled, never wanting him to wait.

"Good luck, cuervo," the woman called after her.

That was how Remedios arrived in a new land—sleepless and unwashed, a blackbird with an intention to burn.

-⸢⸢⸢◆⸥⸥⸥-

They ordered lecheros, coffee with hot milk, and canillas, little biscuits shaped like ship's ropes. In talking with the owner, Benjamin learned they let rooms above the place and took one. After coffee Benjamin slipped the key into the lock of the bright blue door set in peeling stucco. The courtyard smelled of rot, and a bare potted citrus drooped in the corner, but Remedios didn't care. She'd hardly slept on the boat and a headache hovered on the periphery of her vision due to the strong sun and stronger coffee late in the day. When she saw the heavy wooden shutters at the windows of their room, made to keep out the midday sun for the siesta, she felt she could kiss those sentinels to slumber. She closed them, hooked the latch, and turned to unpack.

"That makes me feel cooped up." Benjamin unlatched them and hinged open the glass-paned windows as well. Then he leaned out to sniff the cooling twilight air. "Doesn't that make you feel cooped up?"

If their passage had created a desire for freedom and roaming in Benjamin, in Remedios it had created a desire for privacy and a quiet space in which to sleep and dream.

He paced the room. "Let's find a place for a drink," he said. "Or a walk around the town to stretch our legs more. Will you come?" he asked, jingling a few coins in his pocket.

Out the window she glimpsed the maritime cranes along the harbor and the large ships docked in the port. Veracruz gave her the sense of continual commerce, and as if in punctuation a train whistled in the distance.

Despite this hubbub and the coffee, she was already eyeing the sagging bed with the thin wool blanket like a beckoning paradise.

When she hesitated, he said, "Let's go find where the culture is."

He expected to head downstairs and find the Café de Flore in this port town, only serving tequila instead of Pernod. Typical Frenchman, she thought. Or perhaps he hoped to find a Mexican shaman who would recount to him pre-Columbian tales that he'd use as fodder for poems.

After a moment of her silence, he came and kissed her, the quick peck on the cheek of all quickly departing husbands. And when she heard the door shut, it brought the heart-lifting promise of much-needed privacy. She brought out her tarot cards and the little old book. She'd not gotten them out on the ship. You never knew how people would react to a deck of tarot cards.

Now she closed the heavy carved shutters again and slid the cards out of their linen bag. She relished the reassuring slip of their backs against each other, the snap of them as she shuffled and riffed the bridge and placed the pile on the scratchy blanket folded at the foot of the bed.

She took up the candle. The seller said to light it for the things to be left behind. She didn't have to think twice about what she wanted to banish—war, imprisonment, despair, fear. She'd been living with them for months; they'd been in the background of her life for years. She only just barely kept them at bay in the villa, in that cocoon of artists and friends.

She found a sewing needle in her bag that would work as well as anything, and, holding the candle steady, she felt tears come as she began to carve. They might not have money or jobs or a home, but they were alive in a warm country where Spanish was spoken in the streets. She carved a *W* for war and crossed it with a *D* for despair, depression, deception—her constant recent companions. Remembering Madame Carvon, she tried to make the sigil beautiful as befitting its focal point for power, for change, for harnessing desire and releasing old fears. She turned the candle ninety degrees and inscribed another *D* in the wax, and again until it looked like a monogram of the universe or the symbol of some ancient sect.

She didn't resist crying, in the alchemical realm of salt now as she smudged tears down the candle with her thumb. They weren't the familiar tears of despair but tears of release and exhaustion and cleansing. Any strong emotion would do to charge a sigil, and besides, another thing she intended to leave behind was the tears constantly lurking behind her eyes.

With the candle inscribed with grief and its sister relief, and anointed with tears, she struck the match, the wick lighting up fast and steady. Welcome release washed over her as her tears were transformed into resolve and solace. The flame became a beacon and a purifier, clearing as it burned, lighting her landing in a new home.

She took the *Tarocci* book out of her sack, the treasured object she kept hidden from all, even Benjamin. She'd made it hers now, covering the margins with her notes and observations. The first mark she'd made had felt like a trespass, but once the line was breached, she hadn't stopped annotating.

Next she took up her tarot deck, cut it in half and then in half again, before she turned over the top card. Judgment—the trumpet of angels calling the dead to awaken. A message to rise up, to come back to life. A card of rebirth, reawakening, and forgiveness. She propped it against the candle while the flame elongated, growing higher and brighter.

-⟨⟨⟨◆⟩⟩⟩-

In the morning, the air was washed clean by overnight rain and scented with wood smoke. They sent all their clothes off with a laundry woman the café owner recommended and took turns in the bathtub at the end of the hall after Remedios scrubbed it out with scouring powder they bought in little packets from the pharmacy.

They lingered in Veracruz because they were welcomed. As the days unfurled, they relaxed in the downstairs café for most of the mornings, mainly to soothe Benjamin, who had to be eased into his day and hated rushing of any kind. Breakfast was always muskmelon and eggs with chilis. Then Benjamin ordered a basket of sweet rolls and honey, and a second carafe of strong coffee as they read the papers, mopping up news of the war, scanning the articles for mentions of anyone they knew.

"Read this," Remedios said one bright morning. Despite the relief of their few weeks in the port town, she was beginning to feel restless. Shouldn't they be headed on to Mexico City? Shouldn't they be finding jobs, a place to live even? Benjamin, with his ability to stay focused on the present, seemed content to wander the streets of the port smoking those thin cigars while staring longingly out to sea like some old merchant awaiting the arrival of a schooner.

That morning she passed him her part of the newspaper. President

Cárdenas's policies had established a college in Mexico City staffed mainly by refugees, welcoming intellectuals and artists from war-engulfed Europe.

President Cárdenas's motto was that Europe's loss was Mexico's gain. Mexico's welcome of immigrants was an efficient and satisfying defiance of Franco, a show of solidarity with Spanish Republicans, and a potential boon to the nation.

"Oh, I'll go pack my bags now." Benjamin scanned the article and tossed it back on her side of the table without fully reading it. "Why do I want to create a new generation of Mexican bourgeoisie?" He never failed to make his disdain for employment clear. Jobs were a capitalist tool of oppression and a bourgeois compromise that impinged on his art and his spirit. He hadn't had a regular job in all the time she'd known him. In Paris he had only grumblingly accepted the time she spent at the odd painting jobs she picked up around the city. The only job of hers that he ever approved of was the de Chiricos she forged for Oscar Sanchez because selling them to aristocrats subverted both class and capitalism with satisfying efficiency.

Surely their current circumstances would change Benjamin's stance toward employment, she thought. His old modus operandi of sitting around cafés and raising money from Parisian society ladies hoping to share the aura of the intellectual was one thing; being a refugee in a country where you knew no one was another.

"Lecturing wouldn't be that different from what you did all day at the Café de Flore, would it?"

"Amusing, Rosa," he said without looking up.

"We'll need money."

"Always with the practical." He sighed, folding his part of the paper away. "What do we need money for? Everything here is so cheap."

"You could mold a new generation, foment revolution from the inside." She sipped her lukewarm coffee. "We have enough money for train tickets to Mexico City if we go second class."

"There is no inside. They just become beholden to the system. Complete revolution is the only answer." He struck a match and lit another of the cigarillos. "What do your cards have to say about that?"

When she didn't answer, he said, "I know you have them in your pocket. You don't even go to the bathroom without them. Unlike that fancy book." He held her gaze, as if to say, "Yes, I know all your secrets."

She pulled the pouch out of her pocket.

"So tell me what I need to know," he said.

She'd done this once before, read cards in a café. But that was an ocean away and ended in a police raid. She gave the back of the cards a quick tap to wake them up. As she began to shuffle she asked the universe, or any friendly guiding spirits, to send a message for Benjamin. She stacked the deck on the table and had Benjamin cut. Then she flipped the top card to find the Devil staring up at her.

"That can't be good," Benjamin said.

"The Devil is about self-delusion, self-sabotage, doing things we know aren't good for us."

Benjamin stubbed out his cigarillo with a flourish.

"Not just that. Though tobacco and alcohol can be Devil things. It is more about releasing a state of mind, a thought process, the chains of the past."

Benjamin put a finger on the card, twirling it on the tabletop. "Well, what are we going to do, Rosa?" He sighed. "Linger in this port town?"

That was all she needed. She booked their train tickets that afternoon.

—⟪⟨◆⟩⟫—

It was only later when they were standing on the platform, about to board, that she felt him hesitate. For the first time on all the many journeys that had brought them here, brought them to safety, it was before the final and shortest leg of the trip that she felt him falter.

People jostled them as they blocked the path to the train. She tugged his hand forward, but he didn't move. She could read in his face the realization that they were taking the final step away from his homeland, site of his birth, his fondest place. She didn't think he'd accepted it until then—they were very far from France.

"Rosa," he said in a low voice.

"They're all gone." She brandished the first argument she could think of. "Even André. He's not there anymore. None of them are. It's gone. It's time to go."

This seemed to shake him out of whatever inertia had gripped him, and he climbed the stairs in front of her into the train car, embarking on the final leg of their journey.

SEVEN OF CUPS—
Benjamin Péret

The Seven of Cups is a card of offerings and confusion. It shows a person being presented with seven chalices floating in the clouds, each holding a different vision—a serpent, a ghost, a laurel wreath, a dragon, a tower, jewels, and a head.

Uncertainty reigns over this card. It is a card for deciphering what is real and what is not. It is a card for looking at choices and deciding which, if any of them, are meant for you. It is not a card of comfort. Usually a good amount of anxiety and confusion surrounds this card. There are many cups, many paths, and the first step in choosing the right one is to clarify and examine what the different choices are. It is also a card of unsettled emotion. There can be a lack of focus and a feeling of being lost when this card appears in a reading. Clarifying can be a way to circumvent the disturbance and inertia of this card. When the Seven of Cups appears, if one can scrutinize the offered solutions distinct from the surrounding emotions, the options may become clearer.

I felt a dizzying strangeness stepping out of the train depot and onto the streets of Mexico City. Perhaps it was merely the elevation, which made my breathing feel shallow as the train climbed into the mountains. Despite my hesitation Remedios had convinced me to come here in the end. Her powers of persuasion were matched only by her innate practicality. Something about her I'd always found a little gauche. We were, all of us, striving to transcend such things.

"Yes, but I haven't figured out how to transcend dinner, Benjamin," she'd said to me on more than one occasion.

The juxtaposition of skyscrapers and donkey carts, the women in traditional rebozos with paper flowers in their hair walking past their office-worker counterparts in nylons and high heels, the smell of wet drains and cumin, the hawkers who descended on us with trinkets, the garish billboards advertising toothpaste and dish soap—all of this pleased me, and I thought, for just a moment, that I might be able to live here.

A lottery ticket seller approached us, and to my surprise Remedios bought one.

"For you," she said after she'd handed over some coins.

"What if I win?" I asked, folding the paper into my suit pocket. "Will I have to split it with you?"

She took my arm and tucked herself up under my elbow. "If you win, then I'll stop worrying about the quotidienne," she said. "Can you imagine a better sign for a fresh start?"

We didn't win. It didn't matter.

"This is an interlude," she said, as happy as I'd seen her since we left Paris. "Every life should have an interlude, shouldn't it? To get out. To see another country. Who knows how it will affect us, our thinking, our work?" She stopped again to buy a paper cone of roasted pumpkin seeds. She was always buying things off the street, gathering them like a magpie.

The old colonial buildings struck a low chord of nostalgia against the bright newness of construction cranes as we walked along. And wafting over all of it was the tang of wood smoke and charcoal mixed with car exhaust.

"Did you know the city was founded literally on top of the Temple Mayor, the Aztec capital? We are walking right on top of one of the largest cities of the ancient world."

"Always full of facts," I said. She'd been reading about our new country, holding on to bits of information she found fascinating.

"Bigger than London when Cortés arrived here," she countered.

I was unsure if the mix of Aztec and modern made for the most surreal place I'd ever been, or if it smacked of the triumph of capitalism over older ways of ordering the world.

We knew no one. Had only the haziest idea where to go. The old Russian embassy had been turned into a temporary shelter for recent refugees and became our base. In the next days we started the rounds at the headquarters of the Spanish Republican government in exile, the French embassy, and a refugee agency.

Within a week, a young man with the refugee agency took us to an apartment in the Colonia de San Rafael on the dilapidated calle Gabino Barreda.

He kept up a patter about the fiestas in the neighborhood, as if he were a realtor trying to sell us a new house and not an aid worker showing us the only place available.

We had to step through a huge window on the landing to get inside. The nonfunctional door, heavily scarred and hanging askew on iron brackets, was nailed shut. The floorboards were fuzzed and soft with age and washings, the walls dingy with chipped stucco and water stains. The young man with the refugee agency shoved the keys into my hands before Remedios had even looked in the kitchen, thinking she'd balk because the place was derelict and dirty. But it was all the agency had on offer, and there was no place else to go.

We moved in that same day, and despite our penury, Remedios

rather gallantly was determined to set up a household. So what if there were cobwebs in the corners and mice living in the floor? She took these as signs of life, she told me.

She busied herself with rags and a bucket she found in a closet.

As I stood in the middle of the living room, a tremendous wave of heartache for France, occupied and injured as it was, crashed over me. My morning walks to buy the English-language newspapers and my El Aguila cigars just brought home that I was marooned in a primitive land, where I walked past piles of donkey dung and shards of pottery in the street.

I heaved a suitcase into the middle of the bare living room floor and opened it. As I unrolled the first canvas she came up behind me, as stealthy as the cats she befriended wherever she went, and twined her arms around my waist.

"Did you miss the paintings? Or do you miss their painters?"

I turned my head to kiss her, in acknowledgment of her understanding. She always knew just what to say.

Because I remembered standing next to Max, admiring the collage he'd made and nailed directly to a tree, all of us in the garden of the villa for an art auction. The day had been warm and breezy, the war felt a million miles away, and we all felt a sense of normalcy so buoyant that in a fit of expansiveness Max took down the piece and gave it to me. I'd objected. His work might be devalued at the moment, but we all knew it would rebound when the war was over. He'd pressed it into my hands anyway, saying, "It belongs with you." Yves Tanguy had given me the little watercolor in Paris in exchange for a poem I'd written for him that he used to seduce Kay Sage. And Picasso, drunk and doodling, had dashed off the sketch and bestowed it on me one evening when André and I were drinking at his apartment late into the night before everything happened, before we had to flee and keep fleeing.

Remedios was digging through her suitcase and came back with her well-used sewing kit.

"I figure these will work," she said as she pinned the papers to the wall with needles.

For just a moment, seeing the familiar works on our new humble walls, I could see them for what they were. These were my saints. I'd given up the other kind long ago.

A sagging couch, a rickety card table, two scarred and machine-carved Victorian chairs covered in disintegrating brocade, and a bed covered in a dirty serape had been left behind for us to use. These Remedios scoured; at least our universe would be clean. She washed the serape in the sink until the water ran clear and then hung it out the window to dry. When she was done, the rooms were as clean and spare as a monk's cell.

We'd been living in a single bedroom for a year, a compressed life, albeit in a villa, yet the apartment allowed us to unfold a bit both mentally and physically. I felt a loosening, like a fist unclenching.

In those early days we slept during the siesta, long dreamless interludes in two- and three-hour stretches. A gulf of cumulative exhaustion spiked with worry that pulled us under each day lying side by side until the early evening. But soon we were able to accomplish other things during the siesta, a reunion of the physical between us, which brought pleasure and relief.

It was then I'd often get out of bed, inspired as I hadn't been in months, and come back with a notebook.

"This feeling," I'd say, re-covering us both in the thin sheet. "I was thinking it might be a poem. Or the dream I had last night. The things with dreams, though, it's easy to convey the emotions of them. It's harder to capture the visions that led to the emotions and describe them so the reader feels the emotions without your interference. Then again, poetry's probably the only way to do that."

"You know there's a whole history of writers who recorded their dreams as a way to begin the day. Aristotle and Plato talk about dreams in all their writings."

"Aristotle?" The Aristotelian ideal of the middle way through life was the last thing to interest me.

"Yes, Aristotle. I know things."

She often threw in these little reminders of her formal education. Something I found bewildering as we were trying to transcend and unravel such learning. "The idea that you have to be educated about what you're rebelling against before you're allowed to rebel was meant to keep people in line. Keep them controlled."

She stretched, like one of the languorous cats that had shown up mere days after we moved in and seemed to adopt us.

"Perhaps I should do that as well," she said, nodding at my notebook.

"What? Write?" She'd yet to paint. In Marseilles there was very little time to create. She'd managed a few sketches, that was all.

I tossed the notebook to her and got out of bed, the reverie of our embrace lost. In truth I was annoyed by her interrupting questions and didn't want to show it. "I just started this one. Rip out the front page if you want and make it yours."

She didn't rip it out, but read it.

"You've made me a dark butterfly in your dream," she said. I'd dreamed I was in jail and a cloud of dark butterflies had swarmed through the metal bars, a beautiful menacing. I'd been trying to capture the exact feeling of the dream—of overwhelm and appreciation, fear and attraction, a stifling and an expansion.

"I rather like that," she said quietly.

She began scribbling in the little book at all different hours.

And I admit I peeked in it once she started using it. At first to understand the nightmares that sometimes disturbed her. Dreams in the early morning hours, the hour of the wolf, when she burrowed into my back, waking me, until I put an arm around her and held her in the black as her shaking subsided.

But after I'd looked once, I couldn't stop, astonished by the broad creativity of her mind and the freedom she allowed herself. Her dreams, bits of poems, even fanciful recipes for the things I think she wished she could create. A recipe to dispel bad dreams. A recipe to make one believe she was the King—not the Queen—of England. And the one that made me pause, a recipe to disperse unrelenting melancholy.

She caught me once.

"You're looking through my things." A statement, her flat tone giving away nothing.

"They're just dreams, Rosa."

"I'd share if you asked." She crossed the room and snatched the notebook out of my hand. After that she left it open on my side of the bed with a little note that read, "for your approval."

"Rosa, really," I said, sheepishly closing it and tossing it back to her side.

Did a phrase of hers find its way into a poem I was working on? Did a particular image she conjured linger in my mind and somehow work its way into my work? Probably. If things came from her dreams, or from our conversations, I've long since lost track.

I blame it on missing André and being desperate for the sort of intellectual collaboration we had. I was used to sharing intellectual space with someone, borrowing ideas and refining them. It was like a game of catch. I missed the sharp intellect of his mind, my best friend, my intellectual other half. Talking with André, running ideas past André, debating with André—all these things were as central to my day as cigarettes and coffee.

I felt like an outcast while a party was happening elsewhere. Everyone was in New York, that city looming right out of my grasp. André and Jacqueline were there. They went straight from Marseilles, Max and Peggy too. I'd heard André had managed to set up a little salon of sorts full of bourgeois wallets that he emptied in his usual fashion.

I didn't give up on the idea of joining them and approached the

US embassy here for a visa, thinking I might have better luck than in Marseilles where I was jumbled in with the thousands of people trying to flee. But apparently I'd become notorious, because my application was turned down that same day. So much for a free exchange in the marketplace of ideas, or perhaps so long as those ideas weren't communist. So much for joining my friends.

I missed my life. I missed France.

As weeks turned to months, the apartment could seem lifeless and so we started going a few nights a week to Gunther Gerzso's house. A Mexican painter who'd spent most of his life in Europe whom I knew from the cafés. He always seemed to corral a party. It was there one night when we'd all had too much tequila that Remedios invited everyone to our apartment for drinks in the middle of the week. The invitation and desire to be a hostess were so out of character that I was too stunned to reinforce the invitation. But during the long walk home, I asked her about it.

"Don't you feel that we need people around us?"

I was quiet, puffing a cigarillo. "We do? Or I do? Are you managing me?" I asked, alarmed that she could read me that well.

"I would never," she said, and stopped in the street to reach up and kiss me.

CHAPTER ELEVEN

It was love for Benjamin that made Remedios transform, for a time, into a gregarious hostess. People kept stepping through the window, friends who were told to go find Remedios and Benjamin when they arrived in Mexico City. Somehow the address was passed around through invisible networks. New people came daily.

Her nature was self-sufficient and solitary, but she began welcoming people, cracking jokes, serving tequila and the smoky mezcal that Benjamin preferred as she became known as one of the most charming hostesses in the expat community. Her reputation had little to do with the holes in the floors where she left cheese for the mice, or the cats snaking around the guests' pants legs, or the paltry amount of food. Rather, guests were drawn by the atmosphere she created—the generosity of an open hand mixed with the sort of madcap high jinks André used to start at the villa. She'd start games of cadavre exquis, where she'd take a piece of paper, write a noun on it, and fold it over, then the next person would add a word and so on, with Benjamin calling out the parts of speech until he was satisfied, at which point he'd read the creation aloud to all.

One night, when energies were particularly at an ebb, she brought out her tarot cards, quietly shuffling until Chiki Weisz asked for a reading.

Photographer and filmmaker Emerico "Chiki" Weisz had come by nightly since the earliest days and had quickly become their closest friend, almost a cohost of these evenings. He brought bottles of beer and pastries from the Austrian bakery on the other side of the city that were so close to authentic they brought memories flooding back with each bite.

"I've never had a tarot reading. I think I'm due," he said, as if it were a checkup at the doctor's office.

She sat by his side on the sofa hovering in front of the coffee table, a group gathering around them. Remedios had never given a reading as entertainment like this before a crowd, but Chiki smiled, bright and enthusiastic, and everyone encircling them was a friend. She shuffled and asked the cards to be what they would.

"What's your question?" she asked.

"A question?" Remedios could feel Chiki's defenses go up. "I'm not sure I have one."

He said it in the tone of someone with a weight on his mind. She was certain he had a question that had been bedeviling him for a while.

"If you know everything you need to know and have no questions, then we can do this another time," Remedios said. It was a little harsh, but she wanted to move him along. She tucked her cards together and made to stand up.

He reached out for her arm, stopping her. "Okay, okay," he said, his face a little pleading. She'd forced his hand, but she didn't feel bad. "I want to know." He closed his eyes and then said, "When I'll meet the love of my life."

The crowd around them crowed and clapped. Remedios leaned over and kissed his cheek for bravery, and then she started shuffling again, babbling as she did so to distract from his admission.

"Everyone wants to know this. Of course you do. Who doesn't? Did you know the numbers and symbols on the cards relate to astrol-

ogy and numerology? I leave that sort of thing to the more mathemat-
ically inclined among us, but still, that's all incorporated in the cards
as well. Shall we see what they have to say?" She presented them to
him to cut, which he did in three neat piles. Instead of putting them
back together, Remedios took one card from the top of each stack and
turned them over. The middle first.

"The situation." She turned over the Lovers card. Someone wolf-
whistled. "She is close," Remedios said. "And coming to you soon.
Her energy is already around you. She is the love of your life, and she
is almost here." Chiki grinned.

"What's influencing the situation?" She turned over the card on
the left. "The Queen of Wands. She is sometimes called the witch of
the tarot. Full of fire and alchemical power and life. When you meet
her, you'll know she is the one you've been waiting for. She is able to
transform things, people, and she will transform you."

She turned over the last card on the right. "Where it's going." The
Wheel of Fortune. "The tarot is not usually good with timing, but I
can only take this as a sign that she will be here soon. But you must
go out and find her. Remain active and searching. The Wheel reminds
you that your fate is in your hands. The Wheel is also the tenth card
of the deck. So perhaps ten days or ten weeks until she arrives. Given
the cards around it, I don't think it will be ten months."

"Poor Chiki if it's ten years," someone called out.

The little group around them moved off to refresh drinks. She
heard a word that followed her more and more now, whispered in
the air wherever she seemed to go, and here said with cheer—*witch*.

"When you were talking I realized how much I hope all of this is
true." Chiki leaned back on the threadbare couch. "I was hanging on
every word." He brought his palms to his face, rubbing his eyes.

Benjamin joined them. Chiki sniffed through his nose and inhaled, composing himself. "Benjamin, what's it like to live with a
sorceress?" he asked. "Does she read the cards for you every day?"

Remedios would have read for Benjamin whenever he asked, but it was rare that he did. She'd never given Benjamin a full reading. He'd ask her to pull a card for him here and there. Sometimes he'd ask what her cards had to say as he walked through a room and saw her with them. She offered to read for him recently, thinking that the cards might offer some insights into the long silences from which she could not coax him. He was noncommittal and lackluster in accepting her offer, and really, one needed an engaged participant for the cards to speak, as Chiki had just demonstrated.

These very parties had become a solution, of sorts, to get Benjamin out of his brooding. Remedios knew Benjamin needed people to bounce ideas off, to get his intellectual motor running. The parties allowed her to bring others in to do this work for her.

During these evenings, she would often glimpse the man she fell in love with, the old Benjamin, the French Benjamin. As he held court, expounding his views on the universe, she watched as listeners fell under his spell. He was a freethinker, an appealing revolutionary, and in those moments it hardly mattered that he rarely put his ideas into practice. He was lit up with the fire of theory.

She also felt another presence on those evenings, familiar and haunting—the feeling that André was near, just off in the other room or coming up the street. André's absence had hindered Benjamin as completely as if one of his limbs had been severed. On nights like these, the light would come back into Benjamin, and it was with the acknowledgment of a fact long known but only recently made conscious that Remedios recognized that light had been André. These nights filled with parties, these nights when their friends came around, she could see the faint afterglow of the old Benjamin. It was a bittersweet remembrance of their life in France.

Kati Horna, a Hungarian photographer Benjamin had known only as an acquaintance in Paris, came by and brought her camera with her. She was often lacking for models and asked Remedios to pose that very first night. Remedios found in her a friend who shared the language of surrealism but with a distinctive eye all her own. They drank Carta Blanca in the corners long into the night.

Kati's husband, José, was a sculptor and a fellow Spaniard whom Remedios had known through her student days at the Academia in Madrid, and the two of them spent many evenings speaking in rapid-fire Spanish with Catalan accents.

Gunther Gerzso came, though you got the feeling he preferred being the host. Gunther liked control. Reflexively generous, he'd found work designing sets for the ballet and opera and enlisted Remedios as his part-time assistant to finish the largest of them—an effective way to share the wealth. Remedios happily spent a few weeks designing and painting screens for upcoming performances, which led to her being hired by the upper-crust decorator Clardecor, who needed someone to paint bureaus and drinks carts for their clientele of the upwardly mobile.

A group of artists came by the apartment, seeking out Benjamin to pay their respects. People like filmmaker Luis Buñuel, who was an absolute fountain of gossip about friends in New York, and César Moro, the Peruvian surrealist poet, came as if on a pilgrimage, saying Benjamin had inspired him. Benjamin later admitted to Remedios that it flattered.

These guests always brought the conversation around to André, which soothed and annoyed Benjamin in equal measure. Benjamin felt lauded, of course, that he should be sought out, and talking about his old friend somehow made André feel nearby. But these supplicants also made Benjamin feel like a stone monument to the past where people left flowers and tributes, good for a touch of luck before adventuring, but not a fellow creator.

The hero worshippers paid little mind to Remedios who, quite used to being ignored by men, gathered the wives and girlfriends in the corner ceding the battlefield of intellectual jousting in favor of more authentic conversations. That's where Benjamin could usually find her at any party, off laughing in a corner with the women in the room.

The local boys played soccer in the street below and sent balls flying through the windows, knocking out most of the glass panes so that insects flooded in at night, attracted to the lights. Remedios took to turning off all the lamps and using candles, hoping to cut down on the insect invasion, but it didn't work much. The flying insects became a sort of symbol of their parties.

"A new moth joins us," Benjamin would say whenever someone new stepped through the window.

And so it was that Remedios called out, "Come and singe your wings," one night when Chiki Weisz stepped in, and right behind him, to everyone's surprise, came Leonora Carrington.

"So this is where the last five Trotskyites in Mexico are meeting," she said, and then almost tripped as her low-heeled loafer caught on the edge of the window. Chiki turned instinctively to catch her arm.

And there she was, Leonora, with her windswept hair frizzed around her face and her clear pale skin that belonged swathed in a fine English mist, but now bloomed with vivid pink sunburn across the bridge of her nose and cheeks.

Remedios hugged her, the long, rocking side-to-side hug of old friends. She hugged Chiki too, who whispered in her ear, "The Queen of Wands has arrived."

Leonora spiraled through the party, welcomed like a triumphant hero. Everyone who found their way to the flat was welcomed as a battle survivor, but a special joy greeted Leonora. An enlivening potential arrived with her. They all felt it.

After she greeted everyone, she found Remedios in the kitchen and accepted a cold bottle of Carta Blanca. In Spain when Remedios was growing up, everyone, even the fine ladies, drank beer.

Remedios, cool as a cat and never one to gush, was used to greeting new arrivals with calm. Newcomers, exhausted and often barely holding it together, rarely wanted to be attacked with questions, and she suspected her friend would tell her everything in due time.

"So I've been in New York," Leonora said after she took a long pull on the bottle and belched under her breath. "With Max."

Remedios smiled. "And how is the goat grandfather?"

"Married to Peggy Guggenheim, if you can believe it, and collecting kachina dolls with her money."

Remedios lowered her eyebrows.

"Little Native American poppet dolls," Leonora explained.

But that wasn't why Remedios had looked quizzical. She wanted to ask how Leonora felt about this marriage. At the villa, Max had tolerated Peggy with a silent irritation just barely kept in check. Remedios was surprised to hear they got married.

"I met Peggy in Marseilles before I left," Remedios said, opening up the topic. She took a sip from her bottle, waiting for Leonora to offer some insight. "I suppose Max will do what is required to survive," she said, thinking out loud when Leonora remained silent.

Leonora cocked her head to the side. "How so?" It was something throughout their friendship that Remedios would appreciate, the way Leonora never beat around the bush. She could deploy the most elaborately delicate and nuanced social niceties and small talk when she wished, a skill learned in childhood that once it has been instilled never really leaves. But as an adult, Leonora went through the world with a brisk candor, which braced up everyone around her like cold water splashed in the face on a hot day—refreshing and startling. People snapped up their heads or straightened their backs when they heard Leonora say a simple "How so?" in response to a statement, or the more menacing but crisply delivered "Really? Now why is that?"

"Well, money helps with getting visas and things and of course Peggy's an American, so that helps too," Remedios said and then regretted it. Max and Leonora had been very much in love. It had to wound, this marriage of his. "Kati's been making little dolls recently, maybe they're like Max's," she said, trying to change the subject.

"I'm married myself," Leonora said bluntly. "His name is Renato Leduc. We met in Portugal."

"You're married," Remedios said, bewildered. The man's name was vaguely familiar from Paris days. "Is he here?" She'd clearly come with Chiki, and Remedios was immediately on guard that Chiki might be reading the situation incorrectly.

"We're separated now," Leonora said dreamily. "He took pity on me in Lisbon. Married me to help me get out." She raised her eyes above her bottle, as if encouraging Remedios to comment on her being rescued. So maybe she didn't harbor ill will toward Max, who'd made a very similar calculation and married Peggy. "He was the Mexican ambassador to Portugal, so his diplomatic status saved us. I'd been in a hospital. I had a sort of breakdown."

"You know, I think I heard something about that," Remedios said gently.

"Yes, you were so kind to send me that letter and the deck of cards, that pillow full of herbs. Thank you. You have no idea how helpful they were. I have them with me here, somewhere. The cards, that is. The herbs I burned as you mentioned. That took some doing in the loony bin."

Remedios started at Leonora's slang.

"But I found a nurse who helped me burn it," Leonora continued, unconcerned. "She believed in that sort of thing, you see. And she helped me leave too. Or should I say my family wanted to move me to a hospital in South Africa, out of the way of the war, after I refused to go back to England with Nanny. The family hired the nurse to travel with me, and I gave her the slip quite easily in Lisbon. I knew I couldn't bear another hospital. That's where I met Renato. That's where we got married. The sensible thing to do, given my situation."

It seemed impossible, standing there with their bottles of beer, that the laughing and straightforward Leonora should have come through these trials. But though she'd been ill, she seemed stronger and wiser than the carefree girl Remedios remembered from Paris. It was poignant to imagine the wounds and scars she carried from this transformation.

"I've started to write about it," Leonora said quietly, picking at a piece of peeling paint on the counter. "I don't know why. It's not like I want to relive it, or even remember it. And here I am doing that every day."

"But I've been writing as well. Something I've never done before. During the siesta. I don't know what I'm doing. I don't even know what it is."

"It's alchemizing," Leonora said, making herself stop fiddling. "Digging up the buried treasure, the muck and pain. And transforming it, converting it into gold."

"That's good," Remedios said, nodding. It felt natural, this direct way of sharing what was really going on, a cutting through the small talk to what mattered. Remedios didn't know anyone who could inspire trust and expansion as quickly as Leonora.

"Like a little treasure chest," Leonora said. "You put the pain in a safe and locked chest where it can stay, no one can get to it. And then in the fullness of time, and when you're ready, and if you're brave enough to lift the lid and look inside, you might find jewels or raw lumber or any other building material for art."

"Or you merely find yourself, yet again, looking out at you." Just then, Remedios had the clearest vision of a woman in blue robes at a table, lifting the lid on a small jewelry trunk and seeing her own face looking out. On the shelves behind her were dozens of the same little trunks, and she knew that no matter the difficulty in opening them, she'd only find herself again looking out.

Remedios's shoulders relaxed. She felt that a compatriot had arrived, and an all-encompassing feeling of grace emanated from Leonora and swirled around them both. It was as if they'd picked up from their life in Paris with the same closeness, the same meeting of minds. Many things had transpired, yes, and they'd need to catch each other up on what had happened to them. But the fundamental element of the relationship remained unchanged, a friendship intact.

"Perhaps we should prove it," Remedios said and smiled, feeling that she was in the presence of a true and simpatico heart. "That pain can be alchemized."

"Of course we should," Leonora said, needing no further explanation. "Come by the apartment tomorrow and we'll start."

And linking their arms together, the friends turned to face the party.

TWO OF CUPS—
Leonora Carrington

The Two of Cups is a meeting of the other half in the form of a romantic partner, true friend, or your own soul. The soul can be met through another person or in the discovery of a new side of the self. It is a uniting together of two parts who between them share the cup of emotion. Above the cup is the caduceus of Mercury, a sign not only of healing but of the messenger, the communicator. He eases understanding between two people so that a true meeting of the minds may occur.

If the Two of Cups appears in your reading, pay attention to relationships, neglected parts of the self, and all things that can bring union and wholeness to the forefront of your life at this time.

Upon meeting Remedios again in Mexico, I felt the blaze of her soul. Chiki took me round to her apartment without telling me who lived there. Stepping through the window and finding her standing there in the middle of a party was one of the few moments in my life that made me believe in divine grace.

Her plain clothes, really so elegant, were an appealing foil for her colorful and rococo mind stuffed with the mythical books she'd read in childhood, stories of the Catholic saints, engineering texts, and cosmological treatises given to her by her father. I've never known anyone, before or since, who adopted ideas from such indiscriminate places.

She had beautiful hair. I always envied her lush auburn hair that with her prominent nose lent her a pleasing air of gravitas. I'd later learn that my friend was touchingly self-conscious about her nose, and this too added a kind of appeal that such a formidable creature should be human, too, with a human's insecurities.

Later, she'd paint an absolute triumph of a picture about her nose, which touched me and relieved me in tandem because it showed how she'd come to peace with this distinctive and therefore beautiful part of her face. The painting showed a woman with a veiled large nose entering a plastic surgeon's office with a mannequin in the window—a woman with six breasts, a minuscule waist, and long blond hair—as if the model was on offer in a dressmaker's window like a new dress or a hat. It was funny, a bit triste, and a bit fierce—just like my friend.

Have you ever met someone and known right away that they would be in your life always, in some capacity whether in the center or not?

That's how I'd felt the first day we met in the Paris café with the green-and-white awnings. Remedios had worn a red cloth coat that swung out like a cape when she walked. She offered to sew me one like it, and to my eternal regret I turned her down. She designed and sewed all her clothes herself, claiming male tailors had no idea what to do with a woman's body.

She'll make the suit I'll marry Chiki in. "I know you're British, but you can't get married in tweed," she'll say. Black and boxy, a copy of one of hers that I admired, she'll make a little high-necked white lace blouse to go under it with a thin black ribbon tying around the neck. I'll object to the ribbon when she brings it over, but because she's my friend, I'll put it on. It will be perfect. Of course it will.

Finding her that first night in her apartment in Mexico City was like walking out the door one morning and finding a pirate's chest full of treasure on your doorstep. When she offered me a drink, I read it all in her face. "Oh you're here now," her eyes seemed to say. "Now we can begin." Remedios was always a very solid sort of person, despite all her magic, because of it.

She started coming by the apartment every morning on her way to the market. We'd tiptoe up the stairs to the little room I'd turned into my studio. It was cramped and smelled of cooking from the kitchen, but we didn't care. Its most important feature was the heavy, functional door.

"To have a place all to yourself," she said with admiration when she first saw it, and I was relieved because in truth it was a mess. I'd read somewhere that the messier the studio, the greater the art produced in it, and based on that I'd given up trying to tidy it.

To start we'd make tea, as solemn as two priestesses before an altar. Chiki installed a little gas ring up there for just this purpose. As I lit it, Remedios brought up the kettle of water from the kitchen and we'd stand side by side, without the need for words. As she measured, I readied the cups. We were only making tea, but it was our ceremony.

After that, we would take up the tarot cards. This was our ritual.

Remedios would bring bits and bobs she collected, stuffed in her always oversize pockets—shards of pottery, interesting stones, and the polished crystals she bought from the stalls in the back of the mercado—druzy amethyst to bring forth wisdom, celestine for connection to angelic realms, quartz to harness electrical phenomena. She combined these with the feathers she found in the streets. When she told me that finding a feather was a sign an angel was near, I was reminded that we shared a Catholic girlhood. We would mix all this in with my treasures—candy sugar skulls, abandoned bird nests, and paper flowers. We arranged our loot around us. She would fuss until she got it how she liked it, then she would shuffle and cut the cards. I'd bring over the teapot and the chipped cups, the only type of cups we seemed to have. I'd always warn her about burning her tongue, and she would never wait.

"We should discuss payment for this reading," she'd say.

Of course we didn't charge each other. For anything. In just a few months our households had become interchangeable. Chiki moved in with me, and I was over in her apartment as often as she was in mine.

"What do you suggest?"

"In exchange for today's reading," she said as she ruffled the cards, "you must record your dreams for me tonight."

This was our currency—dares, challenges, requests, games. For my birthday she drafted an invitation to a name we chose randomly from the phone book and then we spent my birthday party in a state of hilarious suspense to see if anyone would come through the door.

They didn't. It didn't matter. It wasn't the point of it, you see.

"But I have something better," I said as I got up. "It's finally finished, I think. From my time in the hospital." I set the thick pile of papers between us as we sat cross-legged on the floor. "Will you read it?" She'd be the first. I hadn't even let Chiki see it, as I knew it would only alarm and worry him. Remedios, I thought, would be able to read it without panic.

She placed a hand on top of the papers, and I knew she was feeling for the energy radiating off the stack, something strange in her face. *Down Below*, I was calling it.

"I can't wait to see what you've done." She riffled the corner of the papers with her thumb, as if taking their measure. "Now, what is your question for today?" she asked, presenting the cards to me facedown on her open palm. When approaching the cards, one must always have a question even if it is only "What do I need to know?" I placed one hand on top of the cards and then reached across and placed a hand on her heart. She then reached across and placed her hand over my heart. In this way we created a figure eight with our arms, an infinity loop, a sacred symbol of the infinite.

"Today I'd like to know about my health." Not a request I'd made before.

Her eyebrows rose for a moment in surprise and then she closed her eyes, calling on spirits and guides, angels and ancestors, sending energy and love and a request for guidance into the cards and out into the universe.

When she'd finished, she placed the cards between us on the floor, and I cut. Then she scooped them together and drew three. The Hermit, the Empress, and the Queen of Pentacles. I laughed. I couldn't help it. And when she looked up I said, "I'm pregnant."

A wide smile broke across my friend's face. "But your news is lovely. When are you due? How long have you known?" Remedios was a gratifying person to share good news with. Not many genuinely wished you well, even friends, especially friends. But Remedios truly wished all good things for me.

"It's very early. I haven't told anyone. Just you and Chiki."

"Well, that explains this. She," Remedios said, pointing to the Empress card, "is the symbol of the divine feminine, symbol of fertility and abundance, though usually not so literally. She"—Remedios pointed to the Queen of Pentacles—"rules over home and hearth.

She is the ultimate caretaker and mother. Two excellent cards for an expecting friend." She smiled.

I pointed down to the Hermit card. "And he is a call to go inside, visit the interior, a turning inward to help with gestation in this case, I think."

She nodded. "You see it the same way I do. He carries with him the light of pure potential." She pointed to the old hermit's lantern. "Self-knowledge, but also the possibility of the light you're creating shining out into the world."

"Being a light for the world is a lot to put on a baby."

"Could be the baby. Could be this." She pointed to the stack of pages. "You've been illuminating your own interior, lighting up the dark places in your psyche. Getting ready to put it out in the world."

"You're the first person to read it, the first glimmer of light."

She swept the cards together into a stack. "And you've been working too," she said, tilting her head toward the rickety easel against the wall.

I'd been conjuring a painting of a walled kitchen garden, three women in the foreground in robes discussing secrets while the spirits of a nearby tree became manifest.

Remedios hauled herself up off the floor. "May I?" she asked before she peeked behind the sheet I'd hung over it. Of course she didn't need to ask, but my friend is as cautious and self-aware as a cat.

When she lifted the covering, she caught her breath—an audible whoosh in. She paused, something I couldn't place on her face. "Your painting has really transformed since last I saw it." We'd been in that group show in Paris—two paintings each, hers a representation of a Valkyrie and another of spectacles.

I stood next to her. "I learned so much from Max, you know, when we were living in the countryside. Not that he gave me tutorials or anything, but through his example. And he through mine. Do you really like it?" I asked.

"It's like looking into the truest part of you, and it's like looking into the contents of my own brain." And then my friend's wide expansive face, usually so open, shut down. "I should go," she said quietly.

I tried to cover over any awkwardness, bustling around, helping her get her things, flipping into the party manners of my childhood.

My painting had somehow unsettled her. "Is everything okay?"

"I need to work. I've been avoiding it for too long."

I knew this feeling, the panic of being behind, being surpassed. That I'd caused this reaction in my friend made me want to give her something, anything, to make her feel better.

I went to one of the teetering towers of books lining the walls and pulled one from the middle, managing not to topple it.

"I've been thinking about ritual," I said, handing her a book by Gurdjieff, who we'd recently discovered was a shared favorite. "That's all any ritual or ceremony is trying to do, to make manifest in the material world an intangible shift in spirit. So I've been thinking that anything can become ritual, painting, or writing, or cooking or making a bed. All of it transforms, makes clean. Making dinner alchemizes disparate things into a whole. I feel like I am always transmuting things. Always changing them. All day long," I said as she practically ran down the stairs. Desperate, I thought, to be away from me. "What about you?"

"Always the generous one," she said at the front door as I placed the book on top of the manuscript she'd taken up, and then she was gone.

⸺⤜⟡⤛⸺

She came back the next morning, and I was surprised to see my manuscript with her.

"I read it in one night," she said, placing it with care on the floor and then putting a group of rocks and crystals from her pocket on top. "Couldn't stop. It's extraordinary. You managed to make me laugh and cry," she said. "It's all true? An autobiography?"

She gave me a gift then, and like all the best gifts it was one I didn't know I wanted but now seemed essential—the gift of being understood. I hadn't known that in writing it, I'd been looking for understanding all along.

"I wrote it so I could just hand it to anyone nosy enough to want me to trot out my time at Santander for their gawking and amusement. I'll hand them this instead," I said, trying for a joke.

"I'm so sorry you went through that," she said with real sympathy. "Of course you should publish it. Others will want to read it."

"No one wants to read an account of my time in a mental hospital."

"What you describe is universal. The questioning of yourself and your sanity. You know, I'm not sure you were even sick. Maybe just sick of the world and overwhelmed by the stupidity of war. That would make anyone act the way you did."

I felt a gratitude for my friend then, someone who would read the best into me.

"And while I've never been in a hospital like that," she continued, "I was in jail. In Paris. It took me back there, but more than that it made me feel less alone, that someone else understands what it's like to be a captive."

This was a shared experience between us, one we rarely discussed with anyone aside from each other. It was too tiring and often upsetting to make anyone else understand. Remedios understood implicitly.

"And I've been thinking about what you said yesterday about ritual. I've been doing something since we arrived," she said. "And I wonder if you'll come with me today. After reading this, I think you should."

I nodded, not needing further explanation. Anything my friend wanted to do was fine by me. We headed to the Mercado Sonora, whose bustle and color and smell distracted us from ourselves.

First, we found the famous stall at the end of an aisle and ate crisp fried churros. She said they were as good as the most famous shop in Madrid. Then she led me back to the left corner of the market past a glass box housing a doll baby with bleeding eyes, the patron saint of the witchcraft market.

Remedios's favorite stall was hung with dried sage and marigolds. The seller, Julietta, kept her herbs in intriguing little canisters, often with a hidden spring or well-concealed button that popped the top with the slightest push. There were decorative boxes too, carved or painted with flowers and Zapotec symbols.

She was no novice, Julietta, she was a born saleswoman, and when she saw us coming she started piling canisters and boxes on the counter. Intriguing jars and sachets with names like "Come to Me" and "Tame Handsome Men." But when we didn't bite, not even at the intriguingly named "Break the Mattress," she placed an ebony box inlaid with mother-of-pearl in front of us.

"But you don't want this," she said, with a push of an inconspicuous button on the side. The lid popped up revealing a fragrant jumble of dried twigs inside. "I just keep it for the Mayan shaman who comes by once a month."

Of course we bought some. Of course it was the most expensive tea in the stall.

As we were walking away, I grew confused, but I didn't want to show it. Buying tea was the big ritual Remedios had been enacting since she arrived? I didn't want to insult her, but it was a little ordinary.

Remedios was in front of me, leading me toward the back of the market where birds squawked in cages along the wall—pale white doves, half a dozen to a cage, with panicked red eyes, bamboo baskets of green parakeets shrieking in fright. Toward the end of the row a pair of glossy crows flapped hysterically against the bars of their cage when we walked past.

Before I caught up to her, Remedios found the seller and started haggling for the crows in quick Spanish.

I walked farther back into a corner, drawn by a black raven on the bottom of a cage, so still and lustrous that I thought it was taxidermied until it unfurled its neck ruff and opened its mouth, panting.

Remedios handed over her bills while the vendor crammed the two crows into a cardboard box. "What about her?" I said, pointing my friend toward the raven.

Remedios peered down, and the crows jumped in the box in her arms. The vendor was outraged when she asked the price.

"The raven is very expensive."

"I'm not rich," Remedios said.

"Neither am I, señora, not after you haggled over a few centivos for that bunch." He gestured at the box. "The raven is pricey. They're hard to catch, comprende? Smart, usually solitary, and this one has a mate. Maybe you've seen it on the phone lines outside the market."

In the end he handed her the raven, cage and all, practically shoving it into her hand as he quoted an astronomical price without looking us in the eye. Remedios took the cage by the hook and fumbled over the money, not bothering to haggle. The seller took her bills, while grumbling—what does a woman want three black birds for if not to use them as her familiars, the messengers of her magic?

I carried the raven in its cage, and she the crows in the box, as we headed out the back of the market, because by then we were attracting a crowd. Out in the parking lot delivery vans and donkey carts unloaded produce, dry goods, and every kind of herb imaginable into the back of the stalls.

Finally outside, we sat on a curb, the air smelling of dank gutter and roasting chapulines, the huge grasshoppers from Oaxaca being sold from a vendor's cart nearby.

"This is what I do," she said. "It's the only thing that seems to make me feel better some days. Like I can breathe. The only thing that seems real."

She opened the top of the box, and a frenzied jumble ensued. The birds jumped over each other to get out. They flapped in her face, and in a flash they were specks in the blue sky. We watched them until they disappeared.

"Benjamin says it doesn't matter. They just trap more."

"It matters to those two," I said.

Heads back, mouths open, we searched the sky for those black dots, and then she announced, "I'm blocked," as if she had a deadly disease. "Of everything. And being with you, creativity is bursting out of you." She gestured toward my stomach, and I instinctively put a hand there, covering. "The painting, the manuscript." Tears shone in her eyes, which panicked my British soul.

I detected no jealousy, rather the despair of one artist reaching out to another, asking for help, for guidance. For a moment I wondered if I dared tell her the truth. Nothing was blocking her except Benjamin and his old views of women—either the innocent or the hysteric, the Madonna or the whore—la femme enfant or la femme sorcière—with very little space for a real woman to inhabit. He kept trying to re-create a Parisian salon here, not realizing that those ways were dead and that he was trying to drag an old system into a new world.

"You're not blocked," I said because it was the truth. Realizing she might feel dismissed by this I said, "I have things to release too."

"It's like there is something clinging to me."

It was on the tip of my tongue to say, "Yes, it's Benjamin," but I reached for tact.

"You're the greater creatrix than he is." She started to argue, but I stopped her. "For all their avant-gardism, every surrealist man just wants the angel in the house." I knew she'd read Woolf. I knew she'd recognize the phrase.

"Creatrix," she said, turning the word over in her mouth like a sweet.

I feared I'd gone too far. I shouldn't have said anything, and besides, one had to figure these things out for oneself. You can be told something, even agree with it intellectually, but it's not until you feel it for yourself with deep emotional knowing that it becomes real. When it's real, then you can act on it. Sadly, there was no mechanism, no way I'd found at least, to engineer the speeding up of this highly individual process.

"I worry that I can't make enough money to support us with my own creations," she said. "In Paris I could only do it by faking someone else's paintings. Here, I take my orders from the people paying me. Obtaining freedom is not the same as maintaining it, this is what I'm beginning to realize."

"We're all blocked at one time or another," I said. "That is part of the path. You're blocked until you're not."

She nodded, and I couldn't tell if I'd offended her. She swiped under her eyes and slowed her breathing, searching for control. I wanted to give her a lifeline.

"I had an Irish nanny who told me that ravens attract energies, all different types. That's all magic is. The focus of will and intention applied to possibilities."

She took a deep breath. "So let it fly."

We were silent for a moment, each of us conjuring an unspoken invocation in our heads, tying all the things we wanted to release to those lustrous black feathers.

Then I opened the door of the cage. The raven remained frozen, as if it had been in captivity for so long it had forgotten it was wild. Or maybe it felt the weight of being tied with all the hopes and fears of two refugees trying to find their way. I thought for a moment about shaking it out. Instead, in two brave hops it was at the door, a tight fit that left one oily feather trailing behind. Then with only a few large flaps, the bird lifted, spreading its wings, feathers edged like fingers. Its friend joined it almost immediately, and the pair soared in a wide looping circle above the market, and then they were away, out of sight, returned to their natural state.

CHAPTER TWELVE

On a bright Mexican morning, Remedios was back in the kitchen preparing a chicken in the way Madame Nouget had taught her, when Leonora popped her head through the window of Remedios's flat and called out, "Come for a ride with me. I have someone you need to meet."

After the food was squared away, they walked through the neighborhood and Leonora hailed a cab, a great luxury, and they drove south of the city, farther south than Remedios had yet traveled.

"I'm fairly certain Diego won't be there," Leonora said. "Which is a good thing, because he takes up all the space in the room and gossips more than my mother."

André and Benjamin told tales of hosting Rivera and his wife years ago in Paris when they'd bonded over their mutual friendship with Trotsky. Benjamin refused to see them now because he was convinced they had something to do with Trotsky's assassination. Leonora, though, had been to tea, invited by Rivera, who found her good company as they knew many of the same people.

"She paints too," Leonora said. "She's better than him, if you ask me. André once said her paintings were like a ribbon tied around a bomb."

The city had given way to jungle, the lush foliage of waxy green leaves shading them until the cab stopped in front of the only blue walls on a street of crumbling beige stucco.

"We're too much in a bubble," Leonora said as she paid the driver. "Seeing the same people all the time."

"She has impressive color sense," Remedios said, thinking the blue of the walls neither tranquil nor subdued, but its own sky, like freedom.

The maid showed them into a verdant courtyard with a fountain in a single spray straight up nearly as high as the second-story roof. A troop of monkeys nattered in the trees and parrots chattered to an old white cockatoo in a cage of woven branches swinging in the shade of a palm. The walls of the house were studded with volcanic rock, giving the whole thing an out-of-time feeling.

"I've been in houses that have this same apart quality," Leonora said quietly. "As if you've stepped out of your life and through a portal to another time. I've decided it is a quality of the occupant. How clear is their vision? How fully have they inhabited their life? The clearer the vision, the more they have allowed it to spread to every corner of their environment, every article of clothing and adornment. The clearer the vision, the more you will feel, when entering their house, that you have stepped into another time."

The maid left without a word, used to leaving guests to gawk as she fetched her mistress.

"It's like something that's always been in my mind," Remedios whispered. "But only now do I realize it once it's come to life."

"Certain houses, castles really, that I visited in childhood felt this way too," Leonora said.

After a long while the maid came back. "Señora says come this way."

They followed her into a room right off the courtyard, the doors flung wide to the plants and the sound of water.

She lay like a perfectly made-up doll in a huge four-poster bed. Her lipstick and rouge perfectly applied, though it couldn't hide her pallor. Her nails varnished a cheerful red. Her hair sat on top of her head entwined in braids, and she wore a white, high-necked lace blouse and a sort of brocade bed jacket of silver and burgundy. She was covered in jewelry, necklaces, earrings, rings. Propped up on pillows and covered from the waist down in embroidered sheets and a homespun coverlet. The maid fussed around her, tucking and fluffing pillows, then asking in a whisper if she was all right.

Kahlo waved her away and reached a hand toward Leonora's stomach. "Mama, how do you feel?"

"Never healthier," Leonora answered, but then her smile faded as if it were rude to highlight her robust physical state.

But Kahlo only nodded and picked up a cigarette burning low on what looked like a breakfast tray, which had been rigged into an apparatus that allowed her to paint in bed. "A great blessing on you."

Photographs and postcards and little bits of paper were thumbtacked to the headboard—some of a much younger Kahlo, recognizable by her handsome eyebrows, and some of friends, a small watercolor of a bleeding heart in the middle of it all. A wheelchair was parked on the other side of the bed in front of a proper easel with a work in progress on it. A jumble of colorful rebozos lay piled in the seat of the wheelchair. In the cab home Leonora would confide that Kahlo's maid lifted her into the wheelchair and then tied her to the back of it with the shawls so she could paint.

"I've brought a friend," Leonora said, and Remedios stepped forward.

"European," Kahlo said after she heard Remedios's accent. "Don't you people know anyone besides other Europeans? You're in Mexico. I suppose you two are friends with André Breton, that old cockroach."

Leonora laughed, and the social training of her childhood emerged. When it served her, her aristocratic social skills allowed her to charm her way out of any awkward moment.

"We know you," Leonora said fondly, kneeling beside the bed

as if they were the closest of friends. Remedios quickly joined her, both in genuflection. "Remedios is a painter too, and I wanted her to come and see how you work." Frida put her hand in Leonora's, rings on every finger like a gypsy. Some were nothing more than chunks of crystal attached to wire, others obviously fine. Leonora caught Remedios's eye and glanced up underneath the canopy of Kahlo's bed. A mirror was affixed there, reflecting back the scene.

"Portraiture," Leonora said.

"So formal." Kahlo turned her head to Remedios. "I am alone a lot. So I paint what's with me all the time. It's not more complicated than that. It's a hassle to get others to come sit for me, and they're usually too concerned with how I depict them. So . . ."

"Ingenious," Remedios said, pointing to the mirror, thinking of nothing better to say.

"Your name. You're the remedy. So we have that in common," Kahlo said. "I was born after my brother died as an infant. So sweet that they viewed you as a remedy for heartache. My father never stopped wishing I were a boy."

This intimate revelation made Remedios think she could ask about the painting on the easel next to the bed.

The fresh painting was a self-portrait, and the rawest piece of art Remedios had ever seen. Kahlo had painted herself nude except for a white medical corset and a white sheet around her hips. Her torso was split open to show her spine made of a crumbling Doric column. But what chilled Remedios the most was that Kahlo had painted herself as pierced all over with nails, tears streaming down her face.

"Self-portraits are the most revealing," Kahlo said, watching Remedios. "Anything else is just a detour on the route to the clearest self-expression."

Here was a better rendition of the pain of metamorphosis than her old painting *Memories of the Valkyrie*. Remedios wished that Kahlo would soon be released from the pain that caged her.

"You should try it," Kahlo said then, startling Remedios. "Forgive me," she said quickly right after. "I don't know what I say anymore. Of course you should paint what you like. You should try to take what is in your head, your soul, and transmit it into the world as clearly as you can. We all should."

Remedios and Leonora were silent in the face of challenge.

Anyone looking at Remedios's paintings could not help but see that she was the main character—long hair, sharp nose, wide-set eyes. She didn't call them portraits and denied it if asked. But Frida's perspective, that one's face was an object to use for the purposes of art, gave her courage.

To see evidence of the sickness and suffering transformed into powerful art using honesty as the alchemical agent enlivened her.

"Tell us how you find the automatic drawing," Leonora said. "Diego told me you were experimenting with it."

"It's a technique for you types." She waved a hand. "You are too cerebral by half. This is why you need your automatic writing. To get past all your learning and techniques. I don't have such burdens."

Remedios had thought the same thing recently. Why was the automatic a more direct route to the real? What about planning? Thinking? Planning a work down to the last detail so that it reflected exactly what you intended. Though Kahlo meant she didn't need the automatic to reach spontaneous depths, Remedios was beginning to think the unintentional was overrated.

"The automatic is about uncovering. I'm more concerned with transformation at this point. This body is nothing but the husk of a caterpillar." Kahlo flapped a hand toward the sheet covering her lower half. "But it will transform into something finer and transcendent even." Remedios felt a wave of horror then of what lay under those sheets—what mangled and twisted pain. "For a long time I have been a survivor, and for what?"

Kahlo had opened up the topic, so Remedios said, "Pain can be the raw material of the alchemist. The prima material we're always looking for."

Kahlo stubbed out her cigarette. "Bullshit. Pain is just pain, stupid and animalistic. And coming for every single one of us in the end."

Despite this denial, Remedios considered Kahlo an alchemist of great power. She knew Leonora did too; that's why she'd brought her there. Kahlo's body, her face, the bedroom, the blue of the house, the courtyard full of monkeys, all of it was in harmony with the very essence of her. All of it she had used and transformed from the base material of pain into the precious metal of her art, her inner spirit made tangible in the real world.

On the table next to a water glass and amber vials of medicine were pre-Columbian artifacts, bits of pottery and shards of clay shaped like monkeys and bats and birds, along with high stacks of books and a slightly macabre miniature bed with two dolls sleeping under a tiny crocheted blanket.

Kahlo picked up a small shard of pottery. "See Tehuana," Kahlo said, holding out the small clay-fired face of an indigenous god. "Me Tehuana," she said, placing it on her heart.

The maid came in then, summoned somehow, or maybe she just knew the interval before her lady got tired.

"Please," the maid said, beckoning them out into the courtyard. It was time to go.

Remedios wanted to leave Kahlo with something. To spend any time with her at all was to recognize the soul of the revolution that lived within her. To thank her for allowing them to see her in such an intimate state. Kahlo was broken and bedridden, and it seemed she'd be gone at any moment. But clearly she was stronger than she looked, judging from the large portrait on the easel that she'd had the strength to paint.

Remedios took out of her pocket the only things she had. A clamshell, two halves that she'd tied back together with red string. She always had talismans and offerings in her pockets as one never knew when they'd be needed. She'd been carrying this one around for days as a symbol of regeneration. She took it out of her pocket now and, feeling a touch silly and a touch heroic, offered it in an open palm.

"What have you got there?" Kahlo asked.

"I thought I might leave it with you," Remedios said, still holding out her hand and feeling awkward.

Kahlo picked it out of her palm with bejeweled fingers. "Thank you. I appreciate this." And she leaned over with some difficulty and placed it just so amid her other artifacts.

ACE OF WANDS—
Elena Martinez

The Wands represent passion and creativity in all its forms. Each ace holds within it the energy of pure potential, and the Ace of Wands is no exception. It is a card of creative change, whether that be hatching a new project or evolving into a new form or phase of life. It is the card of the creator with a calling, a person who can bring ideas into the world from nothing. A person, as represented by the hand, takes hold of the creative fire of the universe, harnesses it, and brings it through them and into the world. The Ace of Wands is a card about the husk falling away and pure divine potential being brought forth, the ultimate card of transformation through creation. When it appears in a reading, consider what is ready to be alchemized and what is waiting to change into divine form.

Why Señora agrees to see these ladies I will never know. One dressed all in black, the other in mannish clothes. If I didn't know better, I'd be offended that they'd dressed for the funeral early. But I've been around gringachos enough by now to know this is just how they are. There's a certain arrogance in it, dressing in plain clothes and no makeup, as if they can't be bothered to make themselves appealing, as if they don't have to. Putting on a little lipstick would kill them?

Or maybe it's just that they are in such sharp contrast to Señora, who every day wants me to plait her hair, to fetch her makeup, to bring her the hand mirror she uses when applying it. Señora has clasped my hand and made me swear that when she dies, for that is the way she speaks nowadays, I will make sure she is immaculate, fresh lipstick and touched-up face powder before anyone comes in to see her body.

I watch the gringas get in the taxi, making sure they actually leave. I've found visitors lingering in the courtyard as if it's a public park, not wanting to depart this special house, and I can't blame them. When invited into the universe Frida has created here, no one wants to leave.

I swing by the kitchen to talk to the cook who is busy making an enormous feast.

"Not more visitors," I say, looking at the heaps of food.

"He's having guests," Cook says with a flick of her head toward Señor Rivera's rooms. "See if you can get her to drink that." A glass of fresh orange juice gleams on the chopping block, and I get a tray to carry it. Yet I know she won't drink it.

As I walk to her bedroom, my anger rises. Cook knows Señora won't drink this, so why is she always forcing such things on her? Why is everyone always forcing her? Señora will try. She always does. She will sit up and sip this. She will attend Señor Rivera's luncheon. It will exhaust her. It all does.

This is what it's like when Señor Rivera is here—constant activity, a stream of guests pontificating about politics and drinking into the night. No wonder he's so fat. He needs reserves to keep up the pace he sets. And then he will leave, suddenly, almost overnight, with cases and trunks and painting assistants and hangers-on, when he is called to paint another mural. He'll leave, and the contrast will be sickeningly abrupt. The house will be as silent as a hospital, because that's what it will become.

I bring the juice into the bedroom as Señora is lighting yet another of a million cigarettes.

"They are so damn intellectual," she says. "I'd rather sit on the floor in the market of Toluca and sell tortillas than have anything to do with those artistic bitches of Paris."

I set the glass on the table. I am always a bit pleased when she speaks to me like this. As if we are equals, just two friends. But I think I also detect sour grapes in the harshness of her tone. One of them would draw Señora's ire in particular, I know, the pregnant one.

Señora has been in pain recently. I can tell in the mornings when I come in and the medicine bottles are near empty and the ashtray overflowing as she's been smoking all night instead of sleeping. She eats very little, hence the juice. There was a time when she supervised the kitchen with great scrutiny, working alongside Cook with the chopping and washing. I know Cook feels the same way about her that I do. Señora makes everyone feel as if they are a friend, and we are all a family in the same household. She's competent too. Her mother taught her how to shop and gave her the family recipes. She knows where to find the best nopales, the freshest chilis, and what it all should cost. She used to talk with Cook after every meal, offering praise or advice. It made me laugh that she took such trouble, because Señor Rivera looked like he'd eat anything put in front of him.

I am here because she trusts me. I am here because I know how to create the facade. It is a type of spell we cast, her glamour, and only when it is intact can she then rest behind the creation of her perfection. There is the fresh huipil, the chandelier earrings, the nail varnish without a chip. She trusts me with her jewelry, though she can be quite cavalier with it, and I've learned not to compliment her on any of it. Early on I complimented a large ring she wore—a faceted hunk of citrine I later learned. Señora peeled it off her finger and gave it to me on the spot. And she wouldn't take no for an answer. It felt macabre and final, and I didn't know how to refuse it.

Señora asks me for her shawl though it's a warm day. She is ever so slowly disintegrating before my eyes. I clear away the things on the bedside table—her enameled pillbox, her eyebrow pencil—Señora still enhances her already thick eyebrows that meet in a point that she tells me protects her third eye, the generator of divine wisdom. An empty coffee cup sits next to a small clamshell held together with a red string. It is probably a tribute of sorts from the gringas. All types of people come to see Señora now, and they bring their offerings with them. People are always leaving little things at her bedside, as if she is already dead, a sainted relic.

Señora peers up over the edge of my tray as I stack the shell next to her full ashtray for emptying. "Leave that," she says, taking the shell back and placing it on the easel next to her brushes. She leans back on the pillows. "They might be bitches, but they have the spirit of creation in them," she says. "Both of them."

And then she closes her eyes to rest, one moment nearer her impending transformation.

CHAPTER THIRTEEN

Remedios and Leonora were silent on the ride home, not wanting to break the spell of their visit to La Casa Azul. But as they pulled up to Leonora's house, she said, "It's a glamour she's casting. Nanny always said a glamour was a spell that the fairies cast so that things appeared more harmonious and beautiful. I never really understood what she'd meant until I visited that house, until I saw how she and Diego live."

They went through the front door, and Leonora headed directly for the kitchen, one hand on her belly.

"I'm never not hungry nowadays," she said. "It's the most disconcerting thing." Her tiled kitchen was always cluttered, always clean, and always slightly chilly, a holdover, Remedios imagined, from Leonora's girlhood in some drafty country manor. Leonora lifted a dinner plate acting as a lid off a clay pot containing a handful of tiny mangoes, each no bigger than a thumb. Chiki bought them for her, knowing they were her favorites. Unwrapping a hunk of soft cheese and a plate of cold tortillas, she sat down with a knife at the kitchen table.

"I'm not kidding that I've never felt healthier. Healthy as a horse."

Two of Leonora's horse paintings had hung near Remedios's at that group show in Paris all those years ago when they'd first met. One a self-portrait with a white rocking horse in the foreground and a real white horse fleeing through a window. The other of a group of horses posed as if in conversation and the title *The Horses of Lord Candlestick*, which must have had something to do with her father.

"With the appetite of one to match, I guess." Leonora cut a thick chunk of cheese.

After the flame of Kahlo, creating from her bed, creating even in pain, and now her friend, in a creation phase of her own, so obviously well cared for by Chiki, who stocked the kitchen with her favorite foods so she could nourish herself, Remedios felt chilled and alone.

Because Benjamin wanted easy things, comfortable things like dinner and his bed made, but he wanted more difficult things too. He wanted that she should never speak over him or interrupt, though he and André had interrupted each other so often that listening to their rapid-fire outbursts, half sentences, and interruptions had been like listening to a foreign language. He wanted her to stop her commercial work and focus on her own art, but he didn't want to work himself. He wanted money to appear out of nowhere.

Yet even a bad day of commercial painting was better than not doing any work, and on the days when she'd had her few hours to work on her own painting, she felt able to do the shopping, the cooking, the cleaning, managing the bills, and balancing the checkbook.

Benjamin offered to take on the banking and bills, but he often forgot to pay, didn't deposit the checks, and quickly they were in arrears. Remedios found it simpler if she did it. Soon she found she'd taken on the whole of the household management.

She tried to explain all this to Benjamin, who'd looked at her blankly and calmly stated that of course she should make her own work a priority if that was important to her. He never acknowledged that their lack of money and their life of constant parties prevented her from finding time in front of her easel. She'd thought of Cinderella. Remedios could go to her easel as soon as she finished a never-ending list of chores.

Leonora looked up and must have read all this on Remedios's face. "Is it Benjamin who holds you back? Does he not want children?" Leonora had always wanted children, always wanted a family. She couldn't imagine any other way.

"I had a procedure in Paris." Remedios sat down across from her. "A long time ago." Leonora's hands stilled above the food. "It wasn't the time for me, we were living in penury, and I . . ." She'd been comfortable with her decision at the time, her need really, to end the pregnancy. What she hadn't expected was the pain, that and the grimy doctor's office. Though if the man had been a real doctor, she hadn't known and had been too scared to ask. "There was a complication." A tiny shake of her head. She'd bled so much Benjamin had finally taken her to an actual doctor, who examined her and gave her the dire pronouncement. "Actually, I cannot anymore."

"Oh, I'm sorry," Leonora said with genuine sympathy, her hands dropping, shoulders slumping. "Remedios, I had no idea."

For Leonora this was a great tragedy, but Remedios didn't think of it that way. Like so many things she'd been through, she'd been grateful to escape with her life.

"I'm lucky to be alive," she said, and then worried she sounded dramatic. But what more was there to say? Leonora too seemed at a loss. Her friend got up and came around the table. Remedios stood, and Leonora hugged her.

The feel of her friend's embrace loosened something in her. "What if I can't create at all?" Remedios asked over Leonora's shoulder. She was so uncomfortable that she had to unburden herself, and being surrounded by Leonora's arms felt like a sudden safety. "Not anything unique, anyway. Not like Kahlo. Not like you. I make advertisements for a drug company and paint fancy furniture for rich ladies. Before that I made fakes." She took a deep breath and leaned back. She'd been lucky to get the job at Clardecor painting cupboards and bureaus, even luckier to get the contract work from Bayer Pharmaceutical. In the ensuing silence, she sat down and dragged the dish of tiny mangoes toward her side of the table.

Leonora went to the bucaro and poured a glass of water for her friend. "You know what I think?" Though Remedios was the older of the two, Leonora sometimes took the tone of a big sister.

"You think I should save myself for my real work," Remedios said by rote.

"No," Leonora said, sitting back down. "I think you need what Benjamin has."

"True genius?"

Leonora smiled. "*You're* the true genius. Benjamin has stagnated here." She held up both hands as Remedios started to object. "Teaching French grammar to college students, which would be fine if he'd also continued with his poetry or started a magazine, or something. As far as I know he's not written a thing since arriving. He's slowly imploding while you're blossoming." Remedios started to interrupt her, to tell her that Benjamin was writing. "What if you had someone to support you?" Leonora plunged on. "Someone to cook and clean and order the world for you? What if you had someone like that? What if you had a wife?"

"We can't afford a maid or a cook."

The two friends were silent for a moment, pondering this irrefutable fact.

Leonora sat back. "Women have been doing these things for centuries. What we need is a way to transform it."

"To alchemize it," Remedios said.

"Take our creativity into the kitchen, the sewing room, the nursery, and make the art from there."

"But I don't like that," Remedios said. "Are we doomed by biology to live in those spaces?"

"Is it being doomed? I don't even know anymore." Leonora started wrapping up the cheese, putting the cover back on the tortillero.

"I feel like I'm going crazy," Remedios said and then stopped short, realizing what she'd just said to Leonora.

"What?" Leonora said with a smile. "I, of all people, can assure you that you're not crazy. And I would know." With Remedios she could be lighthearted about her time at Santander. With everyone else she refused to speak of it.

"Maybe it's where we can find a moment's freedom," Leonora continued. "A space away from men?" She looked over at Remedios. "I'm not saying it's right. But I'm too tired to push against it, and it sounds like you are too. I'm saying, why don't we make it a source of creative fulfillment?"

"That sounds like justifying." Remedios pushed the little dish of mangoes back toward Leonora. "And it sounds exhausting."

"Like anything in life, you can't be forced to do it and you can't do too much of it. Under either circumstance it becomes oppressive."

"Even water becomes a poison if you drink too much of it," Remedios said.

"But maybe expansiveness can be found in those spaces," Leonora continued. "Why is it all denigrated anyway? Child rearing, making food and nourishing, cleaning and ordering. 'Women's work' is what keeps the planet populated and alive. This is somehow the menial work, and all the nonsense of the world is what's important? It's just because it's women's work that it's been devalued, not because it's inherently valueless. Society is inherently biased against the feminine."

Leonora was so rarely political. Despite all the Marxists and rebels surrounding them, the male surrealist view of women was really quite conventional—their theories and desires not reaching all the way to the women in their lives. She leaned in closer as Leonora's insights opened like a gift.

"Why, if I wanted to put on Chiki's clothes right now and go to the market and shop, no one would bat an eye," Leonora continued.

Remedios smiled. "Don't you do that nearly every day?" Leonora was famous for borrowing Chiki's shirts and sweaters.

"But what if he put on mine?" Leonora asked, deadly serious.

"Yes, what if," Remedios said, smiling.

"Yes, Chiki in a dress is absurd because it's someone who's viewed as more powerful in society, a male, adopting the dress of those who have less power, a female. He'd be moving down. While in adopting his clothes I am moving up, which innately acknowledges male power. Perversion of the hierarchy is not allowed."

Remedios nodded, pondering. She felt as if Leonora was testing out a theory in a safe place.

"And why is that? Why isn't the feminine with all its inherent power of transformation and alchemy revered? Just look at our recipes. Taking flour and water and creating bread or tortillas. What is that transformative action if not an act of magic? What are recipes if they're not spells?"

The friends had been entertaining themselves lately by writing recipes—each more outlandish and surreal than the last. Remedios had bought a black-velvet-covered book from Julietta for just this purpose, their grimoire of sorts.

"Shall we make a dish for tonight?" Remedios asked, heading for the cupboard.

"Always," Leonora said, standing up. She reached into the icebox and brought out a small dish of black liquid.

"I've been saving this. Squid ink," Leonora said. "Seems too powerful to waste. I was thinking what if we combine it with tapioca, it might make caviar."

Remedios made a face but understood immediately. "Could we convince everyone it's caviar, do you think?"

Back in France, when Leonora and Max had houseguests in the countryside, she'd gone around to each guest as they'd been sleeping and cut off a lock of hair. She then fed it to them in an omelet at breakfast. They'd been horrified. Remedios had laughed till she cried when Leonora told her.

Now her friend made up a pot of tapioca as she kept up a running commentary. "This is alchemy, a change. Start with one thing, turn it into another. What should our next recipe be for, do you think?"

"Dispelling sad dreams?" Remedios said.

Leonora gave her a sympathetic look. "Of course I'll concoct a potion for you to chase bad dreams away. It'll be the very next thing I do. I can use it as well."

When it was done simmering, Leonora added some squid ink to the tapioca. "It looks and smells like caviar. Think we could fool people?" With her background, she would know what real caviar tasted like. "It'd fool me. Then again, I've always thought caviar was disgusting."

That night, like many others before it, Remedios and Benjamin had invited people for drinks. Leonora brought over the tapioca caviar from the afternoon, and the friends spent a good hour walking it around to their guests, trying to convince everyone it was authentic.

"Poor old, dear old Freddie," Leonora said when they persuaded their friend to try it and he politely proclaimed it delicious.

They tortured him with it rather longer than necessary as he'd brought a guest that night, a recently arrived French former fighter pilot. Jean Nicolle was his name, with hair as thick and black and glossy as a raven's wing. Freddie introduced him to Remedios, and he laughed when their hands met. "After all this time," he said.

"Have we met before?" Remedios asked.

"No, I would have remembered you. I just meant after all I've heard, now we meet. You can't be in Mexico too long without hearing about you and Leonora, the famous expat brujas of Mexico."

"I'm a witch now?"

"Do you object to being called a witch?"

"It depends. What do you think a witch is? Do you think I fly around on a broomstick and wear a pointy hat?"

"Yes," he said with a wide smile.

"Then absolutely, I'm a witch."

He laughed at her teasing and said, "A witch is someone who entrances, who casts a spell with her eyes, her person, her apartment, her parties, her fake caviar."

"Hmmm," Remedios faux-pondered. Really, he was a very handsome man. "Cast spells with their eyes—then perhaps you are the witch, señor."

He was at least ten years younger, maybe more. A rush of desire swept over her, and she felt Leonora watching her from the other side of the room, an amused smile on her face. Remedios wasn't immune to male beauty. Show her a woman who was. When she put her hand in his and shook, it was like putting her hand in a lion's paw, such was the size and strength radiating out of him.

"Out of respect to actual brujas, I can only say I wish I were a witch," she said.

"But this is clearly a house of witchcraft," he said, and she only shrugged, wanting to move off the topic.

"A house of ill repute?" he asked.

"You make it sound like a brothel," she said.

This made him laugh. He was such a contrast from Benjamin, who would have merely nodded, not scandalized in the least at the mention of a whorehouse, as he'd written things far more brazen.

"Is it?" he asked with a glint in his eye. "Is your time for sale?" It was a testament to his good looks that he could say this without a hint of menace or disparagement. Not many men could tease a woman about being a prostitute and have it come off as playful.

The benefit of age was that she didn't blush but said, "We all have a price, don't we?"

"You're not talking about money," he said. "So what is it you most desire?"

"I can't tell you that. You'd have the keys to the castle."

"You can trust me with your keys," he said, taking a step closer to her, coming into her energy.

She studied his thick mustache and lively eyes. "To laugh," she said. "To be free. To fly."

And he lifted his glass in a toast. "To freedom."

KNIGHT of WANDS.

KNIGHT OF WANDS—
Jean Nicolle

Fiery and passionate, the Knight of Wands moves through the universe intent on pleasure. With his staff of fire, this knight knows that he possesses passion and creativity, and with those gifts he offers liberation from the mundane. He encourages expression, communication both verbal and physical, and action based on passion in all its forms. He is lit up with energy and confidence.

If the Knight of Wands comes to you in a reading, you might consider ways to embody his energy and his way of moving through life. He asks you to consider where you find fire and pleasure and how they might come to the forefront at this time.

Freddie convinced me to go to the party. "A little clique of expat artists," he said. "I warn you, they take themselves very seriously, pretending they're still in Europe or something, but it's always good fun when I go. Lots of high jinks and games."

"Games," I said. "I've had enough of games." I'd been depressed since arriving in Mexico, alone and drinking too much. I agreed to go around with Freddie just to have something to do; that and his Americanness cheered me. Full of optimism and can-do energy, Freddie was pleased with the smallest things. Being with him was like being with a well-loved younger brother.

And I knew why Freddie wanted me with him. Nearly every place we went he introduced me as "Jean Nicolle, the French fighter pilot." He liked to drop the pilot thing in, especially when there were women around. At least he didn't introduce me as a war hero. I would have drawn the line at that.

"One of them's very beautiful," he said. "Leonora Carrington. Has an English title and everything."

"What am I going to do with a princess?"

"Not a princess, a title like 'M'lady' or something. You know."

"That's worse."

"Just as well. You'd have to peel Chiki Weisz off her."

"Pas de problème, I do okay when I want to."

"I know you do, buddy," he said with a clap on the shoulder. "That's what I bank on."

The apartment was derelict. Holes in the floors filled with ashes or old cheese, no electricity, cheap paraffin candles dripping on the windowsills. No food, but enough tequila to fill a bathtub.

The men huddled in the corners discussing dreams or theories of the unconscious or something while they smoked little cigars or made a show of packing their pipes. I knew their type—all of the discussion and none of the doing. Freddie told me they were artists, bohemians, writers, and thinkers. But they looked to me like a bunch of tired, slightly drunken salesmen, only they weren't selling vacuums or ency-clopedias, they were selling their nutty theories and ideas.

The whole scene made me even more depressed than I'd been before Freddie picked me up.

But then she was there. All in black with her huge eyes holding en-ergy and fire. Freddie introduced us, and I shook her hand as I racked my brain for something intelligent to say, something that would make an impression. Just looking at her, I felt like a sack of ash I'd been hauling around had suddenly transformed into a phoenix.

She offered me a drink and introduced me to her friend, the fancy Englishwoman, and they set on Freddie like a pair of black-birds and made him eat some disgusting concoction that even I knew wasn't caviar. They had a friendship of inside jokes and rapid-fire slang unique to them alone that reminded me of my sisters at home.

Freddie, earning his keep as a guest, went along with the charade to their delight, swallowing mouthful after mouthful of tiny black fishy balls.

And what should I tell you of meeting her? Have you ever been in the presence of a sorceress?

I'd thought we were the same age, but it wasn't until she was up close that I noticed the fine wrinkles at the corners of her eyes, the few strands of silver in her hair.

When she toasted my glass and said she wanted to laugh, wanted freedom, I thought that I could do that for her. I could take her flying.

She was living with some old man, a poet and a fellow French-man. I met him briefly that night. He seemed off in the clouds and dismissed me with a glance when we were introduced.

When I went by the flat a few days later and found her alone and painting, she told me he taught at the Collegio.

"Am I interrupting?" I asked when I stuck a small bottle of tequila through the window before me as an offering. "I figure I have the keys to the castle, I should use them."

She wiped her hands on an oil rag and said, "Welcome to my realm."

I had to duck to fit through the window, and the whole place smelled of paint and turpentine. "For you," I said, handing over the bottle.

"So you're a gift from the muses in more ways than one," she said and headed off to get us glasses.

In the afternoon light her place seemed to glow. I wanted to see what she was painting, but she'd angled the easel toward the wall. I snuck a peek anyway at her work in progress—a crumbling tower filled with water held a smaller keep with a dark entrance next to a windmill. A tiny woman perched on one of the blades, about to be submerged. I wondered about the woman who looked like she was headed for a dunking and then noticed two more, one running away from the tower and another on a bicycle headed for it. The whole thing looked on the verge of collapse. The colors were dark and muted, earthy even.

Remedios presented herself as appealing and conciliatory as a kitten, but she hid a deeper, more ominous edge.

She came back and handed me glasses and a dish of limes. Then she picked up a sketchbook of rough paper, a fat pencil, and a tiny penknife and came to sit cross-legged on the floor at my feet.

"I don't come by models very easily. The least you can do is earn your keep," she said, whittling the pencil into a fine point with the vicious little knife, shavings falling into a ceramic ashtray in her lap. I poured us both a drink.

She sipped, turned a fresh page, and began silently sketching, occasionally smudging pencil lines with her thumb. Have you ever had a woman pay close attention to you, analyze you with detached consideration as an object, as a mere collection of angles and shadows, all while sitting at your feet?

"Am I a good model?" I asked, joking because her intense focus made heat rise to my face, through my body. When it got to be too much, I preened my hair in jest, opened a button on my shirt, hamming it up to distract from the effect she had on me.

"You are. Your nose is, actually. I have trouble with noses." I thought she'd say something more, but she caught herself. "And you have such a fine nose. Turn to your left, please."

I did as she asked, pleased at her compliment of my nose, of all things. Piled in the corner, I noted, was a heap of rocks, crystals I guess, and looking around the place, without turning my head, I saw them everywhere. They seemed to be placed with purposeful intention in deliberate configurations, one even balanced on the top of her easel, like some ancient spell was being cast. I felt it bewitching me. I leaned down to pick one up, which made her stop and blow out air in a little huff. I'd broken my pose. I hefted the bit of quartz, along with a hunk of dried mesquite.

"I like to practice hands too," she said, standing up and taking the treasures from me. The mesquite had left smudges as if it came directly out of the desert, or had fallen like an asteroid from the sky.

"Hold your hands out like this." She cupped both hands, and I complied. She hunted the room, searching for what she wanted, and came back with a long black crystal, the length and width of a ruler.

"You have nice hands too," she said quietly as she placed the hunk of rock across my palms.

"Do I?" I asked, trying to consider them from her perspective. "How so?"

"Wide palms and square fingers, very male your hands. In contrast to this, which is a very feminine crystal. You support it well. A contrast of different types of protection."

"How do you know all this?"

"Black tourmaline blocks psychic attack. It is a grounder as well. Useful for people who are up in their heads too much."

"Is it useful to you?"

"I like useful things. Things are only beautiful if they are useful and they are only useful if they are right. My father used to tell me that."

"I can be useful," I said. "To you."

That stopped her. "How so? You're proving a terrible model."

"I can fly a plane. Have you been up in one? Much quicker than a train or a bus. You might enjoy the new perspective."

She nodded, turning back to her drawing, somehow unimpressed by my offer.

"Let me take you." I placed the rock on the floor and reached a hand down to bring her to stand. I took the pencil out of her hand and brought an arm around her, pulling her close. She smelled of the peppery tequila I'd brought and pencil shavings and something else that was uniquely her own when I kissed her.

After years of feeling numb, to feel want again, the anticipation of anything, was almost as good as having it. I'd come to Mexico looking for peace, and in kissing her I wasn't sure if I'd found it or banished it. The most ravenous desire—for her, for life, for everything sparked in me. And instead of trying to immediately get her out of her clothes, as I usually would have done, I found myself prolonging that first moment of connection knowing nothing was going to be the same after.

I don't know how long we were there when I heard a shuffle on the stairs, the clearing of a throat. How long had he been watching us before he stepped through the window and went into the back bedroom without a word? A response I'd never understand when it came to Remedios, but one I recognized. The response of numbness.

Chapter Fourteen

Remedios was washing up the breakfast dishes when Benjamin came to her.

"Walk with me?"

"I'm due at Leonora's."

"Take the day off," he said. "I am." He hadn't taken a break from his teaching job at the Collegio since starting it.

They headed toward the zocalo, which always cheered him, but today he could only find fault. He crossed to walk on the shady side of the street, complaining about the sun. He went on a long, uninterrupted diatribe about local politics, which usually provided a source of detached amusement. Today his observations were sharp. Everything annoyed him.

"I've had a letter from André," he said as they crossed the plaza.

This wasn't news, the friends wrote each other near daily, but it was a surprising opening given yesterday.

"The war's over, Rosa. He's back in Paris now. He says you can feel the liberation in the streets."

Benjamin brought Remedios's slack hand to his mouth, not noticing its limpness, a quick kiss on the knuckles. "You feel it too, I can tell. The call to go back where we belong."

They walked past the cathedral, coming into the open plaza.

Parts of the city reminded her of home, the Gothic churches, the colonial Spanish buildings, the porters outside the markets offering to carry purchases. Yet Mexico City remained uniquely itself. Mixed in with the stucco was a rustic, rougher nature than in Spain, as if greenery and lushness were humming just under the veneer of the city and waiting to take over. From the saplings sprouting in the sidewalk cracks to the algae and lichen growing on shaded stucco, nature seemed waiting for the right moment to burst civilization wide open.

Benjamin made it halfway across the plaza before he turned, realizing she wasn't by his side. "What is it?" he called, walking back toward her. She tried to think of something surreal to say. Something that would make him laugh, because she couldn't say this to him, not directly.

She didn't long for Paris. She couldn't sit in another café. Paris seemed built on baroque and curlicue artifice, while Mexico was built on living vegetation that respirated oxygen into her very lungs. She didn't want to go back to sipping innumerable cups of coffee and smoking too many cigarettes while she listened—an acolyte to Benjamin, and therefore to André. She was done absorbing. It was time to breathe.

"Look, Rosa. I know you've been unhappy. I have too. We've . . ." He took up her hand again, held it against his chest as he turned toward her. "Lost ourselves. We need to go back where we belong."

"I'm not unhappy," she said.

He released her hand and looked up at the sun, squinting. "Happier with another for now, maybe. But I think he is just a symptom."

"He's a friend," she said. "I find him amusing."

"And I'm a Frenchman, Rosa," he said, training his eyes on hers.

"So you know how things can happen between two people."

"So for me there is only Paris, is what I mean." Benjamin had been searching for Paris since the day they'd left, had tried to re-create it in Marseilles, in Veracruz, and now here. He'd finally realized that an imitation wouldn't do.

He started walking away, and she had to hustle to keep up.

"Jean's helping me out of a rut. You aren't really leaving me over this." She fell in step alongside him. "He's an ignition. That's all."

"An ignition? That's good. I'm not talking about the pilot." He looked at her out of the corner of his eye but didn't slow his pace. "At least give me credit for being able to see you, you and Leonora. The studio. Your painting. She's enlivened you. I, of all people, understand how friendship can do that, and I understand how rare that type of convergence can be. Plus, you're making money from your painting."

She started to object. She was doing commercial work, not what she wanted.

"I know, I know," he said, waving a hand and picking up his pace. "But soon you'll be painting for yourself. Shouldn't you be doing that in Paris? Not here huddled off in one of the corners of the world. Who will see what you do here? We need to go back to the real world."

She was doing calculations in her head. "We don't have money for passage."

Benjamin stopped and took a pack of cigarillos out of his pocket, fumbling with the cellophane. "André held a show for me. Max, Picasso, Tanguy—everyone donated a piece. They sold it all the first night. He sent me the proceeds. Enough for a one-way ticket." Eyes front, he stuck the cigar into the corner of his mouth and lit a match.

She realized then that he and André had been planning this, his escape, for some time. "For one?"

"I'll send for you. When I get there, I'll be able to raise the money."

She felt a little flash of adrenaline, a buzzing in the brain. The feeling of plots working unbeknownst to her and the shock of their sudden revelation raised an excitement mixed with anger. As they continued walking, she was silent and she realized this bodily sensation was the same as a betrayal, but it had a very different source.

What she felt was a lifting of a burden she hadn't known she'd been carrying. The responsibility she felt, justified or not, to make Mexico work for Benjamin. Though she should have been upset that he wanted to leave without her, and who knew if he would "send" for her as if they were in a nineteenth-century novel, it was no longer her job to make sure Benjamin was happy here. His complaints about the sun or the traffic or the loud music in the streets or the lack of a bookstore with what he deemed a sufficient number of titles in French, these would no longer be her responsibility to solve, to soothe. She no longer would need to throw parties for him, monitor his moods, and try to keep him afloat. She no longer had to feel as if he were blaming her, as if Mexico and the welcome it offered her, offered them both through her, were her fault.

Somehow in the midst of their lives he had come to the realization that he was never going to be truly happy outside France, outside Paris.

And he'd taken action without telling her. All these realizations fell around her like dominoes. Toppling one after another quickly now until her beliefs were lying flat on the ground in concentric circles spiraling outward.

"I owe him everything," Benjamin was saying. He didn't need to specify that he was speaking of André. "He gave me my life, my work."

To have it laid plain, this feeling that often stalked her that André's friendship, not their love affair, was the true center of his life. She felt a sort of exhale at this bare acknowledgment and a rising anger.

"You love him," she said. "But that doesn't mean you owe him. You were a poet before you met him."

"He's the flint that I sharpen myself on. I feel myself becoming dull here. I need to be around him to sharpen my mind."

Tears begin to blur her vision with both relief and resentment. She'd be starting a new chapter, like it or not, without Benjamin's support. It wouldn't be that different from how she lived now. She felt the burden of supporting them both, one she'd carried so cheerfully.

"No, I can't stand to see a sad Rosa," he said, wrapping her in an embrace. "This isn't sad. I'll send you the money for a ticket as quick as I can."

He was gone within a week. The call of home was strong, and their exhaustion was shared. Because of this shared weariness, she could view him with tenderness, even fondness, as they said goodbye. They had no fight left in them, even for love.

The evening after Benjamin boarded the ship to France, Remedios went to Jean Nicolle's.

"I'm ready to fly," she said when he opened the door.

He took her straight to his bed, standing over her with a fiery eye, her own flying ace fresh from battle, with his glorious hair—from the dark crown of his head to the immaculately trimmed mustache, to the fine dark shadow across his chest and the dense trail leading down.

She never thought a younger man, one who wasn't intellectual, could teach her anything, but he proved that night that he had other skills. Her head-based, almost abstract relationship with Benjamin felt frozen in a straitjacket in comparison.

As she walked home in the morning, she felt as if she'd finally landed in her body. Jean ignited all her appetites, and she was hungry for breakfast for the first time in years, it seemed. In middle age she'd found a man who provided a body-based knowing that surprised her as it grounded her in her senses. "This is what we are made for," her body seemed to be saying. "This is what has been humming underneath your skin all along."

She walked into the Austrian pastry shop feeling celebratory and intending to buy some of the crème-filled patisserie of which Leonora was so fond.

"This is a ways out of your way," said a voice. Walter Gruen sat before a pot of steaming coffee and a little porcelain cup. He and his wife had come to her parties a few times in the early days, always bringing new records for the rickety record player Benjamin had bought in a hockshop. Walter owned the best classical music store in the city, located directly across from the pastry shop.

"Can't resist some mornings," she said.

"Join me, won't you? It's so early, and it's usually deserted here. It'd be nice to have company before I open the shop. What finds you in this part of town?"

He had a little smirk on his face when he said it, and she figured her hair must look like she just rolled out of bed. "I have a meeting for some commercial work I'm doing," she said as she neatly placed her cup of espresso on the table. It wasn't a lie exactly. She needed to turn in prints that afternoon. "For Bayer Pharmaceutical. They've been generous." She didn't know why she felt the need to explain to him. Maybe because sitting there, he looked prosperous, a little smug, as if he had everything figured out. "And I've been painting furniture for Clardecor. It takes up all my time."

He regarded her as if he could see through what she was saying. Then he leaned across the table. "You know, you can sell whatever you want."

She tilted her head to the side. "It's a little early in the day for challenges, isn't it?"

"I mean, you can sell whatever you choose to make. I've seen your work. You know that whenever you choose to, you can express your-self and make a living at it, right?"

His abrupt callout was as odious as if he'd placed a dead rat on the table before she'd even had a bite of pastry.

"I suppose you know this because you sell such things, the art of others." He sat on the sidelines as a seller, a middleman, not a creator himself. How dare he call her out?

He nodded, not at all offended. "When an artist finally opens herself up, in confidence and vision, there's no limitation to what she can do. You see it with composers all the time."

She rose and took up the box with Leonora's éclairs. "I should go."

"But I've offended you." His face was crestfallen. "Don't go. You haven't finished your coffee. Of course you should make a living painting any way you can. That's what any artist should do."

"So nice to see you," she said, channeling a little of Leonora and her manners. "Please give my best to Clari, won't you?"

For a moment Walter looked stricken, and Remedios immediately knew she'd set a foot wrong.

"I thought, well, I thought everyone knew. Clari died. About six months ago."

"I'm so sorry."

"Thank you," he said simply, well practiced by this point in receiving sympathy. "Come by the store sometime, why don't you? Bring Benjamin. I have some new releases that I think he'd especially like."

And instead of correcting him, letting him know that Benjamin was gone now too, she simply said, "Of course." The reflex to be defined by Benjamin was as automatic as ever. She was eager to get away now—from the small shop, from death, from the pastries that were like pastiches of the real thing. She wanted to go back to the real thing. She wanted to go right back to Jean Nicolle's apartment.

But she merely said, "I'll tell him." And then she was gone.

–‹‹‹◆›››–

Walter Gruen's words stayed with her during her walk home. Of course it was easy for him to say she could sell whatever she wanted, he was a merchant, a burgher, Benjamin would have called him, which was one of Benjamin's favorite insults for an owner type who made money off the talents of others. What did a man like Walter know about art, really? Benjamin would say. He knew only about selling it.

Moments after she returned to the apartment and set the kettle on, Leonora showed up, stepping through the window on the landing.

Leonora went into the kitchen and helped herself, as the friends always did in each other's house. She often brought recipes she'd been testing, bread she'd been baking, herbs she'd been drying for tea. The friends created recipes for aphrodisiacs, dream inducers, and spells for all manner of things, from inducing visions to banishing painful memories. She was gone for a while, yelling updates down the hallway about her morning, and then she came back with a thick pottery mug of tea in one hand and a plate of sliced papaya in the other. She dropped down on the floor next to Remedios's chair in front of her easel.

"He's napping now," Leonora said, offering Remedios the dish of fruit. Leonora had given birth six months before and had settled into the routine of motherhood with confidence. She picked up the pastry box and opened it without asking, knowing it was for her. She ripped off a large piece of éclair filled with crème patisserie and stuffed it into her mouth. "God." She closed her eyes. "These are the absolute best. But why were you in that part of town? Out walking?" Remedios was as fond of long solo strolls through the city as any cat. She'd disappear for hours, parts of whole evenings, and then reappear with no explanation. Benjamin had accepted it as part of her personality. Leonora had worried about her safety. Neither seemed able to stop her.

"Jean lives near there," Remedios said, popping a piece of fruit into her mouth.

Leonora smiled widely.

Remedios swatted her leg, almost disrupting the pastry box.

"Oh, I see the appeal, believe me." Leonora licked her finger. "I'm just saying, don't let him distract you from your work. A man like that can be derailing."

Nothing seemed to derail Leonora, not even childbirth. She and Chiki, natural parents, had adapted to a baby quickly—the routine in their household impressive. Chiki would lock himself away in the closet he used as a darkroom to develop film while the baby napped. It was then Leonora would come two doors down the street to visit her friend.

Leonora had been reading books on goddess religions during nap times, and she'd brought a thick volume by Kurt Seligmann with her. While Remedios painted, Leonora would read interesting passages out loud. When she'd finished her pastry, she opened the book and began.

Remedios was putting the finishing touches on a painting for Bayer Pharmaceutical. At first she hadn't wanted Leonora to see her doing this commercial work, but her friend's casual manner and perpetual goodwill had neutralized any embarrassment about this paying work. Besides, listening to Leonora's thoughts about the triple goddess was fascinating.

"A moon-based goddess is often based in three parts. That's what I've been learning," Leonora said, patting the book like a well-loved cat. "It's made me think about three-based phenomena. Birth, love, and death. Sun, moon, stars. Analysis, synthesis, and evaluation. Maiden, mother, crone—"

"And if you're not a mother?" Remedios leaned in close with her fine brush on a bit of detail work.

"Mother in the sense of being in the creation time of life. You are creating all the time. Right now, before my very eyes even." She stopped herself abruptly, as if she wanted to say more but thought better of it.

"I saw Walter Gruen there," Remedios said, wiping her brush and nodding at the empty pastry box.

"Dear Walter." Leonora looked up from her book, trying to place him. "The music obsessive, right?"

"Did you know his wife died?"

Leonora nodded. "She drowned. A freak accident. Shocking."

"He said something interesting. He said I could paint whatever I wanted and support myself. Do you think that's right?" Remedios dabbed at her palette. "I don't think that's right." She touched her fine brush to the Masonite panel. "Of course I must support myself and then paint what I like in my spare time."

Silence hung between the friends. Leonora had recently been asked to exhibit her work in a group show at a local gallery while Remedios, overwhelmed with requests for commercial work, had trouble making time for her personal art.

"He's a salesman, Walter," Remedios said, dabbing her brush on her palette. "Reminds me of Oscar."

Leonora was quiet and then said, "He's telling you to be true to yourself. That's different from Oscar, who only cared about what sold."

Just then Chiki arrived with the baby in his arms squirming for his mother. Leonora got up from the floor.

"Hey, Cheeks," Remedios called. "Someone told me that I could express myself and make a living at it. I mean, isn't that what I'm doing?"

"I changed him," Chiki said to Leonora, his camera slung across his shoulder. He kissed Leonora on the cheek and handed her their son. "Sure it is," he said in answer to Remedios.

"And you too. You don't do what you want all the time. You like a bit of paying work." Chiki worked as a stringer for newspapers around the city, taking pictures of car accidents or demonstrations and selling them where he could.

Chiki turned slowly. "Are you calling me a sellout or something?"

She'd tripped one of Chiki's insecurity wires and looked at Leonora with pleading eyes for help. But Leonora just sank to the floor, unbuttoned her shirt, and offered Gabriel her breast.

"No. I was talking about me."

"I think you can do whatever you want," Chiki said offhandedly as he headed out the door.

"You see." Leonora tilted her head toward Chiki's exiting back. "You should make the art you want."

Moments like these were when Leonora sometimes grated on her friend. The daughter of an English millionaire, she seemed to think everything was merely a choice between authenticity and drudgery, audacity and timidity—because for her, everything in life had been. She avoided becoming irritating only because she'd been through her own trials. But there were times when her lack of self-awareness annoyed. She never seemed able to acknowledge the safety net hovering under her every step. That even though a black sheep, with a few telegrams and an expensive phone call, Leonora need never really worry about money if something truly horrible happened. Indeed, when madness struck, her family got her into one of the most lauded mental hospitals in Europe, in the middle of a war even.

This blind spot seemed to Remedios to be her friend's sole imperfection.

Remedios, on the other hand, was solo, making her own way in the world without a man to shelter her. Without Benjamin, she never felt more alone in her life. If something dire like illness or starvation loomed, no one would rescue her. Perhaps her friend, but Leonora had a family of her own. She had a baby, literally attached to her, which was rightly her focus. Helping a friend for a moment might be possible, not for the long haul.

"It's a little like hers, isn't it?" Leonora said, her British accent making her critique sound crisp and businesslike as she tilted her head toward a small gouache painting leaning against the wall to dry. "From the day we visited. The one she had up on the easel."

Bayer had asked for an image for their rheumatism medicines. Remedios's small painting showed a woman in the air as if levitating and being pierced all over with nails.

"It's not," Remedios said, knowing exactly the painting Leonora meant—Frida Kahlo's self-portrait with nails and broken Doric column. "It's different—the background, the foreground, the entire thing."

"You're intellectualizing," Leonora said as she switched Gabriel to the other breast. "If Max taught me anything, it's that the intellectual is completely useless when it comes to art. I'd say it's useless period, but I haven't thought that one through all the way yet. Painting is for the things that can't be said, not a medical condition. It should bring up emotion and feeling, not words, not maladies. If you can verbalize it, then verbalize it. If it brings up a medical diagnosis, then be a doctor." Leonora prattled on, trying to take the sting out of just calling her friend's work at best derivative and at worst a copy.

"I was thinking of Saint Sebastian," Remedios said, but looking at the painting, she could see it too now. Something she'd avoided was staring her in the face. It was derivative, and she saw something else as well.

Both Kahlo and Leonora had managed to insulate themselves in a world where others supported them and allowed them to create. Kahlo through living in her childhood home and resting in the shadow of the famous Diego. Leonora by finding a man who quietly adored her and brought every gift he could find to her door. From these stable bases both Frida and Leonora had started to create, expanding out in all directions.

Not that she blamed them, not exactly. Men had been doing this in reverse for years. Men set up their lives, and chose their wives, in service to their art. Women who would take care of all the details, from the children to the household, while the artist sought the sublime. If the woman was an heiress, someone like Peggy Guggenheim, so much the better. So Leonora and Frida had found that pathway too, but in a slightly different way. Men who each in his own way provided a lifestyle that allowed them to make art. The difference with Remedios was that if she wanted that life, she'd have to create it herself.

"I'm saying you should focus on your own painting." Leonora leaned forward and put the baby on her shoulder for a burp. "And Jean Nicolle . . ." She trailed off. "You might consider him evidence that stability, you resist it. I did too. But stability gives you a base you can create from."

"I don't resist stability. I just don't make decisions guided by safety."

Leonora was quiet, rubbing Gabe's back in soothing circles. "But don't you? With Benjamin, trying to get away from your family, the Church, the stifling expectations? It's a powerful thing, a wedding ring."

At that point Gabe let out a deep belch, of which any man in a pub would have been proud. The friends laughed.

"Well, the trick with wedding rings is not to let them drain all the power out of you." It was a bit pointed, but Remedios didn't care.

"You just came from Jean's. What is that if not . . ."

"If not what?"

Leonora cradled her son. "If not something that will drain you."

Leonora could be dramatic, Remedios knew this, and a little child-like in her assessment of things. Jean Nicolle was about freedom, not imprisoning herself again. Remedios had had enough imprisonment.

Looking at the rheumatism piece, the knowledge came up and revealed itself. "I can't turn this in," Remedios said.

"Of course you will. You won't waste one more second on this type of work. Not one more than it deserves. Give it half your brain. Half your talent. You can do these commissions with one hand tied behind your back and save something for your own work." Leonora's attitude hinted at a snobbery against the commercial, and this grated. It was hard for Remedios to give less than one hundred percent to anything. And really, why? Was this such a lesser form of art?

"When are you really going to put yourself into your work?" Leonora continued, ramping up now. "This is all so controlled, jumping through hoops. When will you come out of hiding? When will you let yourself be seen?"

It was easy for Leonora to say. It's easy to be seen when you've always been supported. "Are you calling me a coward?"

"I think you need to embrace a little of the rebel." Rebellion was one of Leonora's guiding lights and a great source of her charm.

"To rebel against anything means you're still controlled by it," Remedios said lightly as she slipped the dagger in. "Rebelling is really just defining yourself in contravention, instead of assimilation. But the thing being rebelled against still has control. Wasn't your mother's most fervid wish to see you prosperously married and living in the English countryside?"

Leonora nodded and said quietly, "Of course. You know this."

"Surrounded by children and a household. You've essentially done that, haven't you? It's turned upside down a bit, but how different is it really? You're just in a foreign country. We're just penniless." There, Remedios thought as she leaned in, pretending to concentrate on a bit of shading. "Sometimes we think we're rebelling, but we still aren't really choosing." Wasn't Leonora always going on and on about honesty? About how true friendship was based on the clearest honesty with no secrets?

"I think he needs a change," she said after a moment, though Gabe was sleeping as contented as a cherub in her arms. She slowly brought herself up from sitting on the floor with one hand against the wall, and for a moment she looked as if she was staggering from a wound. When she had her feet under her, she left silently without her customary goodbye embellishments and cheek kisses.

—◄◄◄•►►►—

After she was gone out the window and down the hall, Remedios crossed the room and with shaking hands uncovered a Masonite panel on the easel. Her aggression toward her friend—really, she said some rather unkind things—left her with adrenaline coursing through her with nowhere to go. She'd been working on this piece for weeks—an image of a woman, hands tied around a column with a knife in her back. Today she would finish it, she thought. She would do *her* work, not commercial work. She'd show Leonora.

Thinking of where to start, she was struck that the painting almost exactly represented her current feelings. When she'd started, she hadn't understood why she was painting it, but now she wondered—through painting it, had she brought it into her life? Was it premonitory? She cleaned her palette, picked up a brush, put it back down. Opened a tube of paint and capped it again. Chose another, and then another. She got up and sat back down. Forcing never worked well and anger was still pulsing through her, enlivening and distracting.

Was she a painter, or was she not? If Leonora could concentrate in the midst of family chaos, then so could she in the midst of emotion.

But as the high alertness of anger began to recede, she felt the bottom drop out of her energy and self-doubt, that black void hovered, threatening to engulf her.

There was a knock on the shutter, and thinking it was Leonora, a smile came to her. The friends could forgive each other for saying the wrong thing. It was part of friendship, part of loving someone.

"You left before I could say goodbye this morning," Jean said, coming in without waiting for her answer. "I can't stop thinking about you. Don't run away like that again."

And while he looked splendid, she deflated a bit that it wasn't her friend. "I wasn't running away."

"It's okay. I like a little chase."

She had a few hours before she had to be downtown at Bayer. Her momentum couldn't be so fragile that it was disrupted by Jean.

She turned back to her easel, but he caught her up, lips at her neck and hands at her waist that made her forget anything but the feel of him.

"I have to finish, and I don't want to be late for my meeting."

"Your dark secrets, sorceress," he said. "I have to know them."

Looking at the painting of the woman and nails then, she thought it looked fine. Maybe Leonora was right, maybe she should give it her minimum effort and save herself for something real. She replaced the sheet over her work.

Remedios smiled. "First lesson. To alchemize anything, you must apply heat." And she stepped away from her easel and into his arms.

THREE OF PENTACLES—
Hector Delgado, Executive Vice President for Advertising and Marketing, Casa Bayer Pharmaceutical Company

The Three of Pentacles is a card of teamwork and experts. Two people in robes confer with an artisan working on a monumental cathedral. The Three of Pentacles indicates plans, teamwork, building, and expertise.

When the Three of Pentacles comes to you in a reading, you might consider any partnerships that are on offer. They are likely to be symbiotic and valuable. This card can also indicate the need to make plans or that plans already made are currently in motion. This card also offers a reminder of the need for allies in our lives and that some projects require a team of artisans to get them out into the world.

I checked my watch again. Remedios was due here in the hour. She was often late, something I forgave her for.

I sometimes wondered what it was like for her, coming into our lobby of chrome and glass, as hermetically sealed as a hospital ward and a world away from where she lived. In fact, I found myself wondering about her entirely too much.

She was shown into my office looking professional, if a little threadbare, in a black boxy suit that had gone shiny at the elbows, a cheap portfolio tucked up under her arm.

"Sorry I'm late," she said, smoothing her untamed hair back in place as she took a seat across from my desk. "I'd make an excuse, but I can't." She looked ruddy and windblown, as if she'd walked here. I've generally found artists to be a self-obsessed, cantankerous bunch, but she seemed to have social skills, good at pleasing-to-get-what-she-wanted skills, courtesan skills you could call it. I imagined she was catnip to all types of men.

She slid the folder across my desk.

I glanced through to see what she'd done. I'd been encouraging her to sign her work, and today she had.

"Uranga?"

"My mother's maiden name."

"Saving your real name for your real work?"

She leaned over the arm of the chair and dug around in her jacket pocket for a cigarette. Silent in the face of my accurate analysis.

I went back to what she'd created based on what the copywriters had given her. "Of course we'll take them all," I said. She craned her neck to see the one I'd stopped on. Disembodied, heavy-lidded eyes floated in a bare room around a candle as winged insects flew around a flame. A clear representation of the bright loneliness of insomnia. Her rendition was clever and charming without being an illustration or a cartoon. It was what had drawn my wife to her work in the first place.

My wife, she likes nice things. She's a modern woman, always out with her friends. She leaves the kids with the nanny for long lunches in Polanco and shopping. She prefers the modern look, streamlined and minimal. So I was a little surprised when I came home and found a large cabinet painted with stars and what looked like astronomical charts in the living room.

"It's from Clardecor," she said. The decorator she and all her friends were crazy about. "Look."

She opened the little door in the front to reveal a gold-leafed vestibule. It looked like a religious relic, and in the center of it was a painting of a woman on a flying unicycle. I smiled, because of course I did.

"Isn't it wonderful?" she said.

"The hell is it?" I asked.

"A drinks cabinet, for cocktails." She and her friends were serious about their cocktails. "We can keep all the pretty bottles in it."

The painting was well rendered, but what attracted me was the humor in it, not silly but sly, and the otherworldly feeling, as if an enchanted cupboard had been delivered to our apartment somehow and plunked down for us to fill with our favorite potions.

"I saw it in the showroom the other day and loved it. He sent it over this morning on approval. If you hate it, it can go back. But you don't hate it, do you, darling?"

The modern things she loved sometimes felt a little cold to me, but this was the opposite, brimming with warmth and charm. Looking more closely, I could see that the painting was finely done, likely with a tiny brush.

"I don't hate it," I said.

"I knew you'd like it. You have such a good eye."

"You know I'm immune to flattery."

"Oh yes, so manly and immune," she said, and I kissed her laughing mouth.

The next day I called up Clardecor and got the artist's name, which they handed over easily. She'll be glad of the work, they'd said. From there it was only a matter of a few phone calls and a meeting to get her to work for us.

I handed her an envelope now. "Cash as requested."

She blushed, the only time I ever saw her do so. To cover the awkwardness, I picked up the most striking piece in the portfolio. A woman being pierced by nails.

The oddest look came over her face, like a child caught by Nanny. "Something in the ad copy you gave me shook things loose in my head. It's not my favorite either. If you don't like it, I understand."

I leaned back in my chair. She didn't know how rare she was, and it was clear she didn't know how good her work was either.

"I've been approached," I said, "by the government. They're partnering with us to focus on tropical infections—research, therapeutics, vaccines. They need someone to do a series of illustrations to educate the public and a set of more technical drawings for an industry textbook. They're looking for someone to go along on a governmental expedition to Venezuela to study typhoid, malaria, dysentery. Glamorous, I know. But there's a decent amount of grant money, and we'll throw in a little more if you agree to do some brochure work for us." This extra money was something I made up entirely on the spot, hoping to entice her. I don't know why. I wanted to make the offer irresistible. Maybe on some level I knew that sending her away would save my sanity. Or maybe I just had an inexplicable need to help someone so talented and be part of her upward trajectory. "Would you be interested?"

When they'd approached me about the project, I'd immediately thought of her.

"Can I think about it?"

"Not really," I said, a little peeved. I'd offered her a chance of a lifetime, travel, work, all of it paid for and paid well. I'd expected her to jump at the chance. I'd even expected some thanks.

"All right," she said, leaning forward to stub out her cigarette in my ashtray. "Why not?"

CHAPTER FIFTEEN

Remedios reached for the glass on offer from Diego Rivera, who then pulled it back toward his armpit. "First, what's in it?" he yelled over the music.

"Tequila and orange juice if I had to guess," she shouted. That sweet concoction was the famous muralist's favorite.

"Not in there." He handed her the glass. "In there." He pointed at her temple.

Rivera swiveled his head, searching the party. "But where is the other blackbird of Mexico City? Leonora!" he yelled across the room. "Get over here."

The friends hadn't seen each other in weeks, the absence as loud as a scream. Remedios hadn't gone to Leonora's in the mornings, and Leonora didn't stop by at the end of the day for a drink.

Leonora made her way across the party with a light smile on her face, and Remedios felt her stomach twist with anticipatory awkwardness.

"Ah, here she is, my favorite gossip partner." Diego slung an arm around Leonora's neck, his speech a little slurry. "Do you know that we know a lot of the same people?" he said to Remedios as he squished Leonora into his side. "We met through Max Ernst, that constipated schoolboy. Isn't that right?"

Only a friend as close as Remedios would know that Leonora's slight wince wasn't at Diego's crudeness but at being defined, as always, through Max. Leonora avoided talking about her famous lover, and even less did she like being defined by him.

"A couple of European easel painters," he said, leaning back as if taking their measure. "The only easel painter left in the world worth a damn is my wife." Frida hadn't come tonight. They all knew she was home ill in bed.

"Was that rude?" Diego asked, suddenly faux serious. "I suppose I'm being rude. How about this—a couple of imitative European brujas," he said.

"He's calling you witches," Jean said as he joined them, arm threading along Remedios's waist, eyebrows drawing down in concern, though he'd called Remedios the exact same thing.

She was more concerned that they'd been called imitative.

"As if I'll be the first," Diego said dismissively.

"And where are the female muralists?" Remedios asked. She'd become a bit allergic to forceful men of late. "Why is it that women artists never seem to be given those large commissions?" Diego brought out the contrarian in her, just itching to burst the balloon of him.

"Perhaps you'll be the first," he said, laughing at the impossibility of the idea.

"The meticulousness of Remedios's work doesn't translate to that scale," Leonora said. She'd always stick up for a fellow woman, even if things were frosty with her friend. "Huge murals require a certain level of imprecision."

"Did you just call me sloppy?" Diego asked. Remedios couldn't tell if he was pleased or offended.

"I'm just saying perhaps more women would paint on that scale if they were offered that much space to express themselves."

"But there are women muralists," Diego said. "Some of them are even good. Now you, pretty boy, you come and dance with me."

Diego gestured toward Jean. "Before they start asking me for names. You know the zapateado?"

Jean scoffed, which was not the right move with Diego. "I don't know how to dance the zapateado."

"So I'll teach you."

"I'm not dancing with you," Jean said in a surprisingly serious voice.

A look came over Diego's face, heightening what was always there in him—the jolly and the threatening. There was a hint of it in everything, including his art.

"You are dancing with me," he said as he backed away, doing a sort of elegant shuffle as he stamped his heels. Drink still in his hand and he didn't spill a drop, like a highly coordinated bear, graceful for his size.

Jean ignored him, turning to say something to Leonora.

Diego then reached into his belt and removed a pistol. "I said, I'll teach you."

It was Diego's nature that he would insult you one moment, demand to dance with you the next, and then threaten you at gunpoint.

Remedios put her hand out to Diego, as if to dance with him, trying to shield Jean.

"No," he said with a disturbing shake of his gun. "You." He pointed at Jean.

Jean slowly put his hands up in surrender and followed Diego out to the middle of the dance floor.

Diego tucked the pistol away, set his empty glass down on the floor, and clapped his hands in a rhythm that the band soon imitated, getting faster as he stamped his feet.

Side by side the men danced, a sort of Mexican tap dancing with the heels. Jean trying to keep up as the band played faster, Diego clapping to speed up the band.

By the end the two men were sweating, arms around each other's shoulders, side by side as they faced the party and kept time with the stamping of heels. When the song was over, Diego kissed Jean on the cheek and gripped the back of his neck, leading him off to find a beer.

Remedios and Leonora were left alone in an awkwardness filled in by the deafening sound of the horns from the band.

"Jean's a good dancer," Leonora said. "A good sport."

"He's a good sport about most things. Very accommodating," Remedios said in pointed rebuke to what she knew was her friend's judgment of her new lover.

"Look, I'm sorry I stormed out," Leonora said, which made Remedios smile. For her British friend, quietly leaving without saying goodbye was akin to stomping out and slamming the door.

"I'm sorry," Remedios said. "What I said was silly."

"I overstepped the mark. You got sensitive and said things you didn't mean." Leonora in her straightforward way dealt with the weeks of absence between them quickly. "Let's move on."

She made a gesture in front of her solar plexus as if picking something up with two fingers, then she swept her hand to the side and opened the two fingers as if dropping it away. "Done," she said.

Remedios let out a breath she hadn't known she'd been holding. When she was a child, the priest in the church confessional required endless rosaries for even the smallest transgressions. Apologies with Benjamin had been a long, drawn-out affair where she had to earn her way back into his good graces over the course of days, sometimes weeks. With Leonora, rapprochement was done in a matter of moments.

And Remedios, an incorrigible ruminator, was also fascinated that her friend seemed to release emotion so easily. Could that be real? Was that all it took? She mimed Leonora's little gesture of release. Perhaps she could try this new skill too.

"We inspire each other," Leonora was saying, waving a hand at the space between them. "We're lucky to have each other. I can't wait till you're back in the studio with me. It's been awful without you."

"I feel the same." Remedios took a large sip of her drink. "But I'm leaving," she said. She might as well try to be as direct as Leonora.

Leonora's face fell and she paused, then said quietly as if dreading the answer, "Not back to France."

"No, not that. I was offered a chance to go to Venezuela with Bayer. A little expedition of sorts, I guess." Only after she'd said it, and said it to Leonora, did the choice she'd made become clearer. After so much grounding, creating a circle of friends that were like family, creating a home and a hub, she was leaving. And this time she wasn't being forced, she was choosing it.

"I'm ready for adventure," Remedios said. A flicker of something crossed Leonora's face; was it jealousy or something more? "I've never really been on a trip of my own choosing." Remedios continued babbling over the awkwardness, a hopeless habit from being with taciturn and silent Benjamin. "I've never traveled for the sake of exploration. All my movements have been dictated by necessity and fleeing. This is a very different type of trip."

Just then the band stopped playing, and Leonora said into the momentary pause, "Well, that's the end of Jean."

It seemed everyone at the party turned toward them.

The day Remedios came home from Bayer to tell Jean that she was leaving for Venezuela, she too thought that would be the end of their affair.

"So I'll fly you there," Jean had said automatically, as if it were the easiest thing in the world for him to pull up stakes and join her. "I've always wanted to get lost in the jungle with a beautiful woman."

"Jean is going with me," Remedios said now to her friend.

"You're just leaving," Leonora said, something foreign in her voice that Remedios couldn't place. The band took up a new song at a faster pace.

"For a few months, and then I'll be back." Remedios took another sip of the concoction Diego had given her. She was becoming quite drunk. "It's a trip, that's all."

"Aren't you worried that you've been running so long that you don't know how to do anything else?" Leonora said. Remedios wasn't sure if Leonora was tipsy or just being her usual straightforward self.

Remedios felt her shoulders rise. These unexpected glimpses into what Leonora really thought were as jarring as they were unwelcome. And they'd just gotten past a bit of awkwardness, hadn't they? Recently, it seemed every time Leonora opened her mouth, she revealed an alarming viewpoint.

"You think I'm running away from something? That's how you see me?"

"To rebel against anything is to still be controlled by it. Sorry, friend, but isn't that what you told me?" She said it with a smile to hide the knife inside. "Why not seek the authentic?"

"You seek the authentic your way. I'm going to try my own route." Remedios smiled back as if they were just having a friendly conversation.

"I thought we were trying to transcend. I thought it was something we did together."

"You say you just—" Here Remedios mimed her friend's little catch-and-release of a negative emotion. "But resentment is lurking right there, underneath everything you say and do. You're searching for freedoms, but you've mired yourself in duty." There, she thought. If this were the end of their friendship, she might as well say what she really felt.

"You can't really travel, you know, not until you've created a strong enough base to travel out from," Leonora said. And she should know, Remedios thought. Leonora had been born with a strong base. "I thought that was what we were doing together," Leonora continued.

They realized then that the party was looking at them. Jean came over to gently take her arm. "We should go," he said in a tight, quiet voice.

He'd danced at gunpoint, and she and Leonora were obviously arguing. As guests they'd made spectacles of themselves.

As he led her away, she heard Leonora say quietly and to no one in particular, "I hope you find what you're looking for." As if she were invoking a spell. As if they weren't the closest of friends, but two strangers.

⸺≪◆≫⸺

Weeks later she left with Jean for the airfield. The apartment was rented and emptied except for the furniture that came with the place. Remedios shooed the cats into the street. They would need to find new homes. With a refreshing lightheartedness, she closed the window for the last time.

Most of her things fit into the same two suitcases she arrived with. Benjamin had taken all the artwork back to Paris with him. Those pieces were created by his friends, after all. Her second suitcase was packed with her paints and papers and works in progress. Her crystals were nestled in fabric remnants, and her shells wrapped in newspaper, collected feathers of importance lined the bottom of the bag.

On the landing Jean handed her an envelope. "It was wedged in the door," he said, tilting his head to the door they never used, not once. She recognized Leonora's distinctively slanted feminine script. Inside was a heavily tarnished cross with what looked like a halo around the top on a fine silver chain and a tarot card—the Chariot.

R—

I had a nanny when I was growing up who used to tell me fairy tales, a natural witch, though she wouldn't have called herself that. She gave me this for protection. Wear it while you're gone, won't you? It's always served me well. It brought a revelation once. A way to get my life back in order. As did the letter and the tarot cards you sent me in Santander. Do you remember?

For your expeditions and more.

Yours Ever,
LC

That was the thing with Leonora—her generosity was innate and her loyalty was unwavering. Once you were a friend, you were a friend through disagreements and displacements. The tarot card Leonora had sent was the Chariot, considered by some the one true good-luck card in the entire tarot deck, a card of victory. And in this way, she knew Leonora wished her well. The Chariot had another meaning between the friends, and Remedios knew Leonora had sent it for this reason too. It was a card about balancing drives. The charioteer harnesses the power of two sphinxes who pull his chariot, one black, one white, the ego and the unconscious, the freedom of creativity and the routine of structure, stability and inspiration, chastity and sex. Leonora was sending her a reminder about balance as well.

Remedios reached up under her hair and clasped the peace offering around her neck, the cross falling into the neckline of her blouse. Because even if they hadn't spoken, even if things had gotten tangled up in a snarl of misunderstanding, Leonora would always be her friend, and Remedios wasn't in a position to turn down a well-used and powerful talisman. Remedios wasn't in a position to turn down protection of any kind.

"Ready?" Jean asked as he hefted her bags into the back of the taxi.

"Show me," she said with a wide smile.

The plane was small with an open cockpit and terrifying, but she got in anyway. It was on loan from a friend, and Jean assured her he'd checked over every inch of it.

They took off, a wobble and shimmy as they ascended in air. She focused on Jean's wide hands at the controls as he piloted the little plane with skill. It was a cozy contraption, if deafeningly loud, that took them close to the heavens and into the blue.

She looked down to see where Jean had brought her, soaring high. With a deep knowledge that felt like her whole being humming, she realized she had made the right choice, the choice for adventure, for this man. Before she was at the mercy of events and guided always by Benjamin who, for all his talk about release and defiance of societal strictures, held views of appropriateness that were rather small. Leonora called a liaison with Jean self-sabotage and a running away. Remedios knew it was a liberation.

A bit later when he began to descend, she touched his shoulder, and he nodded to reassure her. Flying by sight, he landed in a nondescript field with a small hut by its side. The man in the hut seemed to know him and waved as Jean took her hand.

"Where are we going?" she asked.

"I have to show you something," he said.

They walked to the base of the hillsides, scented with pine, and soon she noticed the trees blanketed in masses of beating orange butterfly wings, so many they formed massive pulsing columns, opening and closing their wings like one living, beating organism.

"The migration," he said. "The monarchs come back every year."

"They're here to mate?" she asked.

He smiled, leered a little. "To overwinter. There is only one generation that can make the journey south. Many generations cycle in Canada, live and die there. And it takes a few cycles of generations to travel south to north. But this is a special group that travels this far, travels home. They come here to create. They're triggered by the angle of the sun."

The long, hanging clumps of insects pulsated where the sun hit them. A few flew in the shafts of light in between the pine branches.

"It seemed like a you thing to me," he said, coming to stand next to her.

If she could ever paint anything close to the feeling that came over her then, she would have succeeded beyond her wildest dreams. She felt it rising in her as if for the first time, the desire to create, a fire rekindled. And more than that, a desire to make this scene a part of her forever. The only way she knew to do that was to take it inside, alchemize it, and make it her own through paint.

"They're vibrant and they fly. Just like someone I know," Jean said with a wide smile, acknowledging his sappiness. She kissed him then, because how could she not?

They were her favorite colors, these butterflies with the orange of flame and the black of mystery. Waving their wings out slowly as if in invitation, a beckoning to rebirth.

DEATH—
the Monarch butterflies of Michoacán

The Death card is the card of endings and subsequent rebirth. While some may put an ominous or literal interpretation on it, the Death card rarely foretells an actual physical death. More often the Death card calls you to consider what in your life is ready to fall away. What no longer serves? What needs to be released so that rebirth is possible? The Death card shows a skeleton in armor on a white horse and those in front of him falling. He carries a black flag fluttering with the white rose of rebirth. In the background, the sun rises between the two towers of consciousness.

If the Death card arrives in a reading, consider the cycle of release and rebirth in your life. Are there jobs, ways of thinking, people, or even relationships that are ending? Don't fear their release, as letting go makes way for new connections, makes way for your own rebirth. Can you help along these endings in your life? If you are gripping onto something that is dying, can you release your grasp and ease it on its way?

We are the generation of travelers. We start thousands of miles away on the edge of the tundra at the end of summer. Our mothers deposited us on the underside of a milkweed leaf, though they didn't know of the journey in front of us. Even they, our sacred mothers, didn't know how to do this navigation. Only our generation can fly such distances. We know where the currents flow and how to find the thermals to carry us when we are weary. When we fly, we are surrounded by our own kind, the survivors, the long-lived. We have knowledge within us of the moon, the stars, and the magnetized energy of the earth.

Before this we were in our chrysalis, appearing to sleep outwardly but inwardly in a cauldron of creation and metamorphosis. It was difficult, demanding work and it looked like nothing from the outside. We literally liquefied ourselves into a primordial soup of creation. Then our imaginal discs elongated into leg and antenna and wing. Have you ever had to turn yourself from one thing into another? Create an entirely new being out of nothing but the raw material of yourself? It requires a safe place to enfold in on yourself while you do your work. On the surface nothing appears to change until one day, you emerge, energy incarnate, ready to travel long distances.

We arrive exhausted in the fir trees of Mexico, content to rest and drink nectar. We aren't part of a cycle. We are the cycle. With every beat of our wings, with all the movement and knowledge we bring here—our only purpose now is to unfold our wings, to let them shine their vibrant orange, to fly.

Chapter Sixteen

Remedios continued sketching Jean while he lounged in the tent on a woven mat. These weekend trips away from Maracay were meant to allow her time to explore botany, but she'd found herself increasingly drawn to Jean as her subject. Whether they were in the apartment in town or in the jungle, Jean enjoyed trying to distract her. If she was working, he'd position himself just on the periphery of her sight line and begin by making small observations about his day, outrageous or made up in order to make her smile. If he didn't get a laugh, he became more outré or funny or seductive. The more she resisted him, the more extreme the experiment became until she put down her brushes and came to him.

Jean was drinking straight rum out of a canteen while she sketched on fragile, translucent vellum, luxuries she could afford now that Bayer was paying her a stipend.

"Is this what you plan to have me do whenever we travel?" he asked. "Model for you?" She'd recently finished an oil portrait of him in fine profile with a little flying contraption in the corner.

"You're not satisfied with your job as my air chauffeur?"

"I'm more satisfied doing other jobs for you," he said with a waggle of eyebrows and then took a sip. "But really, you live this life as if it's real. We both know it's not real. We need to go back."

Remedios sighed. "Maracay is overrated."

"Not just to Maracay. We should go back to Mexico."

Remedios hummed a little under her breath as she smudged out a line for shading. "Not yet."

"What is it we're doing here?" he asked, sitting up and ruining the pose.

"Working," she said.

Bayer had set them up in an apartment in Maracay, close to the laboratory for the Venezuelan Ministry of Public Health in Caracas. Every morning Remedios went to the labs, sketchbook in hand. Still, it took weeks before the scientists trusted her enough to let her peek into their microscopes and then render what she remembered. She was to peer into them and sketch exactly what she saw—her father's admonitions about precision and utility coming to her daily.

After the first few drawings the researchers saw the accuracy and the worth of her work and set up her own microscope. Each morning she fitted the glass with the new specimen. Her drawings remained with the ministry, and a copy was sent to Bayer in Mexico for use in medical textbooks, along with her illustrations for public service campaigns about the dangers of dysentery, typhoid, and other tropical diseases. She was rather fond of the one for dysentery. She'd painted a bowl of lettuce and tomatoes and among them tiny demons with swords meant to lightheartedly show the potential pain of the disease.

Jean took every opportunity to fly away with her. On weekends and whenever the lab was closed, he'd fly them to different parts of the country to explore new terrain. There he'd set up hammocks for them under mango trees and she'd spend her time thinking of her paintings, of her real work, but never doing it. Her scientific observations now mingling with her thoughts about the supernatural. Her ideas about precision and clarity mixed with the ripe, sweet, almost unpleasant smell of rotting mangoes that seemed to hang around Jean like an intoxicating fog and kept her from reaching for her paints.

"You're acting like you have control over all this," Jean said, now with a sweep of his canteen. "And we don't have control. No one does."

He could often be like this—philosophical and ruminative, with a through-the-glass-darkly sort of nihilism that shaded his usual hedonistic stance toward life. Remedios believed it an aftereffect of the war.

She put her sketchbook away and reached for her tarot deck, always near when she worked, and began shuffling.

"Ah, right," Jean said. "There's some control for you."

She shuffled, searching her mind for a question to ask, but nothing came. In such situations she usually sent up a prayer for guidance, a request for knowledge within the current circumstance to be revealed. But as she turned over the cards, they made little sense to her. The connections between them were hazy and unintelligible. In recent months she'd taken to writing crabbed notes in the margins of the cards themselves, but this was only because they weren't speaking to her. She then did what Madame Cherugi advised when blocked, her lessons coming back to her from all those years ago. She started with the basics. She simply described, out loud, what she saw on the card. Hearing an auditory description could sometimes provide insights.

"Lightning strikes a tower on fire while two figures free-fall upside down around it," she said under her breath, but this offered little insight. The Tower is about change, usually a change that has been much needed for a long time. Some fear the chaos of the Tower, but she'd learned to welcome it as the fresh start. Yet there was nothing she wanted to change, especially not the freedom she'd found in the jungles with her lover. Her work was going well, and she was being paid for it. There was nothing to be struck down and destroyed, nothing that needed to be cleared from her life.

"That's why we should live for now." Jean heaved himself up and came to flop next to her, propped up on an elbow. "That is why"—he pointed to the card—"we should get married."

He'd taken her by surprise, and she doubted he was serious. Jean loved nothing more than the grand romantic gesture, like flying her around in his plane. He'd like the story he'd tell, mostly to himself, about a proposal in a jungle tent, about being overcome in the moment. She wondered if he'd enjoy being married at all. She wondered if she'd enjoy being married to him. She flipped the card upside down and slid it back into the stack. "I'm not saying no," she said quietly. "But why?"

"Why, she asks me." He rolled over on his back, staring at the tent ceiling. "Because I love you."

"And I love you."

"Then marry me."

"Am I allowed to think about it?"

"I'm feeling a little bruised here, but yes, you can think about it."

"Don't feel bruised," she said, putting aside her tarot deck and leaning down to kiss him.

--<<<<◆>>>>--

After, Jean lay snoozing next to her in his enfolding decadence that seemed to engulf her like opium. Rolling out from under his arm, she slipped back into her clothes and out of the tent and walked into the jungle toward the twilight sound of rushing water. She'd visited the Orinoco and its tributaries many times, and so far it never failed to impress her.

The migrating birds had returned to the jungle now, called back for their season in a lush river basin. All the migratory animals were being called back, being called home. The waxy dense green of the jungle interspersed with a humidity so lush it felt like steam heat.

She followed the banks of a shallow, slow-running branch of the river as it got wider and shallower again—a great rushing source. She had been buoyed along as if on a river this whole time. Following Benjamin, learning his thought patterns—the two of them buffeted by world events. She had never decided, never actually made a choice.

And here was Jean Nicolle offering another choice, or was it more of a demand? Would she let him distract her? Derail her? The escape from life he offered was delicious. She could see it all stretching out in front of her then. A life in the labs or in advertising using her skills in service to commerce or medicine. Not the worst fate. And coming home to Jean and the type of release and escape he offered. Would it always be like this between them? She suspected they'd be able to go a number of years before their fire died out. And then would she finally turn to her work? Once she'd saved money? Once Jean's passions had run out? Was it then she'd fully express herself?

She waded into the shallows along the bank, only ankle deep and stretching for yards. She lay down on her back, the water sluicing through her hair, soothing her tight scalp. She wanted to hear this from the source.

Leonora's necklace fell down the side of her neck and dipped in the muddy water. Her hair fanned out as the river flowed it downstream. She was making a choice now, to immerse herself in the flow, in the source.

And it was in that moment that she could hear it, the universe was talking to her. She had been seeking this with her crystals, with the tarot, with all the books passed back and forth between her house and Leonora's. She had been seeking a universal experience of the divine, of oneness.

It was there at the source of the Orinoco River that she could hear the flow surrounding her, telling her that she was a part of it. She was one now with it all. She would neither be swept away downstream, nor would she be a passive observer standing on the banks dry and untouched. She was drenched in it.

And she could feel now that Leonora had been nudging her to do this—to finally choose herself. It was there in her objection to Jean, her objection to commercial work. Leonora was right, even if it looked like she made these choices from safety and comfort—she was right nonetheless. And what was so wrong with safety and comfort if it allowed you to make the choices that fed your soul? Perhaps among peace and abundance one could reach out and reach higher. Perhaps there was a certain type of healing that could only take place in the calm of routine.

She has felt this lifting before. When she landed in Veracruz, when she first stepped into the apartment, she hadn't known it, but this lightness was a taste of freedom.

Jean finds her then, crashing through foliage. "There you are," he says as he drops on top of her and she is engulfed in his arms, his scent, his dizzying kisses that blot out everything, even the sound of the river.

But something has changed. She doesn't want to be taken out of the present. She has spent her life running. Leonora was not entirely wrong about that. She can see this obsession with Jean for what it is. A way of hiding, hiding in him. It is time now for her to come out from hiding behind Benjamin and his ideas, and now from behind Jean, it is time to be seen for who she is.

She wishes she could do this and still have Jean in her life, but this, she realizes, is likely impossible. Jean wants nothing less than to possess her totally, as witnessed by his impetuous proposal. He likely has felt this coming in her, even if he's not aware of it.

They create an escape hatch from the present together, a place outside time and reality. There is little space for her work in that bubble, even less for creative thought or for her friendship with Leonora. Being with Jean, as delicious as it is, is still a form of fleeing.

And she has never stopped running—from her childhood, the war in Spain, the Germans in Paris, and even in this land an ocean away. It's here in Venezuela, next to the Orinoco, that she vows to stop. She will no longer flee. She has been doing it for so long, it is reflexive. Looking at Jean and the type of escape he offers and demands, she knows that if she stays with him, she will be subsumed by him. She will, again, get nothing done. She will support them both, as she did with Benjamin. She has always thought that she needed a man to support her. She knows now that she can support herself.

He can sense this in her. Leaning back, he says, "You'd deny me?"

"No," she says. "I'd never deny you."

She gives herself over to Jean there on the banks of the river, one last time, and when they are done and putting themselves back together, she sees a fluttering through the dense green of the jungle—black and orange in flight.

KING OF PENTACLES—
Walter Gruen

The King of Pentacles sits on his earthly throne in his lush garden, contemplating his pentacle. He is a king at peace with himself and his world. He is also a proficient caretaker, as seen by the leafiness and growth surrounding him. The King of Pentacles rules the material world, and he is good at navigating it. Adept with money and well versed in matters of the law, the King of Pentacles travels these worlds with effectiveness, efficiency, and ease. He is the ultimate father protector figure. He is an amasser of knowledge and a superb executive. Fair, calm, and diligent, the King of Pentacles also makes an excellent diplomat.

If the King of Pentacles appears in your reading, consider the ways you might be a better shepherd of your interests in the world. How you might ease your way through life with a working knowledge of money, business, or law. He is an invitation to take care of yourself and your interests with competency and authority.

Benjamin Péret, for all his French sophistication, never cared much about igniting Remedios's creative fires. And Jean Nicolle likely spent as much time staring into the mirror as into her eyes. Neither had any idea what to do with a woman like her, I'm convinced of that.

Of course I found her alluring. Most men did. My wife Clari and I had gone to a few of the parties she used to throw with Benjamin. Most of the expats in Mexico City had traveled through their doors at one time or another. I wondered at Benjamin on those nights, at what it must be like to be so confident in yourself that you could take a woman like Remedios for granted. I supposed it was because he was a Frenchman.

These were nothing but passing observations. I was married at the time, and in love with my wife. But after Clari died, I was alone. I hadn't thought of Remedios in years, when I ran into her at the Austrian bakery across from the shop one morning quite early. Later I would realize that she was coming from Jean Nicolle's apartment.

She went away with him for almost a year. Leonora told me they went to Venezuela. And then she came back without him, which is where our story began.

I ran into Leonora at the Austrian bakery, and in a surge of spontaneity she invited me to dinner that very night. I was embarrassed by her unchecked generosity and was sure she didn't mean it, but she insisted in her very proper British way mixed with all the warmth of her Mexican self and convinced me. I brought her a recording of Pablo Casals as a hostess gift, the six Bach cello suites, which I remembered were her favorites.

What I didn't know was that Remedios was back, and when I arrived for dinner that night, it was obvious I'd been invited to be seated next to her.

She'd been working, she said, as she never had before. Sharing a studio with Leonora, the two of them in a cauldron of creativity. I detected a touch of defensiveness in her voice when she said it, which surprised me, and I noted her use of the word cauldron, which charmed me.

Remedios arrived in my life like a comet out of the sky. I invited her for dinner the next night, and she never really left. Like one of the cats that followed her wherever she went, she seemed to adopt me, though we never formally discussed it. She migrated between my apartment and Leonora's for months, as skittish as a stray. Then she began to cache little stashes of her things around the house. First I found a few rocks and feathers and polished pieces of wood placed around the apartment with obvious intention, then a suitcase with some clothes, then her sketchbooks, and finally her easel and paints.

The last because as an enticement to get her to fully move in, I was able to lease the apartment across the open-air landing, something I'd always wanted to do.

I'd been as nervous as a bridegroom with a ring when I offered her the key to the studio on a braided leather strap.

"I thought it might allow you more space. And me as well. You need your own workplace, and you admire Leonora's studio." I held the key out on a flat palm, as if to coax a nervous fawn. I had the feeling there had been compromises with Benjamin and that she'd fit herself and her work into the corners of his life. Jean was the type who would take all he was offered without a thought for the giving and then ask for more. I'd decided that if anything, I would be a solution in her life, not a problem.

She paused, and for a moment I thought she'd turn me down, but then she took the key and opened the door to the musty room across the landing.

"Yes," she said, peeking her head in. "It's perfect."

She exploded into the studio. I'd watch through the open door as she'd spend the first few moments of any workday placing all her treasures about the room just so, deciding which crystal must face north that day, which plant just about to bloom would keep her company by the easel. Then she'd set down to work. She always kept the door open. She never shut me out.

Her paints she set on the windowsills during the full moon. To cleanse them, she once told me. She claimed she could feel the energies of all her ephemera and that these precise alignments allowed a certain cosmic access each day before she started work.

I worried about her as I left for long stretches during the day to tend to the shop, but Josefina, my housekeeper, reported that she worked silently in front of the easel as if in a trance for as long as eight hours at a time, pausing only to ask for coffee or to send her to the corner for more cigarettes.

Sometimes she'd set her easel out on the landing in the strong sun, the better to see her small, precise brushstrokes.

It was heaven returning home to the smell of paint and varnish and turpentine mixed with the herbs she dried and burned in her studio. When I asked her about it, she told me that at the villa in Marseilles an herbalist had taught her the various uses of different plants. And she told me that as a child she'd believed in the magic of plants, their creation of great living beings out of small seed, water, air, and earth. I started finding bundles of dried twigs in our bed, handfuls of flowery dust under my pillow, bowls of dried marigold heads on the windowsills, and sachets hanging over our threshold. In this way the apartment itself turned into a work of her art with the tiny squiggles and symbols she drew at the thresholds and windows. Small spells she was casting. To me they invoked her constant welcome presence in my life.

Leonora came by nearly every day, in and out of the house so often I called our place her annex. Not that I minded. I knew they were a pair from the start, and Leonora was always the very best sort of company.

One Friday afternoon I'd returned to find Remedios gone and assumed she was shopping with Leonora, a weekly ritual. So I was surprised when Leonora walked through the door without knocking and wearing her usual array of gathered skirt and what looked like one of Chiki's old shirts under the rough sort of painter's jacket she favored, with sensible loafers on her feet. I offered her a drink and prepared to make companionable chitchat until Remedios returned.

"I came early because I need to ask you something."

Of course Leonora knew when Remedios would be gone, knew when she'd find me alone. The friends knew all each other's comings and goings. She'd timed this chat precisely.

Josefina brought in a pot of steaming tea and two pottery cups. Leonora decorously waited until Josefina finished arranging everything on a low table and left. Leonora usually spoke freely, bluntly even, it was one of her charms, and she rarely cared who was listening. That she waited until we were completely alone made me lower my eyebrows at her.

"Name it," I said.

She poured out the tea and handed me a cup, as if we were in the living room of a manor house. "There's a show. She should submit some work."

I nodded.

"But I can't get her to agree."

"Good luck," I said, sipping the tea and scalding my tongue. "She won't let me see a thing. And I don't press."

"Do you know it's been nearly fifteen years since we arrived here?" Leonora got up, her tea untouched. "She's been incubating this whole time." She poked around in the pots of the houseplants, looking at the crystals and shells Remedios kept there. "Commercial work. Never anything for herself. I'm starting to think she's been in a survival state for so long that she doesn't understand it's safe now, safe to be seen. It's been long enough, this hiding."

"She is feeling safer," I said, and Leonora smiled at me. She knew what I was doing as well as anyone, providing a safe harbor for a genius. "The problem is she has no clue," I continued. "She's no idea how good she is, and she won't let anyone see so they can tell her. It's a tight little loop she's living in." I went to the bedroom, brought back a huge scrap of wrinkled translucent paper, and handed it to Leonora. She dusted dirt from the pots off her hands and took it from me with a frown.

"They're the sketches she makes," I said. "Before each painting. Each more meticulous than the last. I rescue them from the trash can, if you can believe it."

Leonora nodded. I knew she'd be familiar with Remedios's process. Leonora looked at me and cocked her head, waiting for the problem.

"She could sell them!" I said. "Look at them."

"She's a painter. She should be selling her paintings. That's why I'm here."

I inhaled deeply through my nose. "My point," I said, "is that she has no idea. No clue that what she's creating is extraordinary. If it were just a matter of being seen, I think you could help her. What I'm saying is she doesn't understand her level of talent. She's crumpling it up and throwing it in the garbage, for God's sake."

It was then the door opened and Remedios herself returned, net bags full of oranges and an armful of the white gladiolas she and Leonora loved but that only reminded me of a funeral. Which, come to think of it, was probably why they liked them.

She seemed to read the situation in an instant. "Have I stumbled on a little cabal?" She snatched the paper out of Leonora's hands. "Have you been snooping in my trash?"

I shook my head slowly at Leonora. "What did I tell you? No idea. No clue."

"It's time," Leonora said, rising to her feet. "For you to show." Her voice was sweet and gentle, as if reassuring a child. Leonora had already had a solo show, which had sold out immediately. Galleries in New York were in contact. But this didn't seem to raise any jealousy in Remedios, nor did Leonora act like the elder leading the lesser. They were what they always seemed to me, sisters in everything but fact.

"They're ready," I said, and I couldn't control myself. "And you could sell these too." I shook the paper.

"Do we need money?" Remedios asked, suddenly serious. And I immediately backed off, aware I'd tripped her sensitive wiring around money. She was always alert to financial problems, some sign from me that she might need to go back to her commercial work. I never wanted her to think she had to support me. The trick was getting her to accept my support.

"No, of course not. The shop is more than enough. I just meant." I sighed here. "These are beautiful. They don't belong in a trash can."

"Then you can keep them all, mi amor," she said and came to quickly kiss my cheek. "Your special collection if you like."

I have to admit, it thrilled my greedy heart for a moment.

"Then that's settled," Leonora said, turning toward the patio garden. "You're showing with me." She pointed at Remedios. "You're keeping the sketches." She pointed at me. "They need four paintings by the end of the week." She hooked a thumb in the general direction of the gallery.

Remedios began to protest—she couldn't create new work that fast, the timeline was too tight, there was nothing to show.

"You have more than those already done and waiting," I said, hoping I was right.

A silence fell, both Leonora and I waiting patiently for her to invite us into the studio across the landing, for her to finally show us the full extent of her labors.

"Fine, you might as well come." She led us across the terrace she'd turned into a personal jungle filled with potted plants and hunks of wood, shells, and rocks. In the middle she kept a huge abalone shell she often refreshed with clear water.

There were six paintings, seven if you counted the one still on the easel.

And they were luminous. The one that drew me instantly, and Leonora too, was called *Caravan*. A man pedaling a contraption while inside his lady love played a piano, created her art. He was both her showman and her caretaker. I couldn't help but feel a kinship between the protective driver and myself, between the woman creating her music in isolation and Remedios.

"I always wanted to run away in a gypsy wagon pulled by a Vanner horse when I was a girl," said Leonora.

"Of course this must go in the show," I said quietly.

Remedios propped the other paintings on the floor, as if they were nothing, not worth hanging on the walls. I knew Leonora's opinion held the most sway here, but she couldn't make a decision either.

"What if we let the cards decide?" Leonora said, picking up the pack Remedios kept never farther than arm's length from the easel.

She shuffled. Remedios cut. Then they each took half the deck and went around the room, placing a card in front of each painting.

"Will it be clear?" I asked. I'd been the recipient of their tarot readings enough times to know that they offered insights and general thoughts, not definitive answers.

"What do you think?" Remedios asked. "Will we know?"

"Oh, we'll know," Leonora said as she held up her half of the deck in front of her like a shield. "What's at the bottom of the pack?"

Remedios smiled. "The World."

"Can't get much clearer than that," Leonora said.

They went around the room, turning over each card in turn, considering them, talking about them in relation to the others. *Sympathy or the Madness of the Cat* showed a woman petting a cat, sparks flying off the animal's fur. Leonora leaned down and turned over the card she'd placed in front of it—the Three of Cups, which showed three women dancing in a circle each holding a chalice above her head.

"So that's a clear yes," she said.

Remedios was standing in front of another piece, which depicted a woman in a checked cloak working at a stylized spinning wheel. In the background it was hooked up to an alchemist's vessel under a cathedral. The round enclosed pot had a thin pipe coming out of it to deliver the distilled essences to the universe. There were hints of the de Chiricos as well as Hieronymous Bosch and a bit of her father's architectural renderings. Remedios stood before it with the Chariot card in her hand.

Leonora came up and stood beside her, head cocked, examining the piece.

Remedios flipped the card to show her friend. "Has to," she said in the shorthand they used for everything.

"Must," she agreed.

The last painting they paused before showed a cloaked figure in a winter forest. A shaft of sunlight illuminated a patch where a flower bloomed. The cloaked figure held a bow in her hands, looking part tree and part human, playing across the shaft of sunlight as if it were a musical instrument. *Solar Music*, Remedios was calling it.

"Casals?" Leonora asked. "Beautiful." Remedios had told me the story of hearing Pablo Casals play in Marseilles. Of course Leonora would know it too. Of course Leonora would quickly put inspiration together with the resultant work.

They leaned down together, almost bumping heads. Remedios came up with the card, and when they saw what it was they both laughed.

"The Nine of Cups," Remedios said, handing the card to me. It showed a smug and prosperous merchant type sitting with satisfied arms crossed in front of nine full chalices. "The one true card of wish fulfillment in the deck," she said.

With that they had decided. Those four paintings would go to the gallery for the show.

-≪≪◆≫≫-

That night Remedios felt like a meteor in my arms, a turning ball of fire getting ready to rotate itself to a brighter flame. It was as if every moment of her life had been bolstering and fortifying her for this time when she could fully emerge and set herself and her vision free. That I might have even the smallest part in it, creating a nest for her, a home base from which she could launch, filled me with purpose and satisfaction.

As I lay next to her in the dark, I pondered this need to protect her. My love for Clari hadn't been like this, and Remedios had supported herself for a long time.

Lying there, I realized I did it because I only wanted to witness it, to hand her the matches and then stand back and watch as she lit the world on fire.

THE WORLD—
Remedios Varo

The World card is the last card of the Major Arcana. It signifies the completion of a cycle and the fulfillment of destiny. The cosmic dancer in the middle of the card represents someone who has come into harmony with her life and her calling. She is in the world but not of the world. The lessons have been learned, and will not need to be relearned. This journey on the wheel of life is complete, never to be traveled again. If the World card comes to you, rest with the knowledge that a cycle is completing and that the knowledge you have gained will travel with you. What you desire will come to you. Peace will be the result.

I clean my brushes, wrap them for tomorrow, and plunge them handle side down into the potted plants where they can absorb the life force of the soil overnight. Then I pull the pots into a line to represent the chakras—red pineapple sage for the root chakra, orange marigolds for the sacral, yellow and white frangipani for the solar plexus, a green philodendron with its heart-shaped leaves for the heart chakra. I bought gladiolas dyed blue from the market for just this purpose, and I place their vase next in line to represent the throat. Next comes the tiny passionflower vine I bought because it was in bloom. Its purple flower stands in for the third eye. Lastly the cutting from a white laelia orchid in a tiny vial stands in for the crown chakra. Once I have them in a line, the botanical power radiating from the formation will infuse my space and the brushes overnight.

I put the paints I'll use tomorrow on the windowsill, where they'll be awash in moonlight tonight. All these preparations make my mornings easier when I am searching for a way back into the work, accessing the vortex, as Leonora and I call it. The place where the world slips away until it is just the paint, the canvas, and me. Once I'm there, I don't want to resurface, even less do I want to do the work to get back in if I'm interrupted. Hours go by, parts of whole days. Leonora understands all this implicitly.

My cosmic preparations also help drown out the voices in my head. The ones that tell me that what I'm doing is useless, that no one cares about my paintings, that I am nothing but a glorified illustrator. My father's voice calls me again and again to try to look objectively. Is that line straight? Is it defined? And the question he would ask most often, the one I have spent a lifetime unraveling—is it useful? And while his voice has plagued me, it has also allowed me to see objectively the sections that are successful, the parts that need more work.

The phone has been ringing all afternoon. Bless Josefina, who answers it and takes down detailed messages. She's kept Walter's house for years, even helped him after Clari died. I believe she views me as some exceptionally fragile treasure of his that she must treat delicately. This I've found rather amusing and not without its perks. I suspect it's the gallery owner phoning now. She calls nearly every day at this time with updates, but what she really wants to know about is progress. Yet another person has come by to put down a large deposit in hopes of being moved closer to the top of the waiting list for a painting. "Quite a well-known collector," she'll say. "Doesn't care about size or subject, just wants to be next in line."

I have learned to let her deal with the politics among collectors, and Walter has stepped in to keep an eye on my business interests. There are requests for interviews, journalists calling from New York City even. All these I turn down. It's given me a reclusive reputation, not that I mind, but it's not intended. I simply don't have time, that and Leonora's ideas have rubbed off on me. Art is for the things we don't have words for. So what is the purpose of talking about it?

I can hear Walter now on the other side of the door, waiting. Only now can I turn and consider what I've completed over the course of a day. I've been working on the fine haunch fur of a creature emerging from a forest, using brushstrokes with my thinnest brush with only three hairs. This creature I've been painting has been leading me down a path, but now the trail recedes. I've been able to access the vortex today, and that means it will be a good night.

I can hear noises from the street below again. I can hear Walter, just on the other side of the door, shift in his chair. If I don't join him soon, he will become louder, he will pour our drinks. He will clear his throat, but he won't open the door.

I never keep him waiting long. Not out of urgency to be reunited as in the days with Jean Nicolle, or out of deference as in the days with Benjamin, who never liked to wait for anyone. Rather, it's out of respect for what Walter has given me—the production of silence, the regularity of meals I don't have to cook or shop for, the orderliness of a house I don't have to clean. He even organizes our social life, though I suspect this is out of desperation. If it were up to me, we'd see Leonora and Chiki and very few others.

I creak open the door, and as I step out I feel a slipping away, as if a cloak I have been wearing falls off and I am Remedios again.

Walter is sitting at the iron table, an ashtray, two small glasses of tequila waiting. Next to them, wrapped in a torn piece of dusty homespun, are two long crystal shards—one black, one white.

"They were left downstairs," he says. "Josefina says that old prospector dropped them off." All sorts of unsolicited and unusual specimens showed up at the house now, hoping to tempt me. Fossils, petrified wood, crystals—my reputation as a collector has gotten around, and oddly this satisfies.

I heft the black one, cool and smooth in my hand. I have an overwhelming urge to bury it in one of the terra-cotta pots where Josefina grows sage and cilantro for the kitchen. It should be returned to the earth, its natural home. Having it out here so clean and naked seems obscene.

"I can't afford them," I say, setting it back with the white one, and reach for Walter's pack of cigarettes. "Besides, it requires dirt around it. I don't like them when they've been too polished."

Walter shrugs. "I believe they're meant as a gift," he says, lighting a match. I lean in and cup his wrist while he says, "Given how much work you've sold, you can more than afford them, if you want them."

Years ago, I'd sold those four paintings in my first group show, the one Leonora, bless her, had practically abducted my paintings for. When the gallery gave me my check, I'd tried to repay Walter, presenting him with a portion of our household expenses. He protested, threatened not to cash it. But then he saw I was serious.

"You don't have to," he'd said.

"But I want to. I want to contribute. I've never not paid my way."

"I'm not a cruise line, you don't have to pay your way." We were silent. I didn't know what to say in the face of this. He sighed. "Maybe you can contribute by redoing some things around here if you like. You could spend your money that way." He was always desperate in those days for some sign I'd stay. He made jokes that, like my cats, one day he'd wake up and I'd have moved on. I think he thought if I put down more roots, that would keep me from disappearing. He shouldn't have worried. "You can change anything you like," he said softly. "You live here now."

Clari's touch was everywhere in the apartment. And she'd had an excellent eye for such things as proportion, balance, symmetry, and color. "If you want to change or rearrange, I understand. Get rid of anything if you want." But I heard the sadness in his voice, the hesitancy.

I went and wrapped my arms around his neck. "I'm not really interested in being with a man who didn't love his wife, you know." And I kissed him. "She did a beautiful job. Why would I change a thing?" He exhaled, knowing that I understood, that my views of the human heart and its expansive ability to love were as large as his. That I wanted to only ever add to his life. Not subtract.

Walter crosses into the sitting room off the terrace and puts a record on. Edith Piaf's voice fills the room.

"She's allowed now?" I ask. Walter didn't often play her, claiming she'd been a Nazi collaborator despite her going before the panels and being exonerated. I didn't mind this ban, as her voice always brought back a rush of memories.

Walter nods. "Is it too much?" he asks. "I can turn it off."

The only thing more evocative of a certain time in my life than Piaf's voice is the smell of smoky wet wool combined with good cognac. It sends me hurtling through time and space so that I am sitting in the cafés of Paris again, an ingénue on the outskirts of the great men, sitting practically at their feet, grateful to be there, grateful to listen. Thoughts I'd had, but never spoken. Ideas they'd detailed but never put into action. Sitting there, with the phone ringing for my paintings, a husband who believes so strongly in my art that he acts as an armored knight between the world and me, my best friend merely a few doors away. Tears well up in my eyes.

Walter moves to turn it off.

"No, it's not that," I say.

I don't want to live in the past anymore. I am here now, on this terrace, in a warm country surrounded by plants and magical stones. I can view that young girl in Paris with fondness, even a little pride for the knowledge she craved, the skills she sharpened, the powers she strove to call down.

Walter raises his eyebrows at me as if to ask, "Is it really fine, or are you just saying that?"

"She sounds good," I say through sips of peppery tequila.

Sometimes, at times like these, the breathtaking luck of all my escapes comes to me in a crush. The potential for capture, bodily harm, ships torpedoed, jail, death—it stops my breathing, panic clutching my chest, heart racing as if I've just outrun some wild beast. Leonora has shared what she does at such times. With the dull end of a pen or a paintbrush, she circles the spot between her eyebrows, site of the third eye. I do it now with the polished end of the white selenite wand from the prospector and feel a deep crunching, as if ligaments under the skin are releasing. Milky white selenite, good for communication and clearing one's intuition, good for breakthroughs of the mind and access to the angelic realms, is good for ushering in calm, it seems too.

"What are you doing?" Walter asks, smiling.

"Releasing," I say. "Seeing. Being at peace."

He merely nods, exhaling smoke through his nostrils, used to my ways by now.

If the crystals are a gift, I'll think of something to give that kind old prospector in thanks.

-≪≪◆≫≫-

It is weeks later that I take the black tourmaline over to Leonora's. Leonora likes anything to do with protection. The white selenite I've left behind, placed on top of my easel, imbuing it with its essence until I return.

Leonora and I meet in the mornings, sometimes very early before our households awake. It is a time when we can be undisturbed. We meet to drink tea, to discuss what we've been reading, to sketch in companionable silence away from the old terrors that sometimes haunt our dreams at night. I will head home before her boys wake, to my studio, to close the door, to begin, to paint.

She is working on a novel about two old women, friends, crones in the best sense of the word. Some mornings she reads me chapters in progress, and I am touched that she has based a character on me, Carmella Vasquez, with thick red hair, who gives the main character, based on Leo, a hearing trumpet and therefore the ability to hear things previously silent. The book is also ruthlessly funny and a little disturbing, not unlike Leonora herself. Her writing is an act of freedom, and listening to it, I can hear her soar.

I am also learning to be free. The lessons and the wisdom, the choices and the obstacles, all of it has come to serve this moment where I live within a very personal amalgamation of what I have gathered—my beliefs, my learnings, my crystals, my cards. Through this I have understood that my life has become a great banquet, not an overladen or gluttonous feast, but a nourishing done by the cosmos, of bones and blood and spirit and essence. These thoughts spin as I feel other things falling away, as the picture is starting to come into focus. Falling away is any form of censorship, especially self-censorship. Falling away is doubt, especially self-doubt, and fear and crippling anxieties from the past born out of war and dominance. Only now, slowly coming into focus, is abundance, and the spiritual life amidst this material fog.

When one painting is done, I am having an easier time releasing it, as I know another will rush in to take its place. With each release of work out into the world, I make space for more. I am painting a great table covered in a white cloth, a golden candlestick sitting still in the middle while cogs of fruit spin around it, levitating, spiraling out. The fruits of wisdom, the knowledge of spirit, and the timelessness of the self bursting forth. All painted with a tiny brush in the sharpest, clearest focus I can manage. Painting is the only way I have found to drive out depression and the dark moods that can engulf me. I am ready to wear the orange robes of the sparks and flames of creative energy that have been waiting for me all along.

Leonora pours us each a final cup of her most recent tea blend, redolent of pine and smoky as lapsang souchong.

"Tell me again what happened up the Orinoco," she says.

This is a familiar request from my friend over the years, but this morning I don't want to talk about the past. "There's nothing more to say. I've told you the whole thing. It was transcendent. I transcended. I saw what I needed to do. I saw what I needed to paint."

"Yes, but tell me again what that means. Actually. Physically."

"You've heard all this," I say, taking a sip of hot tea. "The water changed me. Irrevocably. I can't tell you more than that."

"Exactly," she says, and crosses the room to sit across from me. "It's not for words. These things for which we have art." She fiddles with the Celtic cross, the one I returned to her blessed by the Orinoco.

"So why are you writing?"

"That's different. To create beauty through story is not the same as descriptive writing. I'm not writing a how-to guide, you know."

"Maybe you should. Things are only beautiful if they are useful and they're only useful if they are right," I say, almost by rote.

"But that's ridiculous," Leonora says with a scoff. "Of course beauty is its own justification, filled with inherent value, required for making life livable. Beauty is one of the most important things we can strive for." Leonora says this as if my father's words hold no weight at all. "Beauty is useful, even vital in and of itself. The beautiful is as useful as the necessary. Everyone knows that."

And in that instant my friend sets me free as true words can, when spoken at the exact right time in the exact right combination with the force of love and goodwill. Those true words spoken in friendship aloud by another release and unbind a cage around my heart. Something my own ruminations or meditations could never dislodge is instantly and totally shifted by Leonora's words spoken with grace.

I pick up the tarot deck that sits on the table between us. The cards have become as soft and flexible as linen with the years. Familiar relief and buoying anticipation find me as I shuffle as Madame Carvon taught me. Will the cards hit for me today? Will they provide easy insights or more perplexing implications? I deal three cards out and turn them over. The self-possession and clarity that is the Queen of Swords sitting on her throne. The artisan with his hammer raised in the Eight of Pentacles reminding me that steady work is the way of mastery. And finally, the joy and exultation that is the dancer in the World card.

It is time to go home. A long list of patrons waits for both our art, and I feel the yearning now. It is time to get to work.

I stand and cross the room to kiss my dear friend on the cheek.

"I love you," I say, because my heart is full and because true words spoken at the right time have the force of magic.

"Love you too," Leonora says, slightly startled. "Your presence here has changed my whole life, you know. Now go, get to work."

They are all with me as I walk out the door of Leonora's house and into the orange sunrise street toward home. Leonora burning her own bright light and giving off the warm solace of knowledge that there is another in the world, a kindred spirit so I am not so alone. Jean with his beauty and passion who reconnected me to my body. The monarchs showing me what rebirth looked like. Benjamin, of course, who would always be with me, my initiation into the life of the mind.

He once said he owed André his life's work, and now that I have a friend like Leonora I understand. The life of the mind and insatiable curiosity, the example of how to drill down into what captures me, I owe that to Benjamin. The Orinoco River that washed off the past and launched me, renewed, into my current life. And Walter, who was the first person with whom I didn't have to change at all, the exhale of being myself. And with that exhale came breath and then energy to create as I'd always wanted to in the space of peace that he builds around us.

The ideas are coming now, more quickly than I have time to work on them. I am firm in my technique, assured of my ability to render, confident in my capacity to alchemize.

The universe is pulling at my hair, illuminating my steps as I walk down the street buoyed by friendship and filled with purpose as everything is spinning out in ever-widening circles high into the sky, expanding with love and joy, with true friendship and the man I love, with creation and alchemy in my palms, radiating from my fingertips.

Remedios Varo died of a heart attack in her painting studio on the afternoon of October 8, 1963, at the age of fifty-four at the height of her career. On her easel was her final completed work, *Still Life Reviving*, which depicts a tablecloth rotating like a cosmos while a solar system of fruits, some exploding, and plates spins around a central candlestick. The Spanish title—*Naturaleza Muerta Resucitando*—translates directly to "Dead Nature Being Revived." Unlike every other painting she ever made, it contains no image of either a person or an animal. It was her last completed work.

A Note on the Tarot

I wish I had a glamorous story about being introduced to the tarot that included a raven on a deserted road, or a dusty trunk in an abandoned chateau, or an anonymous package delivered to my doorstep. Instead, about ten years ago I picked up a deck in a local new age shop, and the owner told me they were hosting a weekly series of classes in the evenings taught by a doctoral candidate from a local university with an interest in Renaissance history. The class focused on the history and origins of the tarot, though we also went over the traditional meanings of the cards individually at the end and rather quickly.

As a result, I started pulling cards daily in response to specific quandaries and quagmires in my life, sometimes just with the vague intention of "What do I need to know today?" In this way, I came to know the cards personally.

There are generalized meanings that are widely recognized for each card—the High Priestess as a keeper of esoteric and intuitive knowledge, the Hanged Man as a call to release and stop struggling, the Fool as the freshness that comes when embarking on a new endeavor. However, the tarot is a personal art. Using the cards, you begin to understand their nuances and their personality in your life. To understand that when a certain King shows up in my readings, it's often a reference to my husband. That, for me, the Death card is usually a welcome one, as it often signals a release of something old and stale in favor of space for the new. That the Star card often shows up as a subtle way of signaling that I'm on the right path, like a gentle thumbs-up from the universe.

And while I was becoming more personally acquainted with the cards, I also added to my tarot studies.

I read and reread Rachel Pollack's book, *Seventy-Eight Degrees of Wisdom*, long before I was lucky enough to study with her and Mary Greer at the Omega Institute in Rhinebeck, New York. I participated in Olga Paz's three-month intensive Gestalt tarot study group in Cleveland, which opened my horizons. Some of my favorite thinkers about the tarot are Jessa Crispin, Jessica Dore, and Lindsay Mack. Their books, podcasts, and classes have all added greatly to my understanding and thinking.

The hazy history of the tarot is that it emerged out of a fifteenth-century card game favored in Italian Renaissance courts called Tarocci, which is believed to be the first game to use trump cards. The game evolved to include fifteen additional cards representing the twelve astrological signs and the three theological virtues of faith, hope, and charity. At the same time in France, a deck organized by suit—heart, club, spade, and diamond—was gaining popularity. It's thought that both these decks merged over time to become the first true tarot deck, the Tarot de Marseilles, which emerged in the 1750s and began to be used for divination.

In writing my definitions of the cards, they are influenced by these sources. I also chose to highlight certain aspects of the cards in reference to the person or scene that follows it. For instance, in writing the definition of the Nine of Pentacles, I wanted to emphasize the abundance and luxury of the card. In zeroing in on the hooded falcon as a symbol of thwarted spirit and the walls as symbols of limitation, I wanted to emphasize Peggy Guggenheim's failed romances and her grasping for something more but inability to create or take action herself. Traditionally, other aspects of the Nine of Pentacles relate positively to luxury, abundance, material success, good harvest, and good luck and read the falcon as a positive messenger of spirit. But I chose to highlight the limitations in the card, just like I highlighted those aspects in Peggy's character. In this way I hoped the reader would gain a little insight into how a card can illuminate certain events or people in a life.

Remedios Varo's long interest in the tarot is evidenced in her paintings that reference the cards of the Major Arcana, namely *The Juggler (The Magician)*, *The Hermit*, *The Tower*, *The Lovers*, *Tarot*, *Creation of the Birds*, *To Be Reborn*, and *Tarot Card*. Additionally, she kept a tarot deck, the Marseilles tarot, complete with her copious handwritten notes around the edges. Leonora Carrington made a tarot deck herself, illustrating the Major Arcana, which was reissued during the writing of this book by Fulgur Press. Varo and Carrington collected many books on tarot and the occult throughout their lives and shared them in mutual study.

AUTHOR'S NOTE

This novel is a work of fiction based loosely on fact. I've seen it called faction. It is not a biography. The best and only biography of Remedios Varo's life is *Unexpected Journeys* by the late Janet Kaplan.

Dates and time frames have been manipulated and compressed for the sake of plot. In the name of streamlining, some events and characters were left out completely, and others were combined or invented. Conversations and emotions have obviously been imagined and fictionalized; I intended to ground the basic idea behind them in enough research that they are plausible. My aim was to represent the essence of Remedios Varo's life and in that way engage with what I found extraordinary and singular about it. My hope is that these imaginings allow the reader to do the same.

Leonora and Remedios knew each other only tangentially in Paris. I imagined and embellished these early inevitable meetings until they became a brief but true friendship, given that Benjamin Péret and Max Ernst were part of the same surrealist circle that orbited André Breton. Years later, their well-documented and much-discussed close friendship matured in Mexico City.

Varo's forgeries of paintings in the style of de Chirico are well discussed in her biography. The broadening of her talents to include forging Vichy documents is my invented extension of that skill. The abortion is an educated guess made by a few different biographers and picked up by me here.

Varo's life and work are not well celebrated outside her adopted Mexico, where she is considered a national treasure. This may be because the bulk of her work (as with Leonora Carrington's) is held in private hands and rarely comes up for auction, though that is changing. Few want to part with one of her paintings. When they do come to market, they have garnered increasingly record-setting prices. A sprinkling of her works are held by institutions such as the Museum of Modern Art, New York; the Museum of Fine Arts, Boston; the National Gallery for Women in the Arts, and the Centre Pompidou. The largest collection of Varo's work, over thirty paintings, is held by the Museo de Arte Moderno in Mexico City.

Leonora Carrington's long life is well documented. The biography written by her much younger remote type-of cousin, Joanna Moorhead, provides wonderful insights, as does the memoir written by her son Gabriel Weisz Carrington. The scholarship of Susan Aberth and her book, *Leonora Carrington, Surrealism, Alchemy and Art,* provided much-needed insights. When asked in an interview about her friendship with Remedios, Leonora said, "The fact of Remedios being in Mexico changed my whole life" (p. 313).

Carrington did suffer a mental breakdown after her lover Max Ernst was imprisoned. She wrote an account of her time in a Spanish mental hospital titled *Down Below,* and as a harrowing insight into what a descent into madness is like, I have read nothing even close, except perhaps Charlotte Perkins Gilman's *The Yellow Wallpaper.*

Before Marseilles fell to the Nazis, Varian Fry helped a distinguished list of artists escape, including Hannah Arendt, Jean Arp, Marc Chagall, Marcel Duchamp, as well as the characters mentioned in this novel and many more. Fry's autobiography, *Surrender on Demand,* gives an excellent account of the American Rescue Committee and the Villa Air-Bel, as does Rosemary Sullivan's book, *Villa Air-Bel.*

While there was a housekeeper at the villa named Madame Nouget, her character and skills as an herbalist are entirely fiction.

André Breton's character is based on the surrealist blind spot when it came to the liberation of women. Perhaps I've made him and Jacqueline more odious than they were in real life. André Breton famously expounded on the purpose of art during World War II: "Everything we do is to outwit the anguish of the hour" (p. 93, 143). And he referred to his best friend, Benjamin Péret, as "The Grand Inquisitor of Surrealism" (p. 91).

Benjamin Péret dedicated many poems and volumes of poetry to Remedios, including one dedicated solely to her breasts, "my two hemispheres." The poem he recites at the countess's party is a fragment from "Source," which was included in his 1936 collection *I Sublimate* (p. 124).

Peggy Guggenheim famously came to the villa and bought artwork at the open-air auctions the surrealists sheltering there would have to raise funds for escape. Her autobiography, as well as the cameos she made in Carrington's and Varo's biographies, served as source material for the Peggy who shows up in these pages.

Remedios's meeting with Frida Kahlo is entirely imaginary, though Benjamin Péret did teach at the Collegio at the same time Kahlo taught there. The scene of Diego Rivera dancing with Jean Nicolle is inspired by an incident where Rivera forced Benjamin Péret to dance with him at gunpoint during a faculty party. Similarly, Leonora was friends with Rivera, who liked to gossip with her. Given that the two people closest to Remedios, Péret and Carrington, knew Kahlo and Rivera, I imagined she must have met them at some point, though Kahlo was quite ill by the late 1940s.

Upon leaving the Paris exhibition André Breton organized for her in 1928 in Paris, Kahlo said, "I'd rather sit on a floor in the market of Toluca and sell tortillas, than have anything to do with those artistic bitches of Paris" (p. 217). Kahlo's quote was not specifically directed at Leonora or Remedios. In describing Frida Kahlo's paintings in the Paris exhibit, André Breton famously described them "like a ribbon tied around a bomb" (p. 207).

Pamela "Pixie" Colman Smith is the long-erased artist who created the masterpiece that is the Smith Rider Waite tarot deck beloved around the world for more than a century. In a letter to her friend William Butler Yeats, when describing a recent commission to paint a deck of cards, she famously wrote, "It's a big job for not a lot of cash" (p. 88). For a biography of her life and influences, Stuart Kaplan and Mary Greer's *Pamela Colman Smith: The Untold Story* is a great place to start.

Madame Carvon and her shop are entirely fictional, though Marseilles was long a printing capital and a tarot capital, with the tarot of Marseilles being one of the oldest and best-known tarot decks before the creation of the Smith Rider Waite deck.

The character of Oscar Sanchez is loosely based (with many embellishments) on Remedios's close friend in Paris and Marseilles, Oscar Dominguez. Though he was an accomplished painter, I don't believe Dominguez ever dealt art. He did, however, throw a glass in Paris one night in what is described by witnesses as a jealous rage.

The quote by Remedios's father throughout the book is made up, but is meant to be representative of her struggle to make a living in the world and to make her art. I imagined it as indicative of the worldview of her father, given he was a man of logic and engineering.

The Countess Pastré character is loosely based on Countess Lily Pastré and Marie-Laure de Noailles, the Vicomtesse de Noailles. The Countess Pastré sheltered many musicians in the Chateau Pastré in Marseilles during the occupation, including Pablo Casals and Josephine Baker. The Vicomtesse de Noailles was the lover of Oscar Dominguez and close friends with the surrealist circle.

ACKNOWLEDGMENTS

I would like to thank my friends, family, and supporters who have allowed me to read their tarot cards, show them reproductions of paintings by Remedios in books, and just generally nerd out about my enthusiasm for Varo and Carrington.

I thank my treasured friend, fellow Edith Wharton fanatic, and Knight of Wands Irene Goldman-Price, whose gracious insights into this book reignited my creativity at a time when it was lagging.

I thank dear friend, early reader, and Knight of Pentacles Laurie Kincer, who brought understanding and discernment to my work, which grounded it and solved so many quandaries for me. For this I am so grateful.

I thank deep reader and Knight of Cups Halley Moore, who brings me true friendship along with her insights in a golden chalice. Her close reading made this book better than before. Thank you, dear friend.

Queen of Wands and agent extraordinaire Elizabeth Kaplan offers a range of services, including cheerleading, pepping up, advocacy, bright perception, and genuine friendship, all delivered right when needed.

Trish Todd is the Queen of Swords, bringing incisive thought and an ability to slice through all forms of miasma with a single intellectual blade. I am forever grateful that she sees something in my work and for her team of skilled publishing artisans who assist her.

Acknowledgments

I'd like to thank Natalie Hallak for stepping in Queen of Pentacles–style with verve and enthusiasm to usher this book out into the world.

Flora is the Page of Wands—you're you, that's your superpower.

Mac is the Knight of Swords ready to rush in where others fear to tread and make his thoughts known. Go get it.

Sandy arranges the world to support us all with the grace of a king on his rightful throne. Thank you always for everything, my King of Pentacles.

And Remedios Varo is the High Priestess, the World, and the Magician all in one for me. Encountering her painting *The Call* for the first time was a transcendent experience. It was as if I had been put under a spell that shifted an internal structure within me in an instant. That such a bright comet of a person left behind a collection of deeply personal and powerful paintings is a blessing for which I will always be grateful.

A Selection of Sources

Aberth, Susan, *Leonora Carrington: Surrealism, Alchemy and Art*

Aberth, Susan, and Tere Arcq, *The Tarot of Leonora Carrington*

Allmer, Patricia, *Angels of Anarchy: Women Artists and Surrealism*

Anonymous, *Meditations on the Tarot: A Journey into Christian Hermeticism*

Arcq, Tere, editor, *Five Keys to the Secret World of Remedios Varo*

Carrington, Gabriel Weisz, *The Invisible Painting: My Memoir of Leonora Carrington*

Carrington, Leonora, *The Debutante and Other Stories*

Carrington, Leonora, *Down Below*

Carrington, Leonora, *The Hearing Trumpet*

Caws, Mary Ann, editor, *Surrealism and Women*

Crispin, Jessa, *The Creative Tarot: A Guide to an Inspired Life*

Dore, Jessica, *Tarot for Change: Using the Cards for Self-Care, Acceptance, and Growth*

Everly, Kathryn A., *Catalan Women Writers and Artists: Revisionist Views from a Feminist Space*

Fort, Ilene Susan, and Tere Arcq, *In Wonderland: The Surrealist Adventures of Women Artists in Mexico and the United States*

Fry, Varian, *Surrender on Demand*

Glass, Charles, *Americans in Paris: Life and Death Under Nazi Occupation*

A Selection of Sources

Greer, Mary K., *Tarot for Yourself*

Guggenheim, Peggy, *Confessions of an Art Addict*

Herrera, Hayden, *Frida: A Biography of Frida Kahlo*

Jodorowsky, Alejandro, and Marianne Costa, *The Way of the Tarot: The Spiritual Teacher in the Cards*

Kaplan, Janet A., *Remedios Varo: Unexpected Journeys*

Kaplan, Stuart R., and Mary K. Greer, *Pamela Colman Smith: The Untold Story*

Lane, Mary M., *Hitler's Last Hostages*

Moorhead, Joanna, *The Surreal Life of Leonora Carrington*

Nonaka, Masayo, *Remedios Varo: The Mexican Years*

Péret, Benjamin, *Death to the Pigs: Selected Writings of Benjamin Péret*

Péret, Benjamin, *From the Hidden Storehouse: Selected Poems*

Pollack, Rachel, *Seventy-Eight Degrees of Wisdom: A Book of Tarot*

Riding, Alan, *And the Show Went On: Cultural Life in Nazi-Occupied Paris*

Stahr, Celia, *Frida in America: The Creative Awakening of a Great Artist*

Sullivan, Rosemary, *Villa Air-Bel: World War II, Escape, and a House in Marseille*

Van Raay, Stephan, *Surreal Friends: Leonora Carrington, Remedios Varo, and Kati Horna*

Varo, Remedios, *Letters, Dreams and Other Writings*

Waite, Arthur Edward, *The Pictorial Key to the Tarot*

Warlick, M. E., *Max Ernst and Alchemy: A Magician in Search of a Myth*

About the Author

Claire McMillan is the author of *The Necklace* and *Gilded Age*. She is the 2017–2018 Cuyahoga County Writer in Residence and currently serves as member of the Board of Trustees of the Mount, Edith Wharton's home in Lenox, Massachusetts. She practiced law until 2003 and then received her MFA in creative writing from Bennington College. She grew up in Pasadena, California, and now lives on her husband's family farm outside Cleveland, Ohio, with their two children.